SWEET
KAROLINE

Catherine Astolfo

SWEET KAROLINE

Copyright © 2013 by Catherine Astolfo. All Rights Reserved.

No part of this publication may be reproduced, stored in a retrieval system, or transmitted, in any form or by any means, electronic, mechanical, photocopying, recording, or otherwise, without prior written permission from the author.

This is a work of fiction. Names, characters, places and incidents either are the product of the author's imagination or are used fictitiously. And any resemblance to actual persons, living, dead (or in any other form), business establishments, events, or locales is entirely coincidental.

http://www.catherineastolfo.com

FIRST EDITION TRADE PAPERBACK

Imajin Books - www.imajinbooks.com

July 14, 2013

ISBN: 978-1-927792-07-0

Cover designed by Ryan Doan - www.ryandoan.com

Praise for SWEET KAROLINE

"A deliciously vibrant portrait that realistically muddles good and evil." —*Kirkus Reviews*

"Astolfo's wonderful first sentence in *Sweet Karoline* explodes on the page and resonates right to the end of this twisting examination of dangerous minds. Never have I encountered a narrative voice that alternates more deftly between alienating and enticing." —Mel Bradshaw, author of *Fire On The Runway*

"A deliciously twisted story about the perplexing power of adult female relationships. By turns scathingly funny and darkly insightful, *Sweet Karoline* is a hedonistic journey with all the right ingredients: lust, betrayal, true love and mystery. Grab a glass of wine and have the bottle handy. A compelling read from the start through to the surprising end." —Robin Spano, author of *Death's Last Run*

"In Catherine Astolfo's chilling new novel *Sweet Karoline*, things aren't always as they seem. Anne, the multifaceted anti-heroine in this noir tale takes a fateful journey into her forgotten past, uncovering the painful roots of her childhood. While furrowing for answers, a mystery unfolds, truths swirl to the surface, a heinous murder occurs. Who's the killer? Caught in a tangled web of greed, lies and deceit Anne must come to terms with her past, present and future, and the bleak realization that those we hold close may be the last ones to trust. Compelling, visually descriptive, deftly delivered…Catherine Astolfo's got the goods!" —Douglas Wickard, author of *A Perfect Husband*

"*Sweet Karoline* is a multi-layered mystery, where nothing is as it seems. The story grips you on page one and leads you through a maze of history, twisted relationships, and ultimately the darkness of the human mind." —Liz Bugg, author of *Oranges and Lemons*

"In *Sweet Karoline*, Astolfo has created a daring hybrid mystery that combines elements of romance, history, and suspense in a carefully crafted story that keeps you guessing to the very end. Astolfo explores new boundaries as she extends her reach beyond the cozy mystery in this psychological exploration of the mind of a killer. A unique exploration of guilt and revenge." —Michael J. McCann, author of *The Fregoli Delusion*

"The clever plot twists in *Sweet Karoline* will enrapture you from page one through the last paragraphs of this fast-paced modern mystery. Author Catherine Astolfo exhibits a strikingly perceptive gift for believable dialogue and rich character development. Her dry wit and colorful descriptions will have you howling in laughter at points, but in tears at others as she digs deep into the themes of guilt, race, and relationships. The powers of love and redemption are strong, but does the heart of an Ice Queen ever really melt? Enjoy the romp from Los Angeles, through Canada, to a priceless Italian rendezvous —Lisa Pell, award-winning author of *Who's Your Daddy, Baby?*

For my mother and her life of song and resilience.

Acknowledgements

I am such a fortunate person having my partner, my family and my friends in my life. I love you all so much! My very first manuscript-in-progress readers are also my inspiration: my husband, Vince Astolfo, and my daughter, Kristen Henderson. My son, James Henderson, and his wife Meredith provided not only encouragement but also "LA talk" and tours.

Special thanks to my readers of the first draft for their careful, thoughtful responses and suggestions: Maire Kearns, Melodie Campbell, Sarah Barkwell-Mann, Meredith Henderson, Ruth Ellen Henderson, Frances Daley, Tanya Buchanan and Tara Mann.

A special thanks to Frances Daley for crafting the insightful, intelligent Book Club Questions. Genius!

A huge thanks to the historians in Brantford and Paris, Ontario. I didn't always follow their facts, however. I like to play with reality (as you can tell) and I just had to throw in some family folklore. So please take it all with a spirit of imagination.

I am grateful to the Crime Writers of Canada community, my Sisters (and brothers) in Crime Toronto, my critique group MCM, and my Orenda Writers Group for all their support and encouragement. What a delight being surrounded by smart, creative people.

My appreciation for Cheryl Tardif, my publisher, and her team, grows with every book. I thank them for their advice, suggestions, assistance and most of all, for giving *Sweet Karoline* a home. Special thanks to my editor, Todd Barselow, for his brilliant "polishing."

"Sweet Caroline
Good times never seemed so good
I'd be inclined
To believe they never would..."
Neil Diamond

"The truth is never far behind
You kept it hidden well.
If I live to tell
The secret I knew then
Will I ever have the chance again..."
Madonna

"When the truth is found to be lies
And all the joy within you dies
Don't you want somebody to love?"
Jefferson Airplane

Chapter 1

I met Ethan on the day that I killed Karoline.

Other than a few minor adjustments, I believe that I have handled her murder exceedingly well.

The state of my car, for instance, has become something of a nuisance. Bits of tissue, used napkins, paper cups and pop cans litter the floor at my feet or fly out the window as I drive along. I am invariably subjected to a barrage of honking whenever I reach a red light.

People these days have no patience. They ought to understand that I am busy examining the stray bits in my car. Some of them are works of art. I don't notice the change to green because they are so infinitely interesting.

This study of creative possibilities has become somewhat of an obsession. In the back of my mind I know that all I have to do is clean it up. Yet the thought of actually tackling the onslaught of debris leaves me inert and helpless.

Ethan offered recently to take me to the car wash. He'd help me dump the debris and vacuum the inside, but I have seriously considered the idea that I may be destroying a future Picasso. I have thus far refused his proposition. Not that I have shared my vision of a Picasso with him, of course. I just say that I never have time.

I have acquired a habit of going shopping. I make lists of things in my mind—groceries, toiletries, cosmetics, medicines, vitamins or clothing—that seem absolutely essential to the arrival of tomorrow. But once inside the pharmacy, the clothing store or the shopping center, the bright lights mesmerize me. My eyes blur and I can't for the life of me remember what I have come for.

When I do buy something, I am left vaguely dissatisfied, certain that I could have gotten a better bargain somewhere else had I only looked a little longer. Depressed because I had to use my credit card again and this purchase will become just one more thing to do. Write the check. Buy the stamp. Walk to the post box. Mail the envelope.

The little, unfinished things do sometimes bother me. Dirty laundry is piled up in the closet. The bed is always unmade. In the bathroom, the ceiling is slowly cracking from some unspecified leak that I have failed to report to the superintendent. The drapes in the living room neither open nor close anymore.

At first I tended to watch television all night long, despite the fact that the next day I was a zombie. After I decided to go on an extended sick leave, it didn't matter. I started to sleep all night and all day, never moving unless forced to by some phone call, knock at the door or the call of nature.

I spend hours at the sink. For some reason, the suds and the water are calming. So far I have washed every dish, bowl, and ornament in the apartment two or three times. I reenact advertisements for the latest dishwashing liquid, showing off my lovely long fingers and hands to, well, myself. I speak in a sing-song voice to the imaginary audience, telling them how kind the dishwashing liquid has been to my hands over the years, encouraging them to run right out and buy this product before it disappears from the shelf.

After I've allowed the water to swirl down the drain, I shift to spending hours in front of the little mirror that hangs in my kitchen. People tell me that I am a very beautiful woman. On good days, when I feel haughty and happy, I can gaze into the polished glass and agree with their assessment. On other days, I notice the nose that's a little too upturned. The lips that protrude a bit too much. The dark birthmark above my left eyebrow. The ears that don't lie flat against my head. I have no idea why I am considered flawless, for I have many perceptible flaws, both inside and out.

My father is white and my mother is black with some Native American thrown into her background. My parents have always bragged that I inherited all the great physical features of those races. Their perspective is far less critical than mine. They focus on all the positives. Naturally wavy hair. Large brown eyes with long curling lashes. High, full cheekbones. A small, pert nose. Lips just thick enough to be called luscious.

I am one of those fortunate people who can eat all day and not gain an ounce. Thus I am described as tall and lean as opposed to thin. I have full breasts and a narrow waist. I am a fast runner and good at any sport I attempt. In Hollywood, I am considered full figured.

My skin is a light brown, the color of coffee with cream I guess you would say, that makes me look as though I've just stepped out of a tanning bed. Heads literally turn to stare at me in the street, from across a room, or on the subway. Male *and* female. To me, it's a constant source of surprise, chagrin and exasperation.

Lots of people, especially women, have jealously told me that I should be grateful for my looks. But I hate being identified as beautiful. Men tend to stare only at my chest when they talk to me. Or they show me off like some trophy and do not bother to ask my opinion on anything. I have been approached in bars and stores alike. Even in this land of plastic enhanced faces, I literally cannot go anywhere without being stared at or even followed. Most people, in fact, are convinced I am a movie star or model. These are not careers I've ever wanted.

I have often been stalked, thus the three sets of locks on our door. Our telephone number is always unlisted and has to be changed once some obsessed man discovers it. When you are lovely on the outside, it's always difficult to entice people to look for the true person underneath. I'm learning through Ethan that it's exactly the same for truly ugly people.

Over the years, I learned to live at the surface. It wasn't hard to do in Los Angeles, where even the air is insipid.

I would prefer to be considered intelligent, but that's probably not an attribute anyone would mention when they speak of me. I worked very hard to acquire the position of Executive Assistant at Grace Film Productions, which is where I was employed up until last month.

I was one of the very lucky ones who loved what I did every day and rarely considered it an effort. My former office is surrounded by windows and is fairly well designed. My desk is large and my chair comfortable. The office building, which houses Grace as well as several other companies, is an architectural beauty. All blue glass and steel, round and elegant, surrounded by greenery and topped with a beautiful grey crown that's actually an enormous rooftop patio. The front doors open with a swish. The security desk is classy, the carpet plush. The employees are welcoming and friendly. In the lobby and elevators, hushed music fills the air to calm nerves on the way to hear someone's decision on the success or failure of a movie script.

Grace Films takes a script all the way from the editing stage to production. Sometimes my employers are heavily involved in the resultant movie and sometimes they take an Executive Producer role, basically handing the project off to other producers for the detailed work.

My position requires juggling numerous prickly clients, writers, producers, and even actors, who are either nervous or over-confident artists.

I also organize the lives of my bosses, who have enormous egos and expect everything to be done yesterday. I am able to handle details and disasters with a calm, objective exterior and an inner patience that stems from my adoration of talented people. Or, as Karoline would tell you, my love of power.

I frequently go on set to distract or pacify our clients. I learn about their backgrounds, families, likes and dislikes, and treat them accordingly. Some of my employers have become my friends. Some of the writers and directors and actors are now my dependents.

When my bosses are on location, I am solely responsible for answering the myriad of calls and managing the frantic problem solving. I am able to handle the stress of my position quite serenely. Or, make that, I used to be able to…

I am aware that looks are part of the charm. I can give the clients a smile and they are instantly under my spell. Mine was the first voice they heard. The first face they saw if they got that far. I was often the one to give them the bad or good news about their scripts. In fact, I was the one who often read the first scenes to see if it was worthy of being handed to our producers.

In the good times, I did feel grateful for my appearance. I learned to use it to my advantage. Happiness and overconfidence would swell like the ocean tide warming the shore. I had been taught by my parents to be self-centered and proud. I lived a hedonistic lifestyle, unaware that there could be any other way to live.

In the very recent past I loved getting up in the morning. On weekdays I looked forward to traveling into the city. I would hop out of bed, anticipation fuelling my energy level, already going over the day in my head. Living in Pasadena meant rising very early, but it was worth the long commute, the clogged roads, the incessant weaving in and out of traffic.

Our little section of L.A. County is green, safe and friendly. I'd go for a quick run most mornings. When it was too hot or, infrequently, rainy, I'd swim or work out in the gym. It's amazing the number of people I used to meet jogging on the street, doing laps in the gym pool or running on the treadmill.

Our apartment building is like a village. Everyone knows everyone and all their business, too. When someone dies as ostentatiously as Karoline did, the gossip is rampant. Now my fellow residents avoid me as though I have an infectious disease or have changed places with an alien life form who speaks no discernible language.

On weekends, there was always something going on. Every Friday night I'd be in a bar, toasting and talking over the week with my colleagues at Grace, before I hopped back into the car. In the past, Karoline and Giulio would either come drinking with me or they'd be off with their own colleagues and we'd meet in the parking lot.

Saturdays and Sundays were usually untouchable. Film stars don't want to work on weekends. Whenever Karoline was away for the weekend on business, which was often, I hung out with Giulio or stayed home reading scripts. We had settled into a comfortable, satisfying routine that lasted until Italy. My life didn't often involve worrying about men or going out on a date.

I have not had many happy or haughty days lately, that's for sure. I no longer get up from bed eager to start the day. In my little mirror I see only the lines below my lip, etched by worry and stress. I see the dark shadows under my eyes created by sleepless nights or pills that cause unconsciousness but not rest. I am jumpy and pimples have sprung up out of the unnatural hormones racing through my fearful body. I spend much of the day gazing at the distortions of a face that used to be peaceful, content, ambitious and young.

Recently I hadn't even answered my mother's telephone messages. My mother and father still live in Bell Canyon. I haven't really let Mom in on the aftermath of the tragedy, not the details at least. I don't want to worry her. She is a well-meaning mom, despite the fact that I spent half my life being ashamed of her. I'm not sure she ever knew of my treachery, but somehow I cannot bring myself to turn to her, or to my Dad, for comfort. Although I am not deserving of their support, my main reason for avoiding them is that they are part of the betrayal. They have a mutual treachery of their own.

Another thing I used to love is our apartment. It's part of a Moorish-Spanish designed collection of buildings that boast a beautiful stone façade, light brown stucco walls and rounded bay windows. Every balcony is bounded by gorgeous wrought iron, except for ours, which has rather high stone walls instead. The only drawback is that we have to stand up to see any view.

I used to shiver with delight and pride every time I entered the stone archway that graces the front entrance. Now I shiver for a wholly different reason.

Karoline and I lived in the top of two turrets that face the garden-side of the complex. In the 1940's, her Jah-jah and Boosha—don't ask me the real spellings of the Polish words—came to California to live on streets of gold. As soon as Jah-jah died, Boosha hightailed it back to Poland.

By then, Karoline's mother was already married and residing in Bell Canyon. Halina's brothers went back to the old country, too. Maybe that's why she got pregnant so quickly and so young. Otherwise, she would have been alone.

For years Boosha rented out the old family apartment. The income must have been pretty good, because she never bothered to sell it. When Karoline, Giulio and I acquired jobs in L.A., Karoline wanted to buy her family's old place. Boosha said yes, they worked out a rent-to-buy arrangement and here we are. Rather, here we were.

Unlike newer buildings that are all boxy and small, the rooms in our apartment are huge, aside from the galley kitchen. We have a generous dining area in which Karoline and I used to have dinner parties for up to ten people. Our living room is enormous, with windows that span its entire length. The two bedrooms are in the rounded section of the turrets, which makes them interesting though hard to decorate.

Since her death, I am often reminded of the night I saw Karoline in bed with Glenn. Every time I opened her bedroom door, her eyes seemed to be there still, staring at me with that steely look from beneath the flabby man whose mantra was more porn than romance. For months her door has remained shut. I walk around it, avoiding the waft of air from under the frame.

Mature trees and palms lean toward us from the side garden, giving us cooling breezes that almost negate the need for air conditioners. We can just see the mountains if we peer around the edge of the balcony.

We are tucked slightly away from the busy street, so we don't hear the traffic much at night. There's a sidewalk underneath that runs along a big square yard that residents can enjoy. Across the street on this side is a huge park.

Karoline decorated the apartment because she has—had—a knack for design. She went with bright, bold colors and accessories, big comfy furniture and artifacts from our various journeys spread carefully throughout. Pictures have been placed with an eye for artistic showcasing. We have two carpets from a trip to Turkey that massage your feet as you pad down the hall to the bathroom or through the living room. We even have a small CoJon painting on the entrance wall.

Nowadays, the paint seems dark and gloomy. The nooks and crannies are full of ghosts. The door to the second bedroom remains closed and the balcony is off limits. The yellow crime scene tape still flies in tatters around the railings. I spend my time in my bedroom, bathroom, or the kitchen, terrified to spread out, ashamed to sit on the couch. I skirt around the carpets, my bare feet stubbing the hardwood. I refuse to look toward the windows, afraid I might see her face reflected in the glass.

I would move if I could work up the energy or if I had anywhere else to go.

There's a picture of Karoline on the end table that glares out at me every morning as I slide past the living room into the kitchen. I used to love that image, thought of it as a true portrait of the person she was. She looks very pretty in this particular exposure, although she wasn't really good looking. Her teeth protruded quite dramatically and, unfortunately, she never seemed motivated to get them fixed. Her hair was a mousy brown and had that wispy thinness that made her appear somewhat balding. She was very short with a body that looked childlike when she was young, but gave her a dumpy appearance in her thirties.

Karoline never wore make-up or selected clothing that enhanced her figure in any way. She gave the impression that she had no interest in the external. I loved Karoline for this reason in particular and for lots of other reasons, too.

Dear Diary,

Such an inane, cliché-ish way to start, but I can assure you there will be nothing cliché or inane about the thoughts within these pages. I read recently that keeping a journal is healthy. I am discovering that I love being able to explore random ideas without censure. Put feelings and facts down on paper. Pardon the lack of order, Dear Diary, but it's about me, not you.

CHAPTER 2

Karoline and I met when we were ten. We were both considered immigrants. Karoline's parents had arrived straight from Poland while I was from Canada.

Following the educational wisdom of the time, the school principal decided to promote me past fourth grade directly into fifth. My parents, of course, were delighted and proud. They told me how fortunate I was to have inherited both brains and beauty. I therefore approached school on the first morning of my acceleration with the same happiness and haughtiness that I've mentioned before.

At the gates to the girls' side of the schoolyard I was met by a group of the Fifth Graders. They blocked my entrance with arms linked and faces filled with anger and hate. I stopped in my tracks, heart pounding, shocked and afraid. One member of the group, Shirley O'Connor, stepped forward and assumed the role of spokesperson.

"None of us wants you in our class," she announced. "You think you're so smart and so big. You think you're better than the rest of us."

I opened my mouth to protest that no, I didn't feel that way. I was grateful and pleased, honored to join them, really, not conceited or superior. Honestly, I wanted to say, go past the perfect face and see a little girl who only wants to have friends and do the best I can do.

I gazed longingly beyond them to the Fourth Graders who played happily without me, not even realizing I was gone. I hadn't been in their presence long enough to make mine felt. Tears began to gather at the edges of my eyes. I was unable to clear the lump in my throat to engender any speech.

Shirley O'Connor took my silence as a sign to continue her barrage. "You can't just come into our grade and think that we're going to be your friends. You're not American and you're not even white."

Staring at the collection of fair and red-haired girls, white and pink noses sprinkled with freckles, I was reminded of how different I looked to this small town of mostly Caucasian people. Once again I felt a surge of anger toward my parents, who had not only carelessly created a mixed child, but who'd moved me to this backwoods place.

"You should ask to go back to fourth grade."

I was about to agree with her wholeheartedly when Karoline Mikulski stepped forward. She'd been standing to one side of the group, observing, not part of them, yet until that moment not showing any support either.

"Leave her alone," she said, coming up beside me and linking my arm the way the group had entwined theirs. "She's smart and Principal St. James says she belongs in fifth grade. We'll be her friends if you guys won't."

Right beside her a small thin boy nodded his dark curly head in agreement, though he said nothing.

I paid no attention to the fact that the other girls in the group, who'd been silent until now, laughed and snickered that who cared if Karoline Mikulski and the "Eye-tie" were my friends, no one liked them either. I was eternally grateful to this little imp of a girl who'd defied the majority and marched me off to the classroom with pride and confidence. She was the kind of child who announced in a clear, determined voice to the teacher that her name was pronounced Kar-o-line, like President Kennedy's daughter, though the real truth was obvious.

Later I realized that I'd also hooked myself up with a little Italian boy named Giulio who barely spoke English and smelled of garlic.

We remained apart from the crowd always. Karoline, Giulio and I were a formidable triangle. We went through high school and university together, sharing everything. Karoline's wit, cleverness and unconditional love carried me through. Giulio's serious, artistic and poetic nature led us to adventure and culture that we'd never have explored on our own. I thought that I had given them a great deal of support and love, too. That we were complete and perfect friends. When Giulio left us, Karoline and I prevailed, our friendship stronger than ever. I assumed our duo would last forever.

The day Karoline died, I was not at my best. I was disheveled and beside myself with grief. I know my hair was wild and stuck out everywhere. My face was as pale as it ever gets. My lips quivered. My eyes were red and wet. In other words, I must have looked a fright.

"I'm Detective Byrne, Ms. Williams," Ethan said, sounding like someone out of Dragnet. He proffered his identification, though I couldn't see much through my swollen eyelids.

I gave him my best goddess-in-clay imitation, the look I have perfected for Ice Queen occasions. I am pretty good at snooty and sarcastic when I need to be. My face can mimic plastic surgery with such precision that you'd think I'd actually experienced it.

One ex-boyfriend told me it was always impossible to tell what I was really thinking, let alone feeling, but I suspect that was because he never paid attention to my voice or the slight flush of my skin or the sudden emptiness in my eyes. My breasts could tell him nothing.

Ethan Byrne was different. He loomed very tall in my apartment doorway, silver-threaded hair shining in the harsh light from the hall. Huge round eyes blinked at me from behind black-rimmed glasses. His long bumpy nose and straggly eyebrows lent an almost comic look to his ugly countenance, but I had learned the hard way to look beneath the surface rather than judge by appearance alone.

When I stared into his orbs of dark blue that searched my face, I saw compassion, intelligence, inquisitiveness. What's more, he looked straight into my eyes, despite the fact that I was dressed in my favorite negligee. Karoline gave it to me last Christmas. It was a dark purple silk thing with a very low-cut neckline.

It might seem like an odd gift for one female friend to give another, but Karoline had done some research and discovered that most people sleep better in silk or in the nude. I never could find the prim and proper cover that went with it.

After a long pause during which I said absolutely nothing, Ethan introduced me to the female officer, a thin blond woman in uniform, who stood silently beside him.

"This is Officer Peters. May we come in, Ms. Williams?"

I opened the door and stood back. They halted awkwardly in the living room, taking up all the warm air. I began to shiver.

"Would you like to go and put on something warmer, Ms. Williams?" the big detective asked, his voice a smooth deep baritone that felt as good as a neck massage.

I looked down at myself then. My knees quivered, my nipples stared. Reaching into the front hall closet, I wrapped myself in my scarlet cape. Karoline's matching brown one was left hanging limp and abandoned.

Suddenly I was sitting at our dining room table surrounded by the officers. With his broad shoulders and thick arms, Ethan overwhelmed the delicate chairs, but he managed to look graceful in his dark blue jacket and snow-white shirt. The tie, splashed with pink and aqua lines, looked incongruous with the gravity of his suit.

"As I said," Ethan repeated, "I'm Detective Byrne. I'm following up, now that Officer Peters and her team have completed the first part of the investigation."

The slight lilt to his speech, hinting at origins other than the United States, sent me careening back to high school.

When I met Giulio, he'd just arrived 'off the boat' as our classmates would say. They were proud and superior now that the majority of them were generations away from their own ancestors' immigration. Despite his chronological age, Giulio was immediately placed in the lowest grade the school could get away with. He was tiny-boned and thin, very unlike most of his Italian paisans. Feminine and soft voiced, he fit in with no one.

Karoline had instantly adopted him. Their own little weird unit of two had immediately embraced me.

At first it was difficult to understand Giulio. Over time, however, I was able to relate to his gestures, recognize a few words and interpret him as only friends can. Giulio embraced his new language slowly and never fully spoke without a thick and stumbling accent. This may have explained Mrs. St. James's erroneous judgment that he was slow.

Karoline, on the other hand, was almost instantly fluent in all three languages—Polish, Italian and English—as though born to absorb words.

My mother was delighted with my friends. A fierce and loyal Canadian who'd been forcibly transported to the United States by the man she loved, she embraced differences in culture and race with a showy, dedicated flare. She became decidedly more African in her roots, which I found embarrassing. She invited Karoline and Giulio over to savor her native meals and desserts, recipes handed down from ancestors so distant that I doubted they were even hers.

Struggling to be so accepting and open made her look pathetic and false in my eyes. I was appalled that my parents were mixed race, leaving me in a limbo between the two. Not only that, they'd moved me to a town where the vast majority of people were white. While cultural differences piqued my mother's interest, I was at the opposite end of the spectrum. I wished I could just be like everybody else. White, ordinary-looking. Unworthy of stares, adoration, curiosity and hatred.

The kids at school stayed far away from us in the cafeteria at lunch while Giulio munched his sausages and capicolli. Years later, when garlic became the rage, I would remember the sweet salty smell of Giulio and laugh to myself as the spice was 'discovered' by the rest of our acquaintances.

Once we reached high school, Giulio confided in Karoline and me that he was gay. We were the only ones he told. Giulio was our friend, our mentor, our guide and now he was a safety net all in one. He promised that, should he or we not find our true loves, we would live together into old age. But that was before our trip to Italy.

Dear Diary,
Maybe it's their inheritance and upbringing that has caused them to remain so childlike. One a pampered little boy, the only son, surrounded by doting females who did everything for him, the other a contradiction of appearance and concept.

CHAPTER 3

I returned to the present with Detective Byrne's prompting. I noticed that he was staring at me curiously. He cleared his throat.

"Ms. Williams." His accent mingled with the throaty southern syllables to produce a voice that was commanding even in soft tones. "Can you show us where it happened?"

I took a moment to understand what he meant by 'it'. I mumbled something like 'sure, come this way,' or some other expected comment. We crossed through the living room to the center balcony. I stood against the wall, far from the edge, terrified I would see 'it' again if I looked over. Ethan and Officer Peters put on gloves and leaned over the wall, up on tiptoes, as though they too would hurl themselves into space.

She looks like a jigsaw puzzle with a couple of pieces gone. The line from the song zigzagged through my head.

Ethan looked around and back at me, his eyes searching and quizzical, and at first I was afraid that I'd sung out loud.

"How did she make it over?" he asked, his voice catching in his throat, as though every time he looked at me he wanted to sob or cough. "This wall is pretty high and she's awfully short."

I responded first to his use of the present tense for Karoline, then to the curiosity and suspicion that infused his words. My heart ached. My eyes filled with tears. Self-preservation and fear prevented me from breaking down and telling him everything. I forced my Ice Queen voice to reply.

"How would I know that?"

"Thought you might've guessed. Or maybe there was a step stool here and you moved it. Just one of those automatic things, ya know?"

His deep blue eyes looked straight into mine. Where mine were icy and swirled with layers and depths that hid my feelings, his were soft and bright and forthright. He would never be able to hide any emotion. I don't know if that was the moment when I realized he was achingly, strikingly ugly. So ugly that the attractive parts of him—his eyes, his large lanky frame and thick curly, salt-and-pepper hair—acted as lightning rods of appreciation.

I do know that Officer Peters scarcely registered with me, so perhaps it wasn't until later that I noticed the juxtaposition of Ethan's appearance.

He is tall and wide-shouldered, narrow at the waist. But his nose is crooked, slightly off-center. His face is hound dog shape. His ragged thick eyebrows furl unexpectedly. His hair, a deep rich black with strands of silver, often pokes straight up from his head. Ironically, he has the same problem that I have. People pay unwanted attention, albeit for different reasons.

"No. No step stool. No guess. I really don't know."

I continued to stand by the wall, but my knees were suddenly very weak. I could feel my body shake from the inside. My face must have gone very pale, because Ethan was immediately at my side. He held my elbow and directed me into the apartment.

When I shied away from the couch, he left me sitting at the dining room table with a cold glass of water nearby. I put my head down on the cool surface, my mind swirling. The voices of several dozen dinner parties echoed from the wood.

"Religion has always caused more problems than it has solved," Daniel declared, swirling his wine and taking a large swallow. "Think of all the warfare that would have been avoided without religion."

"You're just quoting John Lennon," Vicki sniped at him, a good-natured grin on her face.

"No, seriously, think about it. Starting with the Crusades and up to the present, most wars have been among people of different religious beliefs."

"I think war is just built into the male psyche," I said.

I was being half playful, half serious, but the four men sitting around the table sat up straighter in their chairs and stared at me.

"I really believe you'll find any excuse to pummel one another. Look at male children. They start off right from birth wanting to play guns and whack each other over the head. Religion doesn't really have anything to do with it."

"Give me a break!" Joseph guffawed. "Males are no more warlike than females. Maybe we're a little more physical, but women find devious ways to annihilate one another. Females are just as likely to set off a nuclear device as males. They might not be as likely to go into all out hand-to-hand combat, but they would find a way to express their aggressive side if males weren't there to do it for them."

"But getting back to religion..."

And so the debates would rage. Half or even wholly drunk, we'd express opinions and ideas that had little to do with fact and more to do with our own experiences or grievances. It was usually Karoline who would take us off into a different direction each time.

"Only people in our positions can afford to debate whether religion causes war. The poor and the disenfranchised are usually the ones who suffer from it or are entered into it through no other choice. We can sit back all we want and fling our words around..."

Off we would go into what the world should be doing about the poor. It didn't matter whether or not we knew much about the topic. Any thought or comment was savored like a candy, tossed around in our mouths and then flung back out in a different shape. Sometimes we'd get loud and obnoxious or even allow the debate to deteriorate into an argument. But Karoline would always put us back on track. She'd remind us that the debate was about the issue, not the people involved. She'd offer an opinion based on fact or a recent news item that would put the argument in perspective. Properly chastised, we would sail off into intellectual sparring once more.

Giulio also referred to her as 'capo tosta'—hard headed. Her arguments were always so fierce and strong.

If only he had seen how her head had hit the pavement, splitting open like an egg, spewing red and white and grey yolk all over the sidewalk.

It seemed to me at that moment, my head bent over the table, that Karoline was always the anchor. I would surely sail off course forever now. Especially because I was solely responsible for Karoline not being here any longer. I was unable at that moment to see how I could have done it, to understand the reasons behind that savage unthinking act that had resulted in her crumpled body lying beneath our balcony. I really had proven to have the dangerous soul that Karoline had protected me from. If only she'd protected herself instead.

Ethan came back into the room and gently touched my hand. It was a gesture that I found reassuring, yet I jumped back from the heat of his skin and glared at him.

"I didn't mean to startle you, Ms. Williams. I just want you to know that we are finished here for the moment. I'll be down at the...with your friend. Officer Peters has some questions for you and then I'll be back upstairs. Are you comfortable enough?"

The compassion in his voice threatened to break the dam of my emotion. I wanted to fling myself at his feet and sob and beg forgiveness. Instead I merely nodded, keeping the tears away by biting the inside of my lip. Immediately, the little blond policewoman was there, her pen at the ready. I allowed my fear to flow into resentment of this officious person at my side and her annoying questions. A hot rush of adrenaline caused my limbs to tremble.

I pressed my fingers against my thighs under the table and tried to concentrate. *Karoline's full name; Karolina Maria Mikulski. Date of birth; June 30, 1950. She'll be thirty-two next month, I almost said. We're getting to be old maids, Karoline would have joked, but she would have meant it, too, being proud of our single state. A woman of the eighties thinks ba-king and fuc-king are two cities in China... Her next of kin? Oh God, what will Halina do? Halina Mikulski, her mom, she lives in Bell Canyon. No, her dad died years ago. Yes, she has two older brothers. How will Halina be told? Oh my God, what will she do when the police come to her door? Religion? Really, why do you need to know that? Karoline was agnostic. Her mom would say Roman Catholic, I suppose. Height, weight. She works for Stewart and Stewart. She's a legal secretary, an executive assistant for Daniel Stewart. She's very smart. What will Daniel do without her? What will I do without her?*

To this day I have no idea how I responded to Officer Peters, whether I said all of this aloud or whether I kept most of it to myself. I must have given a few right answers because somewhere in the middle of the interrogation, Halina was on the telephone. She sobbed and asked me over and over how this could have happened.

Officer Peters still sat at the table writing in her notebook. She attempted to appear as though she were not listening.

"She was so happy. Wasn't she happy, Anne?"

My head filled with a cloud of anger and guilt. I hated Halina at that moment. I hated that she had known me since I was a gangly little girl. Halina thought she understood me better than my own mother did. I hated that Halina seemed to always wish that I had been her daughter and not Karoline. Of course Karoline was happy, I wanted to shout at her. Of course she hadn't wanted to actually die. She didn't choose death. I chose that for her.

Naturally I shouted none of these things. Instead I gave sympathetic responses. Halina continued her litany for what seemed an eternity. Was it an accident maybe? She couldn't have jumped on purpose, could she have? If she did, was Karoline so unhappy? Did I not see any signs? Why didn't she, her own mother, see any signs? Where was I when it happened?

I provided reassuring answers. Words that Halina would expect and need. I couldn't remove her sorrow, though I fervently wished I could turn back time and put Karoline on the telephone.

I recall Officer Peters' look when I replaced the receiver. I gathered the Ice Queen within me and forced her to give the bitchiest response to those raised eyebrows.

"That was not very pleasant," I told the officer. "I certainly don't appreciate your being here and listening to every word."

I began to rub the table top, noticing some spots like fingerprints on the shiny wood. I got up and looked under the sink for the cleaner and polishing cloth. *Karoline will not be happy about this*, I thought, wondering who the hell had spilled something. I shook a little of the liquid cleaner onto the surface and began to rub it in large, light circles. Just the way Karoline demands it. "You can't be rough and sloppy when you want to clean something properly, especially wood," she always says. "You have to concentrate even though it is a menial task that doesn't engage certain parts of your brain…"

"Ma'am," the police officer said, quite loudly, staring at me oddly.

I remember that I smiled at her. I think I said something like, "Yes? Is there anything further that I can do for you?" I do know that I made my voice purr, as though I were talking to a particularly dense client or some ignorant man whose eyes were permanently glued to my tits.

I had to maintain the anger. It was the only way I could survive. Inside, my heart knocked on the door of reality, threatening to open everything to the world. I tamped down the tears. Stomped on the terror. I couldn't call Karoline to help me, speak for me, or tell me what to do. That side of Karoline had been lost to me for some time. Now she was gone forever.

Only Ice Queen Anne, the one I had nurtured for those times of self-preservation, could be with me now. No matter how ugly or horrid she sounded, she was here.

Officer Peters asked the same question that Halina had posed. "How do you know it was suicide, not a terrible accident?"

I stared at her, trying to work out the scenario I had rehearsed, but somehow the words would not come. Finally I said the only thing I could muster.

"Well it's not like we put Christmas lights out on our balcony."

The woman appeared to be confused and who could blame her?

"In other words, it's not as if she would be up on the balcony wall taking down Christmas lights or anything."

Again there was a pause as she scribbled in her notebook.

"I understand," she answered.

"Do you? And besides, am I the one who said the word suicide?"

"As a matter of fact, the call to 911 stated that someone had just committed suicide."

"What other conclusion could there be? As I said, I don't think Karoline was trying to put up decorations in May and I sure as hell know she wasn't taking any down."

"Where were you when the accident or suicide happened?"

This time, I tried not to pause. "I was asleep in bed, where most people are at that time of night."

"What awakened you?"

Rehearsed this! You can do it!

"I really don't know. I'm a fairly light sleeper and I think it was some noise. Just something out of place. I—I woke up suddenly, unable to define what awakened me. So I got up and looked in Karoline's bedroom but she wasn't there. That surprised me. So I kept going into the living room and I saw that the balcony doors were wide open. So I went out onto the balcony and she wasn't there, but I just—I can't tell you why, I just looked over and then I saw..." ...*a jigsaw puzzle with a couple of pieces gone...* "So I called 911."

Other than too many 'so's' and 'justs', I thought I delivered the speech quite well. It wasn't terribly logical, which was why they would probably buy it.

"You didn't go down to see if she had survived?"

I wanted to claw at her eyes, those big green eyes staring at me so directly, pen poised in the air, smug little mouth forming a judgmental line. I wanted to say, "No you fucking bitch, of course not, I knew she was dead. Did you ever see what someone looks like when they've fallen seven stories and landed on their head on a paved sidewalk?"

At the same time I wanted to faint at her feet, break into sobs, tell her I loved Karoline and please, please, please bring her back.

"No," I answered and was disconcerted to feel my eyes dart away from hers. Deliberately, I looked her straight on as I embellished.

"I was so shocked I couldn't even stand. I barely made it to the telephone."

I stopped polishing the table, stood up to put the cleansers away, wiped my hands on the finger towel, and sat down again.

"Is there anything further, officer? I have to call a great many people..."

"Just one. Did Ms. Mikulski appear to be depressed? Do you think there was a reason for the suicide?"

"That's two questions," I wanted to say, but I answered carefully. "She...lately, Karoline has had a rather bleak take on life. I don't know if you call that depressed or realistic."

"So you would categorize her as unhappy?"

I hesitated. Unhappy enough to want to die? No, definitely not.

"I guess. You don't usually jump over a balcony if you're pleased with your life."

Peters jerked with shock at my response and I knew Ice Queen had gone too far. My head buzzed with the voices of fear, regret, grief and self-pity. I hated myself for those last words to Karoline. I wanted to spread loathing all over this room so I wouldn't have to face the reality of the police in our apartment. Of the absence of my best friend.

"Detective Byrne will be back up to speak with you as soon as he's finished at the scene," was all Officer Peters offered. "There may be further questions that he will want to ask. Plus we will need a written statement quite soon. Do you have someone that you would like us to call for you?"

Yes, I felt like saying. "Call Karoline. Tell her to come back." That I didn't mean it. I didn't realize that it would be forever, that I couldn't do it over again and this time, do it differently. I wanted to stand up and tower over the officer. I'd show her how my nipples stood straight forward because my body felt like ice in this skimpy gown that I was too stunned to replace with something more dignified and warm. I'd pretend I was haughty and confident. I'd pretend it wasn't Karoline who had kept me on course.

But I knew that my knees were soft. The muscles in my thighs trembled every time I got up. I was afraid that the next attempt might plunge me forward onto the floor. What I did say was that I was perfectly fine. There was no need to call anybody. I was the one who had to do some calling if she would just leave.

It seems to me that shortly thereafter—though the sequence of events may be totally skewed in my memory—Detective Byrne reappeared to tell us that 'the body' had been removed. He went into some details that I have never been able to remember. I'm pretty sure that he even sat down at the table again with the officer and me, because I have a remembrance of warmth and heat and the thrill of male proximity.

I began to realize that Karoline was not there on the sidewalk any more. In fact she was nowhere. I put my head on the cool surface of the table once more. Listening with half an ear to the officers' inane details, I heard other voices again, this time our little group of philosophers discussing our favorite topic.

"So what about sex then? We used to believe in free love. But what does that mean?"

Daniel was more than half drunk. He clutched the glass of red wine and swirled it thoughtfully. The ruby legs flowed up and down the transparent sides, glistening in the light over the dining room table. Our favorite topic was not simply about sex. It was an exploration of the last two decades, the ones when hope and innocence intermingled with drugs to make us believe we'd change the world.

"Well, I personally define sex as any contact with another body in order to pleasure yourself," Vicki said. "Free love is any pleasure you don't have to pay for."

Raucous laughter ensued.

"But love ought to mean some kind of relationship," I pointed out, feeling high and pleasant and argumentative.

I knew everything at that moment. I was complacent and ignorant, mistakenly enjoying a life I thought was real.

"Free love is a misnomer. Maybe we should call it getting your rocks off without entanglement. I bet everyone would understand what that meant."

"Most men would." Vicki's lips were covered in the foam from her latest margarita.

The males laughed as though they wanted to confirm her indictment.

"Hey, most people would. I don't agree that men and women necessarily see sex in different ways. That's just societal expectation. Like calling sex 'love' instead of just plain sex. Women are supposed to want romance and marriage and babies, not an amusing romp in the sack. So that's what we pretend to believe," I shot back with the adrenalin that comes from depressing one's usual inhibitions.

Though I noticed Karoline's quizzical stare and unusual silence, I kept going.

"I for one have never believed that sex is just about reproduction. In that scenario, women are merely receptacles and incubators. I really think sex is essentially a very good time."

In response the men laughed again. Giulio gave my hand a squeeze.

"Don't say that too loudly," he said with a huge smile. "You're far too gorgeous. You'll be having a lot of fun every night if you don't watch out."

I don't know if anyone else heard Karoline, but I did. She sat at my right and whispered in my ear. I assumed she was teasing me. "Not much different from now."

"We're getting off topic," Daniel complained. "We're not discussing Anne's sex life in particular, although I probably shouldn't object. The original question was, what has happened to free love? How do we define sexual relations? Are the eighties bringing in a new prudishness?"

"I think we should define sexual intercourse, not relations. 'Relations' gives it a confusing element. People think of the word in terms of relatives or relationships. But sexual intercourse is different," Joseph proclaimed.

THE CASE OF THE MISSING BRAIN

Review copy

Compliments

of

Erika Chase

(Linda Wiken)

"Is it really?" Karoline asked. "I think intercourse is just as confusing."

The group began to laugh here, but she cut them off.

"Do we mean any mode of relating or connecting when we talk about intercourse? I mean, since we're having oral dialogue here about sex, does that qualify, too? The word means contact, interaction, communication. Doesn't that cover all the senses, including hearing?"

"Well, I like it," Daniel answered. "That means we can have sex any time we want. Which means love is definitely free, since it's in the air. Clearly we don't need to fear the eighties after all."

And so the discussion went on, philosophical, erotic, almost clinical in turns. Again, it would be Karoline who would bring an end to one angle and start us off in another direction. She always had quotes and references stored in her head. She made good use of silence and appeared to wait until we'd ventured into ridiculousness before she offered her sane, researched opinions.

When I reflected on the discussions the morning after or weeks later, I wondered if she did this on purpose. Was her mission to show us how stupid we were? Guilt would banish that thought from my mind.

Detective Byrne asked me suddenly if I was okay. I raised my head from the table, which was no longer polished or gleaming, but steamed and greasy from forehead and finger patterns. This time his gaze pored over my scantily dressed body, while I stared at the oddly chiseled features of his face. I wondered idly if he was any good in bed. There must be something to redeem that face.

I was too numb to actually feel anything though. I certainly don't remember any more interrogation. He reiterated what his companion had told me. They'd need to ask more questions very soon. I'd have to sign a deposition of my information. Would I mind if they searched her room once more before they left? Was there anyone they could call to come over and be with me?

After the police officers departed, I heard, for the first time, a deep and absolute silence in our apartment. The utter complete lack of Karoline. Even when she was quiet I was aware of her aura, her smile, her smell. For most of our years together the apartment had been filled with music.

We were eclectic in our tastes. Any decade, any style, as long as we liked the words and could dance to the music. We loved to sing along, boogie through the hallway and the living room, do the dishes to the rhythms that boomed from our stereo.

Now all of that was gone. Along with her physical presence, Karoline took the music with her. A ringing started in my ears that replaced the swish of her movements, the creak of her bed, the slam of her doors. The rumble of her pen across the endless pages that she had written. Letters that I discovered later. Letters that destroyed us.

I returned to rubbing the table, which had once again been contaminated with the officer's notebook and the dots of my saliva as I lay breathing and thinking on the wooden surface. I spread the cleaner further and further over the wood. Around the Murano cut glass bowl that we'd picked up in Venice. Around the gold-plated candle sticks that we'd bought in Florence. Around the tray with the salt and pepper shakers we'd brought home from Milan. Karoline would expect me to use the gold revitalizer on the candlesticks by next week. We'd bought it specifically for that purpose and we made sure it was done on schedule. The salt and pepper shakers were full. From now on I would have to remember all on my own to dust everything.

Our jobs not only had prestige but paid well, too. We had lived relatively frugally but we travelled high and often.

I thought about that fateful trip to Italy, the days we had with Giulio and the days we subsequently lost.

Dear Diary,
I love her, but I have never met anyone so shallow. That goes for the Eye-tie, too. They're silly, lazy, too easily satisfied. I am always the one who has to do everything, make things happen. They plan and organize but they don't follow through, so what's the use?

CHAPTER 4

"Buon giorno, signorina! Desidera le valige?"
"Ciao, Marco!! Come stai?"

Giulio's arms circled the other man, who responded with kisses. His face showed every bit of his unqualified joy in his cousin's presence.

Giulio's eyes glistened with tears as he turned to us and waved at a small group of smiling people. "Ti la presento mia famiglia."

Everyone beamed and shook hands and picked up our luggage, laughing loudly as they led us to their cars.

What followed was a round of visits to eat and drink wine. Karoline was much better at picking up the nuances of language than I was or ever will be. She understood what everyone said despite the unfamiliarity of the words. I was left to nod and smile as I met 'la zia, lo zio, il cugino, la cugina, il nonno, la nonna'. On and on it went, house to house, dining room to dining room. They devoured huge pots of pasta and enormous bottles of red wine everywhere we went. Very quickly, after being squeezed between short, round people on couches for photo after photo, my mouth was tight and tense. I found it difficult to smile.

Karoline, however, had never seemed so alive. She laughed and talked and waved and hugged in a manner that I'd hardly ever seen and certainly have not seen since. My little dumpy friend who saw herself as homely and plain was suddenly the star of this group of homely dumpy people who didn't seem to mind an extra pound or two around the waist, as long as it meant you liked to 'mange'.

With me they were overly polite and solicitous. The women didn't seem to register my presence while the men rarely raised their eyes to my face. Sometimes I caught them elbowing each other as they looked in my direction. The women did this surreptitiously while the men giggled openly even in Giulio's presence. Once I saw my friend's face go red. He appeared to give his Zio Alfonso a mini lecture, which Alfonso completely forgot the next time he was face to face with my breasts.

Karoline was the center of attention. For once I felt quite ignored and was, I must say, very content with that. My major problem was that I had become completely bored with family visits. I could have stayed home and done the same thing. I took to walking up and down the beaches. I poked in shops, ferreting out all the tourist attractions that each little Marina or Alta had to offer. In Silvi, a beautiful little town by the Adriatic Sea, Giulio finally noticed my boredom. He assigned his cugino Paolo to take me up the mountain to Silvi Alta, where some beautiful little churches could be toured and lovely vistas could be photographed.

At first, the only thing I noticed about Paolo was that he was much shorter than me. As I walked along to the car, I could see the top of his head. I was suddenly embarrassed that I had worn the red shoes with stiletto heels. His hair looked wavy, clean and soft, as though begging fingers to trail through it.

Just as this thought crossed my mind he looked up and smiled a white, inviting smile. His deep brown eyes sparkled with energy and sensuality. I stumbled and he caught me with a firm grip on my elbow.

The energy in the car after that was difficult to ignore. As though to distract us both, Paolo kept up a running commentary in his lilting if limited English. He described the medieval village to which this winding pathway led.

"You see the wall, here, here," and he pointed to the stone border that hugged the road, "that is how the old town is, you see. It is like a...like a crown on the hill. The stones are like the jewels all around it. But you see it is not for the decoration but for protection in those days. It is very high up this mountain. You will see."

I was trying very hard to see, as he kept repeating the phrase, but all I really noticed were the hard muscles in his bare arms, the soft black hairs curled against his brown skin.

"From up there, you will smell the salt of the ocean," he said, his voice soft and caressing, "because the breeze, it always carries the sea to the mountain."

But all I could smell was his aftershave, his slight perspiration and a sexual musk that had nothing to do with the ocean.

When the little car, somewhat protesting the final slopes, had finally made its way within sight of the village, I was gratefully distracted by its charm. Beautiful arches of stone gave way to small rows of homes dotted with colorful flowers and trailing vines. On nearly every corner one could enter a dark, hushed church and savor its art and history. We walked all around on the flat cobblestones, soaking in the atmosphere.

Paolo stopped and spoke with several people, introducing me to some. I actually nodded and smiled and said, "Buon giorno," trying my best to trill the r's and not sound quite so foreign. Every one of the villagers grinned and shook my hand, some toothless and wrinkled, some young and contemporary. The vigor in the little place was seductively friendly and happy. I snapped dozens of pictures with what I thought was artistic abandon.

In the early afternoon, when the sun was extremely hot on my foolishly bare head and my idiotically clad feet were on fire, we stopped in a café for lunch. Paolo seemed to know the owner. He indulged in a short conversation with the host and hostess who glanced over at me once in a while. Finally, the woman smiled slightly and showed us to a table with an astonishing view.

Slightly elevated, the restaurant provided a vista of the hills on one side and the ocean on the other. The sun blazed above the canopy and glinted on the green and blue patches of the scenery. Inside the café, people gathered around glasses of wine or beer and mounds of delicious food. All about us the stores and streets had gone quiet for lunch followed by siesta.

Paolo at first kept up his running commentary on the people or the grape varieties or the food, all the while his eyes on mine. He pointed out historic sites that could be seen around the valley from this vantage point. He asked questions about the United States and our life there, which I answered in as little detail as possible.

As the afternoon progressed, the small line of sweat across my upper lip was not from the heat of the day. My entire body was electric with the nearness of him. I could feel darts of excitement run from my breasts to my inner thighs to my toes. I tried very hard to focus on his words but all I could hear was the rhythm of his voice. All I could see was the plumpness of his mouth as he formed words or as his tongue spread over his lips to lick away a drop of red wine.

The hostess continued to serve us carafes of wine until the sun began to make its way over the highest hill towering to the left of where we sat. My face was flushed with the wine and the desire coursing through my body. It seemed that there was no one else here but us.

When I leaned over and brushed my mouth across his soft thick lips, the electricity of his touch radiated to every part of me. I shuddered with want. I was completely flesh. No thought other than having him could penetrate my brain. I followed that touch with a passionate kiss. My tongue probed the warmth of his mouth. I felt him shiver with excitement. He pulled back very quickly, his hand holding only my finger, as though afraid he might burn himself on my desire.

He whispered, "Andiamo," in his soft musical voice.

Suddenly I noticed that the village had become alive again, hours ago perhaps. The stores and streets bustled with people once again. The hostess stood there with the bill, her face dark and cold. I barely registered the fact that her eyes were thunderous. What's more, I don't think I would have cared if I had.

I followed Paolo out of the café, my hand tucked in his as he led the way. I barely noticed the narrow streets or the people as we made our way, silently, back to his little car. Once there he folded me into the passenger seat and climbed hastily into the driver's side. Only the sound of our breathing betrayed the urgency of our departure, for he was careful as he wound the car down the steep road.

I closed my eyes and relished the feeling of coveting him, of the sexual vibrations that sang in my groin, of the tingling in my breasts that made my nipples press against my blouse. By the time he parked the car in a small clump of trees, I was wet and scarcely able to breathe.

Once again I followed him. He grabbed a blanket from his trunk and led me to a little clearing. Though the temperature was no longer sweltering, there was no wind and the evening was warm. My desire kept my skin hot to the touch. He laid me down on the blanket and began to kiss my neck while he undid the buttons of my top. I stroked the back of his head, tangled my fingers through his soft hair, traced the outline of his back and shoulders through his silky shirt. He gently released my breasts and began to lick and suck them, his tongue supple and wet. The thrill rocketed through me, causing me to moan and begin undoing his belt.

Once unconstrained, his penis was large, thick and honeyed. Moaning, I moved my hand up and down on his hardness while he lifted my skirt and began to play his fingers inside my wetness. I could feel the spasms as I responded with orgasmic tremors. I was transported somewhere else when voices suddenly infiltrated the fog of pleasure.

Drunkenly, I lifted my head as the faces began to appear more distinctly before my misted eyes. They were very close, standing just at the edge of the clearing. They certainly would have an unobstructed view of my companion's hairy curved ass as he bent over to pleasure me. I had to shake him and point over his shoulder to get his attention.

Once he looked in the right direction, Paolo scrabbled to his feet. His penis became limp and ridiculous in the fading light. I pulled my legs up. I threw my skirt over my nakedness, unaware that my breasts continued to shine in the moonlight. There stood the host and hostess from the café. Their arms literally held up a young woman who had dissolved in tears.

A huge roar of Italian resounded in my ears as I pulled my panties up. I straightened my skirt and quickly readjusted my bra once I saw that my breasts were in full sight of the entire clan. At my side, Paolo had swiftly pulled up his pants and was redoing his belt buckle. All the while he roared back in his language at the same volume.

I brushed the grass and bits of twigs from my clothing and hair. I began to walk toward the little car, leaving the foursome to scream at one another. Still dazed from the ferocity of our encounter and the rush of adrenalin that left my heart pounding, I stood and stared off into the darkness. The voices behind me intruded on a soft and luxurious country night.

Before I knew it, the host from the restaurant, a rather large, dark man, silent and grim, had climbed into the driver's seat of the car. He gestured at me to join him via the passenger side. Chastened, I did as I was told. I watched as Paolo followed the younger and older woman—in the streetlights I could see that they were obviously mother and daughter—to another car. Evidently abandoned hastily, it waited crookedly at the side of the road. Paolo climbed into the back while his accusers took up the front.

The older woman sprayed gravel noisily onto the hood of Paolo's car as she raced away up the hill. My driver turned the wheel and sped at a frightening speed back down the mountain, his lips set in a harsh line. Even if he could have understood me and I him, I knew he would not speak.

So I sat in stunned silence, feeling rather like a child who'd been caught in an evil deed. I tried to work out what had happened. Obviously the younger woman was Paolo's girlfriend. I wondered why he'd taken me to the café in the first place. Perhaps he hadn't planned our rendezvous at all, but had succumbed to the same power that I'd felt.

I was never a person who felt that sex was any different from sharing a scrumptious meal with someone. I didn't have any qualms about having a sexual encounter with a person I'd never see again. I could remain friendly with a man with whom I've had a torrid affair. In those days I assumed the only protection you needed was birth control, though I changed that stance over the years.

Before Ethan, I'd never really been in love. I still have no illusions about fidelity. I don't know if I can actually do it for a sustained period of time.

It was blatantly obvious to me that night, however, that the poor young woman, the daughter of those café owners, certainly believed in fidelity. She was devastated by Paolo's indiscretion. Of course that caused me to feel a certain amount of guilt. Especially when we reached Giulio's uncle's home. The grim father-of-the-injured-party leapt from the car, leaving me to fumble out of the passenger side. He raced into the house where he promptly, with lots of shouting and hand waving, told the entire story, round hirsute ass and all.

When I reached the doorstep, I could see their faces. The whole group of aunts and uncles and cousins turned to look in horror at me. I imagined what I looked like. Disheveled, flushed, clothes askew, I was unable to hide a glimmer of sexual aura. In other words I was a Western Tramp, a putana. Giulio's eyes, when I caught his glance, were the worst. He signaled disappointment, shame and disgust in such poignancy that all at once I was overflowing with remorse.

"I didn't know…" I tried to say, but was prevented from finishing by Karoline's firm hand on my elbow.

She steered me back outside away from the shocked hush of Giulio's relatives and the continued flow of invective from the aggrieved café owner.

Karoline hurried me down the dusky pathway to a bench overlooking the ocean, a spot I would have reveled in at any other time. After we sat down, she grasped my hand and turned my face to look at her with firm fingers on my chin. "So tell," she said, and I did, though I left out the details of the sexual experience in question, afraid I would be too flowing in my description and therefore not at all contrite.

"I had no idea he was attached to anyone," I said in my defense. "He never mentioned a girlfriend."

"It's a fiancée. Apparently that little clearing is a secret rendezvous of theirs. So the parents are really upset. Not only is it obvious that Paolo is a cheat, but he's also been screwing his intended. I guess virginity is still revered around here. The wedding takes place next week, or at least it's supposed to."

She let go of my hand. "It's one of the major reasons we're here. Giulio is the best man. Or did you forget that part of the itinerary?"

I stared off across the water, listening to the soothing sound of the waves, wishing I could disappear. "I guess so. I thought we were going on a tour of Italy, not a family visit."

I know I sounded childish and selfish, which is in fact exactly the way I felt. Karoline, as always, was sympathetic.

"This really hasn't been what you expected, I know that. Maybe you and I should just go off on our own. Maybe very early tomorrow morning."

I gave her a sheepish smile. "Yes. Sneak out of town before dawn. I get your meaning. But you really don't have to come with me, you know. You are enjoying this immensely. I truly don't want to spoil it for you. I could join a tour or something. I honestly wouldn't mind. If I were on an organized group tour, I'd be safe so you wouldn't have to worry."

She looked at me as though actually considering the suggestion, but I realized quickly that she was making a decision. It was a choice. Her original, cherished friend Giulio or her other, in some ways more valued friend, Anne. In the end, the selection that she made ended her life.

As it turned out, we did leave before anyone was up the next morning. Giulio didn't come to say good-bye, although Karoline admitted later that he'd kissed and hugged her before she left. I was the one he didn't want to see. I had mixed emotions as we climbed aboard the bus to parts unknown. I was suffused with guilt only because I'd hurt Giulio. Certain that he would forgive me at some point, I found that I was not enormously sad. In fact, quite the opposite. I was thrilled to be free.

Karoline and I spent four weeks traveling through Italy. We made no plans, pre-booked nothing. Karoline had her own ideas about sightseeing. We never trod on the path of common tourists. We went south to the romantic Amalfi coast where we fell in love with Sorrento and Capri. From the cliff tops, we gazed out over the navy blue water, watched birds sail the winds in every direction, soaked in the salt air. We avoided the gift shops and instead traversed little winding alleys and roadways that led out to sheer drops. We marveled over dazzling stone cottages. We ate in quaint cafés that were tucked under trees or behind a house, away from mainstream scrutiny.

We went north to Florence and stood on bridges to gaze at the domes, steeples and baptisteries. Under Il Duomo's spell of green, peach and white angel carvings and gold tales of hope, I almost entered the hallowed ground, until Karoline reminded me that, throughout history, organized religion was responsible for too much war and death. It would have been unconscionable to appear to admire this monstrosity. We found little shops in the alleyways, far from the tourist marketplaces, with treasures made by hand from stone, marble or glass. We ate authentic Florentine meals, drank heavy dark wine and enjoyed the flow of Italian words and laughter all around us.

In Venice, just north of the Three Bridges, we discovered a square that was a young adult night scene. Surrounded by student residences on all sides, giant old red-bricked buildings with wrought iron Juliet balconies leaned with approval over the scene. We sang and danced with the locals, drank beer, ate panini and took a ride on someone's speed boat up the canal.

All the while, I assiduously took pictures of every step of our adventure. Our albums stand all dusty and ignored now. They had once proudly graced a coffee table and have been pawed through more times than I can count. Karoline and I look happy, excited, rested and young. We are together in most of the photos, arms around each other, laughing, pointing, posing. Neither of us had ever had so much fun.

I had three more lovers after Paolo, two native Italians and one transplanted German. These secrets I never shared with Karoline, though she must have known where I was. She never asked so I never told.

Nor did I ask her about the waiter she flirted with and who took her on a late-night stroll, nor about the boat's captain who seemed to spend a very long time with her in his cabin.

Dear Diary,
She thinks I don't know about most of the men she has fucked, but I know every single slimy one of them.

CHAPTER 5

In the clear light of hindsight, I can see that we had begun to simply avoid certain sides of our lives. We became reluctant to explore the enormous chasm of difference that existed in our two philosophies of life. I didn't believe that I had to be my fellow creatures' caretaker, while Karoline had a drive to help others and make their lives better. All that Karoline's philanthropic urge did was cause her guilt, as far as I could see, since she never really acted upon her desires other than giving a large percentage of her salary to charity. Which she promptly used for tax deductions.

When I look back now, I wonder if Giulio and I were her 'hard luck cases'. Perhaps she felt she was already dedicating her life to good. Without the burden of these two absurd friends, Karoline might have been a crusader, a nun or a leader in the war on poverty. A politician perhaps.

Sexuality was only one of the topics we began to avoid discussing intimately or privately. The topic still figured in debates with others, along with charity, politics and religion, but there ceased to be any sharing between the two of us. Those discussions would have come too close to placing our fractured relationship under a formidable microscope.

Since Karoline's death, I have polished the table to a sheen that resembles very old wood, even though the table is one that she and I bought new. It was the single most expensive piece of furniture either of us had ever purchased. At first it was a source of pride and excitement. This was where we ate either alone, together or with our friends. This was the focal point around which our heated debates took place. This was the displayer of our most prized souvenirs. This was the center of our life.

Karoline religiously kept it clean and polished. She dictated its care, as she did with the Turkish carpets and the other artifacts we brought home from our minstrel wanderings. Her obsession with keeping the souvenirs clean and polished was a good thing, I'd thought. I for one immediately abandoned them and would have sent them off to a closet, alone and neglected. Under Karoline's rigorous attention, the mementoes still looked new and I was appreciative. I could look at them and remember each step, each breathtaking view, every moment that we stood shoulder to shoulder gazing over a place or a building or a world wonder that I'd only read about in books.

Over the years I began to believe that those journeys were like the men in my life. I loved visiting them for the first time, feeling the newness of their surface, getting to know a little bit about how they came to be, intrigued by their mystery and mystique. Soon after that initial visit I would get bored, anxious to get on to the next world wonder. Already thinking about future possibilities and places to see even as I stood in their midst. Unlike the towers and ruins and statues, which appeared unmoved by my indifference, the men would often cry, beg or storm away angrily. Perhaps to them I too was an unfeeling relic. All of that changed with Karoline's murder and the advent of Ethan.

The day after Karoline died, Halina and my parents arrived unannounced on our doorstep. Still in my silk nightgown, my hair was frizzier than ever. My eyes red from lack of sleep. All I remember was the suffocation. The hugs, the housecoat thrown around me. The coffee pressed into my hand. The endless questions, the tears.

My mother is an enormous woman. Folded under her belly and boobs are layers of jiggling fat that swim underneath the sundresses she favors. Always colorful with prints, flowers or joyful patterns, she wears them in winter or summer. Her long hair—once dark black and now striped with grey—is usually tied in a bun at the back of her head. Her eyes are a startling combination of light and dark brown flecks. Wide and guileless, they give her face a beauty that distracts nearly everyone from her size.

Vera Williams fills up a room in more ways than one. Gregarious, loving and loud, she is the stereotype of a black mama. She loves to cook, entertain and wallow in other people's dramas. She is fond of retelling the story of her roots, the American slaves who came into Canada and married Indians. Vera, she would have us believe, was a Mohawk-African Princess. She treats me as though I were a trophy, sculpted to honor the roots of both royalties. I, in my hidden and secret self, am utterly ashamed of her flamboyant, in-your-face personality. She smothers me with adoration. Yet I am aware of a distance that keeps me from believing in her love as genuine.

Halina is the polar opposite to my mother. Tall, slim, polished, Halina is completely self-absorbed and couldn't stand her daughter for turning out to be short, homely and stocky like her father. Gordon Mikulski died very young, when their only girl was just a baby. Probably to get away from Halina.

Neither Karoline nor I really talked about it, as per usual, but we both acknowledged somewhere deep inside us that we didn't have normal mother-daughter relationships. When our two mothers were in the same room, no one else could speak. Their words flowed over one another like ocean waves, now and then smashing up against each other in a roaring crescendo. In their life and in their conversation, everything was about them, from their point of view. They allowed no intrusion from others.

My mother isn't actually *self*-absorbed. She is merely consumed with my father. She didn't really have anything left for me or my sister except her native traditions, which she dishes out to everyone in general. Thus I, like Karoline, never felt special or unconditionally loved. We were both pretty much ignored.

My father is tall, slim and extremely good-looking. I never could understand his obsession with Vera, but he lives that old adage, there is no accounting for taste. When he is near her, he cannot keep his hands off her. They always hug, kiss or touch in some way. Originally my bedroom was next to theirs, until I grew older and figured out what the nightly bumps, moans and thrashes meant. I convinced my father to make me a room in the attic and slept far more soundly after that.

My sister Elizabeth is very similar to our mother, though she would probably not approve of that statement. She's more like our dad physically but she has the same exuberant personality as our mother. She's the consummate hostess. A store greeter. A woman whose phony sweetness feels like cardboard dripping with syrup.

The dichotomy of our half-and-half appearance doesn't bother her. Ten years older than I, Elizabeth is much lighter skinned. When our parents moved to the U.S., Elizabeth was old enough to choose, so she stayed behind. Later she married a black man and had three children who nearly cover the whole spectrum of skin colors. She appears to be comfortable in both worlds. Perhaps that's the Canadian way. Certainly my mother proclaims that her birth country is as perfect as her first daughter.

With my swarthiness I am often, ironically, mistaken for Italian. By the time I moved with Karoline and Giulio to Los Angeles, I'd gotten over my shame and confusion about my own heritage. I learned to simply ignore it.

All these years later, I can see what lured my father to move from our small Canadian enclave to the United States, even notwithstanding the financial considerations. The place we landed in was fairy-tale perfect, at least from the outside.

Bell Canyon is ringed by hills dotted with lush native plants and rounded boulders. Huge sycamore and oak trees cover the area. Their enormous limbs straddle the roadways and hillsides like giant muscular legs.

Bell Creek, a lovely, peaceful blue stream, winds its way through the community. It's known as a 'horse community'. Most of the homes are enormous. A lot of them include stables and paddocks for the horses.

Originally our house belonged to my grandparents. They bequeathed it to their only son with the stipulation that he live in it. Ten years after their death he would be allowed to sell, but that time frame has come and gone and my mother and father are still in the Canyon. From their house my parents have a breath-taking view into the valley. The place isn't one of the larger residences, nor a part of the gated upper class, but it is huge in comparison to our home in Canada. So spectacular are the sunrises and sunsets that they are causes for celebration each and every day.

When Karoline, Giulio and I trekked through the Canyon Trail, we encountered deer, hawks, squirrels, foxes, woodpeckers and quail. We'd often spied coyotes from afar, but we'd been taught not to investigate. The area is a stunning combination of modern sophistication and country wild.

The Mikulskis did live in one of the more ostentatious houses. A white southern-style mansion with a wide porch that stretched all the way around the front and side, the place sported big, airy rooms with tons of windows. The hardwood was always shiny. A wooden staircase, the same deep brown color as the tree in front, wound its way from the entry to the landing and then up to the floor with all the bedrooms.

It was a romantic and mysterious house to little girls. Outside Karoline's window the slanted roofline of the porch led to one of the fat white columns gracing the outside. When Karoline first talked me into sliding down it in the middle of the night, I felt I'd desecrated something holy.

Behind the house an old barn that contained empty horse stalls served as a storage and tool shed. It had one magnificent secret. A closed-in loft became our clubhouse. Even Karoline's two older brothers never discovered the hidden door to our hideout.

Despite its stuffy heat and cobwebs, Giulio and Karoline and I spent hours in that attic. We read, played games, made up jokes and tried cigarettes. The sweat poured down our faces in summer. We shivered inside our jackets in winter. We told stories of the places we would go and the things we would do.

Once, we went through a spurt of shoplifting, snatching whatever was at hand when the storekeeper's back was turned. We hoarded our stolen wares in the leftover hay inside our loft. We blatantly styled ourselves as The Young Thieves Association, or the YTA, but we were neither brave enough to enjoy our plunder nor smart enough to steal something useful in the first place.

For a very long time I thought that the Mikulskis were rich and that Halina was cool compared to my mother. I thought of Vera's tight curls, her plain brown face, her stubby fingers and wide girth and I decided Halina was a movie star. She paid a great deal of attention to me, too, which naturally added to my childish worship. She always gave me tips on how to wear my hair, the kind of lipstick and make-up I could use once I was old enough and whether or not a blouse looked good on me. With enormous effort I learned enough Polish to please her.

Halina played our music. She even smoked, painted her nails and wore bright red lipstick. She drank something that made her breath smell sharp. Her accent was exotic. In her kitchen we danced and sang to Elvis, the Beatles and every other popular fifties and sixties band. Karoline and her mother were happy together while we wiggled our butts and hollered the lyrics. As the attention Halina lavished on me splashed over onto Karoline during our frenzied dancing, my friend floated. Later our own apartment sang with the same joy, often fueled by the same alcohol stimulus, even the same tunes.

I never could understand why Karoline completely ignored her mother at any other time. It only occurred to me later on that it was actually the other way around.

Karoline's brothers were big hulking shadows who grunted and ate their meals sloppily and speedily. They didn't go to school once they turned sixteen but joined their father in whatever mysterious work he did. When they were in the kitchen, however, they invariably picked Halina up in their huge arms and swung her around. She would giggle and flush the same way I did whenever a boy I liked said hi.

I didn't remember Karoline's brothers ever paying attention to me or to their sister. Halina was the center of their world. When they grew up they married women who looked exactly like her. In fact, the wives were younger duplicates of Halina in personality as well. To focus and keep the attention on themselves they moved their husbands hundreds of miles away from their mother-in-law.

Much later I discovered that the house was rented and that the money source was Halina's mother. Unfortunately, Karoline's Boosha was a traditionalist. In her will she gave all of her estate to her sons, creating a rift between Halina and her brothers that, as far as I know, never went away.

Imagine how angry Halina would be if she knew that Karoline had received a significant sum from Boosha just before the old woman died. An amount that paid off the mortgage on the apartment.

Bell Canyon, the town where we grew up, prided itself in being far enough from L.A. to be considered innocent yet close enough to be sophisticated. The population was largely upper class. Many made their livings in the city, especially in the film industry, but absconded to the boonies to have their children or hide from their fans. As a result, there were a great many families who, during the week, were husband-and-fatherless, and some wife-and-motherless, because they worked in Smog City while the rest of the family stayed at home.

My father, Ian Williams, was born in the States, but he'd been brought to Canada so young he didn't remember Bell Canyon. Like Elizabeth, he'd been old enough to choose not to leave when Granny and Gramps moved back to the U.S.

I met my paternal grandparents exactly four times that I can remember. Suddenly they were both dead of cancer a few months apart and our lives were irrevocably changed.

Dad, the only child, inherited his parents' house and a monthly stipend from their investments that could keep our family in an elevated status. In Canada my father was a teacher and my mother was a nurse. Neither profession was well paid in the United States.

When we were transplanted to the U.S. to take advantage of the inheritance, my mother and I were, in the beginning, very unhappy. My mother was unable to work as a nurse. My father, with his dual citizenship, landed a plum job in L.A. teaching at a college, so he was gone all week like many of the others. And we missed Elizabeth's calm presence.

At nineteen she was already grown up in her mind—and mine—and engaged to her high school sweetheart. Both my mother and I grieved for her every day until Karoline became a fixture in our household.

Suddenly Mom and I replaced Elizabeth as easily as changing our clothes. My sister was such an independent, self-confident creature, whereas Karoline was warm and lively and fiercely connected. She nosed around our house like a pet, doing a loyal bulldog impression with her beady eyes and protruding teeth. She had an interest in the minutia of daily living that was contagious. Karoline was confident in her intelligence, in her ability to know or discover the answer to every question.

In our youth and up to the incidents over this past year, I worshipped Karoline. I thought of her as the smartest person on the planet. When our relationship disintegrated I realized that I had never told her how much I admired her. Now I never can.

By the time Halina and my parents arrived, Karoline's mother had the funeral already planned. The casket chosen. The cemetery in Bell Canyon would provide the space for my friend's new residence. Halina must know how much her daughter would have hated living forever back in that boring little town.

Halina put Karoline away in shame and horror. Shame that she had committed this selfish act of suicide. Horror at the idea of jumping from a balcony. So ignominious. Thoroughly thoughtless. At least she could have taken pills. A far less messy result, easier to explain to the neighbors. Or Karoline could simply have gone home and buried herself under Halina's grasp. At last the ugly little duckling had done something worthy of Halina's attention, even if it continued a misperception of Karoline and me.

Of the funeral and the reading of the will and the burial, I remember very little. I allowed my parents and Halina to haul me around that week. Back in Bell Canyon, the pillow in my old room afforded me no rest.

People stared. Their mouths flapped. *Everybody's talkin' at me, I can't hear a word they're sayin'.* They touched me with ice-cold fingers, patted my hand, my shoulder. I wanted to scratch out their eyes, their ugly piggy eyes. The rage inside me pounded against my skull, hammered in my chest.

I lowered my own eyes so the people would think I'd been crying. I didn't want them to see the hatred and fury that would surely turn them to ashes on the spot. Karoline would detest this ceremony. She would roll around in that grave for centuries to come, writhing with contempt. Here she was, back in the Canyon, the little white bread community from which we had escaped. All the people whom she had scorned now looked down at her both literally and figuratively. A disgraced suicide. My sin and her humiliation.

Dear Diary,
She often reminds me of a puppy dog. Curled up at your feet at night, completely oblivious, licking your hand for attention, jumping and rolling over when you tell her to. Attached to her master for no real reason other than animal comfort. If someone came by who offered her a better treat, she'd be off like a shot.

CHAPTER 6

The old adage that time heals all wounds didn't work for me. My odd behaviors began to betray me as the weeks went by. It was as though my wound became infected, filling my whole being with pus, clogging my thought processes.

Karoline and I co-owned a sporty little red convertible whose roof we rarely saw. The air going past was thick, noisy and smelled of fuel, but we didn't care. As long as it was warm and a bit of sun shone through the smog, we had the top down. Scarves tied jauntily around our heads like 1940's movie stars.

For the first couple of weeks after the funeral I drove to work as though everything was still the same. I imagined Karoline beside me, chatting, sharing breakfast sandwiches and coffee.

"Did you see this article about the murder in that movie theatre? Gruesome or what?" she might say, peering over the newspaper at me.

Her nose was far too turned up, so you could see right up her nostrils when she lifted her chin this way.

"What do you think about that smarmy old councilor? Do you think he's really guilty of fraud?" or "I hate these bloody ads. Look at that. Advertising sanitary pads. Is nothing sacred?"

Her opinions were always sarcastic, always designed to get a reaction. More often than not, Giulio and I responded to her comments with a smile, a giggle or a shrug, but sometimes we'd get into a merry old discussion.

I adored being with Karoline at the end of work because I was always the one doing the talking. Almost every day I would be asking her opinion, getting her advice, telling her about my clients, nattering on and on. Mornings, Karoline was the passenger. Evenings were my time while she drove.

Before Italy Giulio was there, too. He'd always sit quietly in the back seat. Looking up now and then from his reading, he'd smile indulgently at our babble or join in with a pithy comment or two. Those were the days when we shared everything. Or at least, I did.

Until Karoline was gone I had forgotten how blatantly the commuters paid attention to me. When I stopped at a red light or crawled along in insect trails of traffic, someone was bound to look over and whistle. Or ask me out. Or ask me who I was. Stopping dead still was like being under a spotlight. It was Karoline who had shielded me from their intrusiveness. She'd give them her famous stare, which froze people in their tracks, as Giulio always said.

I remember someone referring to Karoline's eyes as beady, her look witchlike. I thought her eyes, small and framed by bushy brows, mirrored intelligence and an I-don't-care-what-you-think-of-me attitude. Her hair was plain, her dress commonplace, her demeanor unassuming. No one stared at her. I admired the fact that she wasn't noticed, and respected that she didn't care. I was so imperceptive.

The staring eyes on the freeway were piranhas piercing my armor. I was at their mercy without Karoline.

I didn't really think I was speaking aloud to Karoline-not-there. At first I was convinced my fellow commuters were reading my mind. They stared at me even more ferociously as I gabbed away inside the convertible. There wasn't anyone else but Karoline to whom I could voice my complaints or my opinions or tell about my day, so I deliberately imagined she was still there listening raptly. I decided I needed to confide in my friend as though she could hear me. I needed her to tell me what to do as she always had. What could be the harm?

Once I began to talk to Karoline again I suppose I paid less attention to the road. Particularly in the evenings when it was her turn to drive. Sometimes I pretended it was three years ago and the oddballs were still an indestructible trio. The Polack, the Half and Half and the Eye-Tie lived and worked in the most fascinating city in the world, traveling every day to our amazing, challenging, well-paid jobs. We had left Shirley O'Connor and our small-minded hometown far behind. We had prospects. We knew lots of important people. Most of all, we had each other.

Until the incident when I ran the car up onto an embankment, I hadn't realized how preoccupied I was with our conversation. On that day I realized abruptly that I had stepped over the edge, the one that takes you from the shore of daydream to the sea of nightmare without noticing that you're wet.

I also hadn't realized how utterly, completely and definitively I had eventually shut out every single other person in my life. For all my years in school I'd been part of a trio. When we graduated we acquired jobs close to one another. Giulio lived two blocks away. Karoline was my roommate. They were my friends, my confidants, my travel companions. More often than not they were my dates on a Saturday night. I didn't need anyone else. I was safe from the terror of establishing relationships, looking for love, finding the right man.

Only the drive for a sexual encounter ever led me to go out with men. As Karoline and I regularly discussed, those liaisons often caused tears over the agony of unrequited devotion. Or they resulted in obsession and stalking. And not from my side. There were ways, Karoline said, to satisfy my sexual urges by myself. Over the years I slowly began to refrain from dating. We made a pact with Giulio to father our children should we ever want them but Karoline and I came into our thirties with no ticking clocks. We were too busy with careers, travel, shows, openings, parties and dinners.

Then Parris Jeffrey, followed by Glenn Simpson, entered our lives.

Dear Diary,
Everything was so perfect. We didn't need anyone else in our lives. Then those two started to fuck up big time. I've been patient a long while and I don't see how I can put up with it much longer. Am I the only one with brains?

CHAPTER 7

Parris is a tall, lanky girl with long red hair and luminous blue eyes, two years younger than I. Not quite beautiful with her beefy thighs and knobby hands and freckles smeared all over her cheeks, she is nevertheless the kind of woman to whom attention is paid. Men follow her hearty laugh down a street or a hallway and watch the sway of her hips. She has thick lips that she paints bright red and she uses her long black eyelashes without compunction. She looks and sounds lusty. Parris can tell an off color joke, curse or fart in public and get away with it. She makes everyone laugh and brings everyone into her circle.

Parris worked for me at Grace Productions. These days she has my desk.

At the time, I was thrilled to acquire an assistant. We had a huge number of projects on the go and I found tracking all of them exhausting. Joseph Grayson, one of my employers, approved hiring someone to groom and mentor as well as assist. Grace Productions was expanding. There was even talk of a branch in New York City. For our business, the 80's recession passed right over and flung us toward the future without a blip. Thus I had no thoughts or concerns about competition from a new hire. I sat in on the interviews. Parris was our number one choice.

She immediately proved that we had been correct in our assessment. Smart, funny and personable, she handled the clients like a pro. She asked questions, watched carefully and requested help or advice when she needed it. Parris was a dream. Before I knew it, we were having lunch together or going out for coffee at breaks. She told me her thoughts, ambitions, about her family and her love life. In time I told her some of my secrets, too.

Very slowly it dawned on me that Parris wasn't simply a colleague. She was a friend. It also occurred to me that she listened to and shared far more of my thoughts and opinions than Karoline did. Where my lifelong friend and I were drifting apart, this interesting, younger female was edging closer. It was like a husband and wife who'd become estranged.

Karoline noticed, too. "So you had lunch with your assistant again today?" she asked on our homeward commute, peering at me sideways as she slowed for traffic.

"I did," I replied happily because I had no inkling that I should not. "Remember I told you about that project, The Silver Fox?"

"The screenwriter who's a prick and the story that sucks but somehow Joseph loves?"

"The very one. Parris and I have been putting together a plan for handling him. The screenwriter that is. I think it just might work."

"She sounds rather manipulative."

I looked up in surprise at the criticism, but Karoline's eyes were on the car in front of us.

"I don't think so," I said, making it a definitive statement with my tone. "Diplomatic maybe. I know we have to be somewhat controlling, I guess, but only for the sake of the film. We simply have to get it up and running, even if we have to do end-runs on the writers."

"We? Isn't she just your assistant?"

I was silenced at the strength of dislike in Karoline's voice.

"I like her," I said finally.

Karoline gave me her beady stare.

The following week I decided I should introduce Parris to Karoline. Maybe they would hit it off. I knew there was an underlying aversion to my assistant from my best friend's corner, but once they met in person I was certain Karoline's reservations would disappear.

She was just looking after my interests, I knew. She probably thought Parris was overly ambitious, trying to move in on my position. I had to prove to Karoline that such was not the case. Parris is lively, bright and down-to-earth. Surely no one could dislike her for long. Maybe she'd be our new third.

At the last minute, as we were setting up for a dinner party with the usual suspects, I told Karoline that Parris was coming, too.

"Joseph and Vicki are going to bring her with them," I said. "She lives near their building."

Karoline continued folding the napkins. She loved real cloth napkins. We had collected a dozen or so from different countries, so the table was always colorful and eclectic.

"Okay. Seven napkins then. Seven plates. Seven dwarves."

"You'll like her, Karoline. She's really not trying to replace me at work, you know. In fact the place is expanding so much that we'll probably have lots of room for Exec Assistants. Vicki will soon need one of her own, instead of splitting me with…"

Karoline laughed. "Sweetie, I never thought she was going to try and take your place."

"Oh." I was stunned at the mocking tone, the way Karoline tossed her head as though I were a complete idiot. "But…why don't you like her then?"

"Who said I don't like her? You think I'm jealous or something?"

I stared at Karoline, confused, but she was too busy getting plates out of the cupboard to look at me. "Of course not."

"Then stop sneaking around having lunch with her and inviting her over for dinner without telling me."

Stunned, I couldn't find any words to describe the odd feeling in my stomach. Karoline never talked to me like that.

She turned around and smiled at me.

"I can't wait to hear what Daniel has to say about the new tax regulation the city just passed. He's going apoplectic. You watch. He'll be the first to arrive, full of piss and vinegar. C'mon, don't just stand there, let's get this shindig on the road, girlfriend."

True to her prediction, Daniel was not only first at the door but he was also rambling from the start about the controversial city regulation, none of which I understood. He arrived with his wife in a colorful flourish, brandishing a huge bunch of orange and yellow flowers, two bottles of wine, one red, one white, a checkered shirt and pink cheeks.

Daniel Stewart is not a stereotype for a lawyer. He's thin, very short, freckle-faced and has unruly brown hair that often sticks up in a cowlick. He looks young from afar, but up close you can see the lines around his eyes and the furrows of his oft-frowning forehead. He's extremely wealthy and often sent Karoline out to art auctions on his behalf. He's very fond of the artist CoJon, the one whose mysterious past is almost as famous as his colorful swashes that form themselves into ethereal scenery. Our CoJon was a bonus to Karoline for a job well done.

Luckily Daniel is not a trial lawyer. I can't imagine that a jury would side with his child-like demeanor. Not to mention his bullfrog voice, which is frightening the first time you hear it emerge from that small person. I like Daniel, though. He is intelligent, charming when he wants to be and he adored Karoline.

When Parris, Vicki and Joseph arrived a few minutes later it was in a flurry of hostess gifts, wine, shoes, glasses and places at the table. Vicki, one of my bosses, is a tall commanding blond who appears mannish in her style and dress, but whose voice conjures up a stereotypical femininity that includes shopping and spas and pampering. Blessed with an aura that demands attention and oozes confidence, Vicki has industry heavy weights lining up at her door to sign a contract with her.

Joseph, soft-spoken but genius in a conversation, brilliant at targeting a client's career in the right direction, is her perfect complement. They live together but have never officially married. Neither has any interest in progeny. Their company, Grace Productions, and each other fill their lives completely and utterly.

Unless confronted by stress or an unscripted event, they are satisfied and enthusiastic. Any glitch in their plans can turn them both into melting chocolate, helpless, gooey and messy. Which is where I come in.

Or used to.

That evening, Parris was a vision of burnt orange and almost as hot. Reddish hair, matching blouse with flounce sleeves, flashing brown eyes, she was, despite being rather tall and large boned, stunning. Not shy, she jumped into every conversation with alacrity and defined opinion.

Everyone talked all at once. The cacophony of voices muffled the tension that soon settled in over dinner. I was, Before-Italy and Before Parris-then-Glenn, completely oblivious to hidden agendas or underlying tensions. Karoline would always point them out to me. I was inevitably the last to know that so-and-so was having an affair or that such-and-such hated their business partner. I had no idea that Giulio was in love with his cousin or that his cousin was engaged. I could never have predicted that Giulio would remain in Italy, would leave us without good-bye, or would leave us at all.

I realize now that I had reacted viscerally all my life. Through my senses, through what I saw, heard or smelled. No jumping to conclusions, no intuition. No feelings in the pit of my stomach. My approach always worked well with the film industry bunch because they live completely on the surface, shallow and predictable.

That night, the fluttering in my chest and the squishy feeling in my belly were foreign to me. At first I didn't recognize the symptoms. I thought I was reacting to the rich meat sauce. Then I began to tune into Karoline, the tone of her voice, the choice of words, the topics, the way she lifted glass after glass of wine. I realized with a shock that the tremors were coming from the earthquake of Karoline, an upheaval that was about to rearrange the landscape of our relationship.

"It's similar to Beverly Hills Cop."

There had been a lull in the conversation between Daniel and Karoline. Vicki and I had taken a breath. Chewed our food. Left a hole in the noise. Thus Parris's voice, its lustrous timbre somehow earsplitting in the quiet dining room, echoed across the table.

"Just what we need," Karoline said, "another vacuous movie about idiotic people. A great contribution to our national culture."

We'd had these debates in the past. The difference between film and movie, art and entertainment, literature and pulp fiction. But there was something vicious in Karoline's tone that made everyone stop dead still. Instead of taking part in the argument, the others were shocked into silence. Their faces reflected uncertainty about how to enter this new geography.

Parris, because the dart had been aimed at her, continued innocently into a perceived discussion.

"I think there's something to be said about making movies purely for entertainment. Just to be able to go out and have a laugh…"

"Laugh! The characters exhibit inane, ridiculous behavior and are clearly people none of us here would want to know. If we're laughing, if we find that nonsense in any way funny, it's because we're mocking these morons. This movie is encouraging us to make fun of other people."

"Karoline, you can't think the characters in that movie are meant to be seen as real people. They're like cartoons."

Parris gave a small laugh, still believing she was debating, just as I'd described the amusing exchanges of words around this table in the past.

"Ahhh, cartoon people."

The silence from the rest of us was a wall of disbelief through which none of us could speak and of which Parris appeared unaware. Later I felt terrible that I hadn't intervened, hadn't somehow pulled Parris and the rest of us out of the pool of venom that leaked from my roommate's mouth. Hadn't somehow foreseen that Karoline was about to unearth a deadly disease of hatred that would infect us both. That would poison the air forever.

"But aren't you film people all cartoonish? Aren't you vapid and shallow and ridiculous? People who manipulate and steal in the name of so-called art and then trot out movies like Beverly Hills Cop and expect the rest of the population to support you financially?"

Karoline pointed her fork toward Vicki and Joseph. They sat with pale faces and question mark frowns, considering whether or not to laugh or get up from the table, impaled like dried flowers in a frame by Karoline's stabbing fork and her malicious tone.

"I've known Vicki and Joseph for years. They are the epitome of insipid and superficial. Definite cartoon characters. But you don't see them up on the screen for us to laugh at. In fact, I usually sit very politely and pretend their conversation is stimulating and intelligent."

"Karoline."

Daniel spoke her name quietly, reverently, almost like a question. Where did you go, Karoline? Who is this person who has taken your place?

As though she'd been under water, Karoline's eyes became clear again and she shook her head. Carefully replacing her fork, she shoved her chair backward, causing it to smack down on the hardwood floor. Then she walked, shoulders back, toward the exit. She grabbed her brown shawl and disappeared into the hallway, slamming the front door as she left.

I picked up the bottle of white wine that Karoline and Daniel had been sharing and shook it, peering inside as though I could see mysterious contents lurking.

"Okay, Daniel, what did you put in this bottle?"

Early the next morning, after the guests were long gone, the dishes cleared, the chairs back on their exact spots, Karoline appeared in my bedroom. I rolled over to blink up at her hovering over me, her lank hair damp and wild, her eyes round discs of a drug called madness. It was not a Karoline I recognized.

"You'll be sorry, Anne," she whispered. "Sorry about everything."

She staggered off to her room, her shawl clinging to her rounded, old-woman shoulders. I heard her bed shift as she flung her weight onto it, heard those sounds for the first time, the invectives and taunts that would eventually, literally, put us both over the edge.

Dear Diary,

I have always believed that friends are far easier to love than family. The saying that 'you can't pick your family, but you can pick your friends' has always rung true for me. What I don't understand is how they could betray me like this. For years I have been the one to guide them. Without me, they would be nothing! They never had any self-discipline or logical sense. They could never make decisions, or budgets, or career plans, or even figure out what they should eat for optimal health. I loved them, provided for them, and gave them everything. And this is how they repay me?

CHAPTER 8

For a very long time after that night, I tried to ignore the changed world in which I now lived. I did immediately realize that I had no one in whom to confide. No Giulio, of course. I would have felt too guilty talking to Parris about Karoline. My mother and I had never acquired the kind of relationship that fostered discourse of any kind, let alone 'girl talk'. She maintained a distance, a motherly stance that she thought was appropriate for our difference in age and role.

Karoline had been my sole confidante for so many years and now she was the one I wanted to discuss.

Alone, I didn't have the tools to fix Karoline. So I pretended I didn't notice her increasingly sleepless nights. I ignored the fact that she suddenly began smoking. That she'd sit on the balcony for hours staring at nothing. That she no longer asked me questions or appeared to be listening to my rants. She refused to answer me when I asked her what was wrong.

Slowly, like scum forming on a pond, the dancing, theaters, clubbing, parties and dinners faded away under a film of unease. For a time I chattered on. For a while I bought tickets for the movies, said yes to outings and openings. I marched forward, Karoline muttering beside or behind me, unkempt and disinterested.

Instinctively, I avoided parties and dinners. There were no more discussions around our beautiful wooden dining table. Soon there were only nights of mumbling from the balcony.

I didn't know what Daniel thought because I didn't ask. Of course I didn't invite Parris home again. We went to lunches and business affairs, dinners with our clients and bosses. My wall of cheerfulness and everything-is-okay remained intact and solid.

One Friday night Karoline didn't show up at the parking lot. I had the keys, but I didn't want to leave without her. I went back into my office and tried her office phone over and over. I left frantic messages on our answering machine. Where was she?

It was dark by the time I finally decided to drive home without her. I wasn't particularly quiet as I entered our apartment. Nor was I a bit shy about heading straight in to push open her bedroom door, which was slightly ajar, to demand an explanation. For a few moments I stood astonished, frozen to the spot.

Karoline lay on her back while a man moved slowly and languorously above her, his hips and buttocks smooth and black in the semi-darkness. He was moaning softly, whispering fuck me, Karoline, over and over, his voice husky with desire. I could smell the musky, moist fragrance of their bodies and the saltiness of sweat. I watched as he began to pump harder, his hands on both sides of her, his face dipped to her breasts, sucking and moaning, faster and more abandoned with each thrust.

At that moment Karoline opened her eyes and looked at me. She stared with disdain as I heard him tell her that he was coming inside her. She began to chant fuck me, fuck me, her eyes never leaving mine.

I closed the door.

So began a six-week sojourn with Glenn Simpson. On our couch when we came home, eating from a barrel of ice cream. Shouting at the television as basketball players streaked across the floor. Smoking with Karoline on the balcony. Beer bottles piled in the kitchen. Coffee cups in the sink. Frying pans with sticky grease spots sitting on the stove. Behavior that Karoline had never before allowed in our apartment.

Glenn was a huge, flabby man whose skin was so dark it looked purple. His rounded cheeks pushed his eyes back into his head, making his black orbs little pinpoints of malice. He wore enormous sports shirts and jeans that rode on his ample hips, often displaying his disgusting butt crack. Whenever he bent over, a shiver of revulsion raced through me. He was at least ten years older than we were, but he acted like a spoiled teenager.

He used the kind of speech patterns that I detest. In my opinion, it was a throwback to slave talk. He had been born in New York City to a middle-class family and had a university degree, this much I knew. Yet he behaved as though he'd just been released, ill used and uneducated, from the shackles of a cruel white master.

"I been done work" was an oft-repeated phrase. He'd decided, he boasted, to live off the system for as long as he could. Showing up in L.A. with his paltry experience in New York amateur theater, Glenn had expected the film industry to immediately embrace his unusual, dramatic looks, his shiny bald head and sneering mouth. I didn't know how he could expect that they would. There were thousands of his type getting off the bus at Hollywood and Vine every single day.

Not only that, he criticized me constantly for not properly embracing my black roots. My experience had been so different that I refused to engage with him. I thought I knew far more than he did about the true American dream. What was his version? That he ought to be handed whatever he wanted just because he was black and thought he was unique? He was like teenagers who all dressed the same yet proclaimed to be different. And when the 'Jew film moguls' didn't adore him after all, he decided he would just play the system for as long as he could get away with it.

I began to quarrel with him but they were senseless arguments that sounded like children squabbling. Karoline would not participate. She'd give a wan smile or simply take him into her bedroom.

"Get your bloody shorts off the coffee table, asshole," I'd say. "Why don't you get a job? Aren't you ashamed to be a useless prick?"

"Listen up, asshat, you can't be dissin' me," he'd say, or "You a hemorrhoid," he'd reply, then proceed to explain his remark, sometimes betraying his Black English. "See, an asshole or a prick has its uses, whereas a hemorrhoid…"

"Karoline, why are you putting up with this bastard's bad manners?"

A shrug and a thin-lipped smile.

"I can't stand this anymore. Get him out of here or else."

A look. Or else what?

A question I was unwilling to answer.

I began to go in early and stay late at work. To have dinner with Parris. To take the unreliable transit, several buses and even the subway rather than travel with them by car. By the end of the six weeks, I rarely saw the couple who ostensibly lived with me. When I came home they would be in the bedroom, or out somewhere unknown. I spent most of my time in my room, as did they. The living room was a deserted wasteland, the kitchen a dump, the dining room an echo of a recent past.

When I think of Glenn Simpson now, I am unable to separate him from that final destructive act. The last straw after an accumulation of straws of which Glenn was only one. The explosion after the long wick was ignited.

I remember those weeks as living in two worlds, two polar opposites, two planes that I would never have believed possible if anyone had foretold it. On the one hand, there was my life with Karoline and her man, which had become a tense battle of wills. On the other there was my satisfying career and my friendship with Parris. The dissonance ate away at my sanity.

Long after the funeral, on those insufferable commuter drives alone, I slowly began to unravel. The only way I can describe it is that I had no narrative left. There were no voices in my head to guide me. I no longer had Karoline's steady, confident opinion about the minutiae of daily living or the bigger pictures of worldly decisions. Self-assured, arrogant, sarcastic Anne was gone, too, replaced by a hum of confusion and guilt. Hesitant, unglued, vulnerable Anne walked through Los Angeles and prowled our apartment in a daze of denial and indecision.

The progression is fairly easy to see in retrospect. I had no choice but to face my state of mind once I wrecked our car. Apparently I was not cooperative after the accident. I can't tell you exactly how I behaved, since I have no memory of that incident. I don't remember driving over the embankment, which luckily headed uphill instead of down. I don't remember the police arriving at the scene.

What I do recall is sitting in the back seat of the police car. Its roof light languidly painted the night red. I sat staring straight ahead, listening to garbled messages on the radio. Up front the two policemen whispered to each other, spoke into a microphone and waited. Within a few minutes, an unmarked car pulled up and the officers got out. After a brief conference I was transferred to another vehicle.

"No problem, sir," the young male policeman responded to someone outside as he opened my door and helped me out.

He was speaking to Ethan, who reached for my hand and gently tucked me into the front seat of his car. The warmth inside, the soft silk of the leather seats, the scent of his aftershave, made me hunch over in tears.

When he got behind the wheel, he placed an enormous yet gentle hand on my shoulder.

"It's all right, Ms. Williams," he said. "I'm glad you asked for me."

I have no memory of asking for him, but something inside me responded to the comforting tones in his voice. I folded into his side. He put his arm around me and let me cry.

We reached my apartment some time later. The moment I opened the door, I was embarrassed by the odor of mustiness and disuse. This apartment that was so accustomed to laughter, discussion and song lay dusty and ignored.

I led him into my bedroom. He lay down beside me as though this was a natural position that we'd experienced with one another a hundred times before. I told Ethan everything about Karoline and me. From our meeting in childhood to our life in L.A. I told him everything except the end. He used the word suicide, the official word for her death, and commiserated about that terrible experience.

That first night he left me sleeping, but reappeared the next morning armed with muffins and coffee.

"I want you to know that I've never done this before," he said. "I mean, become friends with someone involved in one of my investigations. If you are uncomfortable with my being your friend, just tell me."

But I didn't feel uncomfortable. I felt the opposite. His use of the word friend filled me with a feeling that I recognized as hope.

Later that morning I reluctantly called Joseph and Vicki to ask about a leave of absence.

"I know you've been...struggling since Karoline died," Joseph said. "We've been worried, as you know."

Had I known? Had I seen myself, this fourth-dimensional shimmering of the previous me, at first behaving just slightly off balance, then seeping more fully into the other world? The day Karoline died, the life I knew, the 'me' I knew, went over that balcony with her. I no longer got up from bed eager to start the day. Ultimately, I might no longer have a job.

Slowly I chased away my parents and most of my acquaintances. My looking glass, heretofore the perfect Magic Mirror, reflected a dazed uncertain face. I stumbled in a fog, unwilling to admit that I was lost. Not until I'd wrecked my car. Not until I'd been publicly humiliated and frightened by my own loss of control.

"But you're our family, kiddo." This time it was Vicki's soothing voice, thick with emotions that I'd never before heard displayed. "You take as long as you need. Your job will always be here."

"We'll come see you when you're ready." Joseph had taken the receiver again.

All I could do in response was weep, a sound they'd never heard from me, the calm and steady one, the fixer, now unable to fix myself.

Thanks to Karoline's management skills I saved a great deal of money and invested wisely. I now owned the apartment outright, in large part because of Boosha. In a move that both shocked me and compiled my guilt, Karoline bequeathed the place to me in her will. I knew I could live at least a year without working, but I was comforted by the fact that Grace Productions would welcome me back.

These days I feel as though I am traipsing unprepared through a foreign country. I haven't packed. I don't know the language. I don't have the appropriate skills or any of the requisite equipment, but I'm on the journey nevertheless. Not to mention that I have no one at whom I can rage. I am the one who got on the ship and sailed away to unknown shores.

As the weeks go by, I get to know Ethan Byrne. He exudes a charm and quiet confidence that are captivating. He is completely unaware of his physical shortcomings. Quickly I begin to see the finer side. The layers of color in his eyes. The lopsided grin when he is about to tell a joke. The gracefulness of his hands.

Soon I don't notice the crooked nose, the unruly hair, the shaggy brows or the too-square chin. Protected by his athletic prowess, the beauty of his eyes, the tenor of his voice and the generosity of his spirit, Ethan grew up knowing that his looks really don't matter. For the first time, oddly enough, I begin a relationship with someone for whom the outside is unimportant. He doesn't fall in love with the long legs, perfect breasts, gorgeous hair and dark eyes. He falls in love with me.

How he sees the real me through the weeks of sleeping, cleaning and shopping, I will never know. The person who was folded in a dark cave slowly emerges, changed and exhausted. I tell him I will always be grateful that he sees a future me, a goodness in me.

Dear Diary,

I have always thought of her as a false goddess. So charming on the outside, so inept and incapable within. She has none of the ability to rule over herself, let alone be a deity for anyone else.

CHAPTER 9

After a time I almost believe in Ethan's vision of Anne. As long as I never think about the night Karoline died, as long as I vow never to tell him my truths. Ironically, I trade a superficial lifestyle for an introspective one, as long as the layers I inspect never touch my deepest sin.

Ethan tells me all about his move from Dublin to Los Angeles when he was thirteen. His story so closely mimics the Kennedy legend that I know Karoline would have been proud. Irish parents loaded with determination and intelligence land in Hollywood and make a fortune. His family owned several textile plants back home and around England, but Ethan's father has taken the company to where the sidewalks are paved with gold and multiplied its profits beyond any of their ancestors' dreams. Edward and Teresa Byrne became so well connected and famous, that Karoline and I had heard about them long before I met Ethan. Who knew that the gangly, ugly detective at our door would turn out to be their son?

They were not happy when Ethan became a police officer, but Ted and Teresa have not abandoned him. Probably because they know he wouldn't really mind if they did disown him, at least from a financial point of view. Money definitely does not matter to Ethan. He does care, however, about his parents as people.

Another disappointment for Ted and Teresa is that Ethan has never married, though he came close a couple of times. His sister Marianne is a wife and mother of three and she's a year his junior. Of course Marianne wed a millionaire film producer, someone whose credentials have even more weight than her own family's.

However, Ted and Teresa aren't very happy with me as a potential daughter-in-law. They are appalled that Ethan has become involved with someone from a case. Not to mention I am obviously unwell, jittery and odd, unable sometimes to form a coherent sentence. I cling to their son. He is my life raft and it's noticeable.

He's not simply my savior, though. Ethan is a gift that I unwrap, layers of surprises, complex yet simple. A man with ribbons of feelings, intellect, insights and generosity. A man infinitely interested in Anne the complicated woman. Not surface Anne, but someone who has depth. We both become prospectors of Anne's other self.

Over time Ethan wakes me up, takes me out of the apartment and my grief over Karoline. Slowly I begin to smile, then laugh again. Energy seeps back. I stop talking to myself or to my dead friend. I no longer shop, sleep or wash dishes obsessively. I clean up the Picassos. I begin to make decisions.

I rearrange the furniture in the living room. Cover the couch with a soft green throw. Put a lacey tablecloth over the wooden surface that needs too much polish. Except for the CoJon and a few other treasures that I love, I put or give away most of our souvenirs. I am able to occupy the space. I even open Karoline's bedroom door, though I haven't yet disposed of her belongings.

Halina took a few items, but she doesn't want to deal with her daughter's clothing or other things. Halina has left that up to me. Anne, the best friend, the sister Karoline never had. The beneficiary of her apartment. Halina seems oblivious to that last detail. Perhaps she assumes that we paid for the place as equal partners. Certainly she will never know about Boosha. Not if I can help it.

I have dinners with Parris. We go to movies. Wander around parks and the zoo. Slow, quiet activities that she senses will allow me to heal. She invites, never pushes and always accepts when I need to be alone. Her big open smile has become a source of joy. Her arms are a comfort zone. I am astonished by her generosity, her easy-going ways. She models for me that friendship doesn't have to smother.

I am alarmed that former Anne still reemerges occasionally. I walk around with two selves, the one I am discovering and the one who now and then whispers nasty things in my ear. She sets me off balance. I thought she was gone.

I often feel as though I am acting without a script. I am bereft and confused. One Anne is the same haughty selfish bitch that she's always been. The only people that I'd ever really allowed into my head and heart were Karoline and Giulio.

The other personality is soft and weepy and vulnerable.

I am not certain which of these personas is the real me. I am not certain I like either of them.

Dear Diary,

I have begun my strategy. Wheels in motion, as they say. They will both learn the hard way, but they've left me no choice. Neither of them will survive this war intact. Maybe then they'll obey. They'll look and see the real Queen and say, yes your majesty. Ha ha ha. Seriously, though, it's all for their benefit.

CHAPTER 10

Ethan and I make love after many months of exploration. Hours and hours of conversation, dinners and outings, handholding as we walk the beach. His lips are always soft and full, promising, but I don't allow the shiver to extend to my toes. I've never held out this long, never thought too much about jumping into bed with someone I fancied. With Ethan it's as though I am a romantic and must wait until everything is perfect.

Jesus, you are turning into a maudlin asshole, Ice Queen Anne whispers, but I fling her aside. As time goes on, I dare to think that the best side of me is becoming stronger. Perhaps Ice Queen Anne is suddenly afraid and tries to take over now and again. I vow not to let her, but I know I have a lot of work ahead in order to bury her.

Ethan's arms feel different from any others who have held me. His care feels different. He doesn't tell. He gives options and suggestions. He doesn't force, he inspires. There's no judging. His eyes display acceptance, giving and taking, acknowledgement of an inner me that even I have trouble seeing. Until he leads me into my bedroom, I'm not certain that I haven't conjured a dream man.

Ethan removes my clothes tenderly. Touches me soothingly. Massages my arms and back and neck. He picks me up off my feet and lays me on the wide mattress, then climbs in beside me, still fully clothed. His big hands begin to feather over my skin. Not a touch but a buzz of electricity from his fingers, up and down my legs, over my belly and arms, my breasts, shoulders, head. I feel the tingle in the deepest parts of me. My physical being links with my thoughts.

Then he begins to kiss me and the sensual thrill is like nothing I've ever felt. His lips are a caress, a warm connection that is both a soothing bath and a wash of desire. When we are face-to-face, he looks into my eyes. I see a version of myself that I do not recognize. I gently remove his shirt, his pants, his underwear. It's my choice. He gives himself to me at my request, not as a result of his desire alone. When we join in lovemaking, I feel as though I have entered his skin, tucked myself inside him. I am fully engaged, no longer dismissive and apart.

I suddenly know the meaning of the words, 'and the two shall be as one'. Not subsumed, but made stronger, more complete, better.

When Ice Queen Anne begins to whisper that she is about to OD on sugar, she is suppressed by all five senses, which are awakened and dancing with excitement.

All that night we touch one another, physically and spiritually, passionate and heated, soft and exploring. We take turns sleeping in one another's arms, cocooned and strengthened, comforted and safe. I have never felt so treasured.

For the next few weeks I travel another new landscape. I am still uncertain and shaky. I watch my feet and tread carefully, looking for potholes, enjoying the soft sandy parts between my toes.

It takes a huge burst of courage to reveal some of my secrets. But somehow I know that this is part of the hard work. The end goal will be worth it; a new Anne, a life with love will emerge.

We sit on the couch, facing one another, touching and talking. I decide I have to tell him. I know what I have to do and I don't want to approach it without his support and knowledge. Again, this is a far different Anne that I'm contending with. I'm not sure she knows what she's doing, but I have to trust her. She's the one that this man loves.

"Ethan, I want to show you something."

I pad in my stocking feet into my bedroom and retrieve the packet from under the mattress. Seated back in the living room, I stare down at the thick pile of papers held together with a blue ribbon.

"This is what I found in Karoline's closet. I need you to read the first three."

He spreads his fingers through the papers. Reads. Stabs the pages with his big fingers as though angry with the words and not the writer. When he is finished he looks up at me with anguish in his eyes and fury on his face.

"Have you read them all? Is any of this true?"

"Yes and yes."

"They were in Karoline's closet?"

"Yes. In a trunk she kept there. Some of the letters came in the mail, but even though they were clearly sent to me…"

"…you never knew about them."

It isn't a question and he isn't shocked. I think I should explain. Excuse.

"We had different household duties. Karoline got the mail, mostly because I always forgot and once I misplaced the key. The landlord charged us fifty bucks to replace it."

These last few days I have noticed that Ethan gives me odd looks whenever I speak of Karoline, but until tonight I chose to ignore them. I am afraid of where his insight might lead.

"She never showed any of these to you?"

I shake my head, allowing the tears to slide down my cheeks. I draw in a stuttering breath and try to regain control.

"Never. I found them when she was breaking down. I searched her room, looking for anything that would explain…"

Explain what? Her insanity? The sudden appearance/disappearance of Glenn Simpson? The gradual disappearance of the real Karoline? I'm uncertain about giving him the details. Karoline's incessant scribbling, her mutterings, her days-long absences from the apartment. I grasped at any explanation, finally digging through her trunk, the one she'd buried in her closet years ago. I didn't know what I expected to find, but I definitely did not expect the letters.

A tense silence keeps us immobile for a minute. When he finally speaks Ethan's melodious tones are measured, controlled. He delivers a concise theory that he's clearly thought about for a while.

"Anne, you were in an abusive relationship for years. You became a classic abused spouse, submissive and emotionally crippled. This is the most glaring, most manipulative example."

He stabs the pile of papers once again.

"I'm not happy about what happened to Karoline, don't get me wrong. But I am glad she's gone from your life."

I begin to shake. From the terrible honesty. From the terrible lie.

Ethan doesn't know how complicit I was in shaping my life with my friends. My parents, probably without meaning to, raised me to be a narcissistic Princess, haughty and self-absorbed. They protected me from a world that might've used me. I learned how to use beauty to my own advantage instead.

My mother gave me lessons in how to remain emotionally distant. I went from that overprotected discipline to Karoline's regime. I never really thought about others' feelings except how the consequences related to me.

Like how to deal with the writer in tears who was aghast at the way the screenplay had twisted their main character. Or how to manage the man who lay weeping at my feet when I broke up with him. How to avoid an emotional bond with the guy I'd just slept with. How to replace real discourse with intellectual sparring.

I ignored the fact that my very best friend was disintegrating right in front of me.

From Parris I have started to learn true friendship. From Ethan, real love. But it took the unraveling of Karoline for me to reach out beyond the nest we created. If Karoline's demons hadn't swallowed her, would I ever have noticed my shallow existence? I don't think I would have.

I would describe myself as content, self-absorbed, privileged, coddled. I equated these feelings with happiness. I mistook laughter for joy and arguments for conversation. Saw overprotection and control as love.

I was capable of vicious thoughts, of cold betrayal, of a terrible, final act. Do I still retain that Ice Queen Anne, the one that I was? I must, or surely her voice would have been completely silenced by now. Can a person really change? Or am I a monster hiding under this bandage of love and attention until my wounds heal?

Tears spill down my face. Ethan encircles me. Rocks me like a broken-hearted child. He kisses my wet cheeks, my blubbering lips.

"Anne, I love you," he whispers at my ear, nuzzling my neck, kneading my back.

"I know, but I'm not sure you should," I tell him, anxiety cracking my voice. "You don't really know me."

He doesn't know the complete me. He can't have glimpsed a fully lovable Anne under the layers of odd behaviors and insincerity. Is he like all the others, assuming beauty and goodness because of the surface perfection? What will he do if he ever discovers what I did, what I was, what I might still be?

"And I have only just started to learn what that word really means. You've been teaching me, Ethan, but I still can't trust it."

Or myself. I shake my head, refusing to slip down the mountain into that valley of self-hatred once again. I sit up and hold his eyes with mine, squeeze his hand so he won't stop me from my confession. I must find out.

"I didn't tell her I'd found the letters. Instead, I followed the trails, at least up to a point. I need you to know everything."

I stumble on the last word, aware that there is one secret I cannot tell just yet. Perhaps never. There are so many missing pieces of myself that must be replaced. I am a crossword with obscure definitions that lead to empty spaces. I am half and half in skin and mind, not whole of anything.

"I can't remember the first four years of my life. It's a blank. The only person who ever knew about that was Karoline. I didn't even ask my mother. I assumed that everyone forgets their early childhood. Until Karoline pointed out that mine is far emptier than most. There are no glimpses, no half-remembered scenes. Nothing. But I never wanted to investigate. Clearly, Karoline did."

It's my turn to stab the letters.

"After I found these letters, I decided to visit my sister Elizabeth. I took a week off work, told Karoline nothing. Disappeared just as she had begun to do."

Dear Diary,

Today I want to talk about trust. The dictionary defines it as, "reliance on the character, ability, strength, or truth of someone or something". For years there was complete trust. Total reliance. Unfortunately, it's the truth part that has begun to fall apart. Fucking assholes. What's that song again? When the truth is found to be lies and all the joy within you dies?

Chapter 11

Although I'd been to the Toronto area several times over the years I'd always arrived with my parents leading the way. There'd been different purposes then. A different feel. The visits were about the birth of a child, a christening or a graduation. I attended ostensibly happy family occasions while half of me remained in California. They were an interruption of my real life, an obligation.

Often Karoline would accompany us, turning the event into a gabfest for two best friends. I realized that this was the first time I'd ever visited my sister on my own. Usually I was on the periphery of my mother and my sister's duo, buzzing around them with Karoline or sauntering off by myself. Not really there. My thoughts ahead or behind. Back in Bell Canyon and later, L.A. Always afraid that if I were gone too long, my world would alter profoundly in my absence.

This time I was fully present. I saw the Canadian skyline with wide-open eyes, navigated the broad roadways with rapt attention. I scrutinized the differences between here and there with a fully engaged mind. Perhaps influenced by my mother's preference for her homeland, and maybe some long-ago childhood memories of my own, I always saw this side of the border as cleaner, smarter, newer. Canadians appeared to either replace the old or scrub them up more often. In Los Angeles we revered the past with an obsession that made the present seem inferior.

Here they used words like maximum speed rather than interstate limit, in that snooty Canadian style. Buckle up became fasten seat belts. Lodging was now accommodation. Of course miles were 'km', which referred to kilometers—with an re. No signs mentioned Chambers of

Commerce. Instead there were lovely pieces of art on the roadside, announcing Lake Country with a flourish of blue and white and yellow. Lots of symbols became a kind of universal language telling me where to find gas or food. Though I admired the Canadian sensibility, I loved my American home, our unselfconscious manner, our brashness and assertiveness. Especially the egotistical cocky air of L.A.

I carried California with me in a different way this time. There was no worrying about what I was missing, as though the currents of my life would navigate new territory without me. Move on to levels that I would no longer be able to reach. Switch channels. Those changes had already happened while I was present.

I zipped past the Lester B. Pearson Airport and glimpsed the CN Tower pointing at the sky. Its sister buildings glinted in the distant sunlight. Along the highways, not freeways, I headed east and then north. The rental car was a sleek little grey thing, easy to manage, perfect for a city girl who usually drove a sporty vehicle that fit into any lurking parking spot however small.

At first my heart pounded with the apprehension of so many shocks to my system, leaving my city, heading to unknown territory both physically and emotionally. Navigating customs, the airport, the suitcase and the rental all by myself. No Karoline buffer, no parental guides, no obvious reason to be here.

It was a warm spring day, one of those perfect days that I thought of as Canadian. Fresh air scented with evergreen and burgeoning hay. None of the stifling but familiar smog of my city back home. Fields, miles of them, on either side of the highway. I knew I was traveling at a good time for traffic but I still thought of the road as somehow innocent of congestion. I slid the sunroof open, cranked the music and felt free.

It wasn't until I'd reached the city of Barrie that the anxiety began. Elizabeth had no idea her younger sister was about to enter her contented sphere with questions that might be an earthquake with aftershocks. Would she even admit that she knew the answers? I hadn't warned her I was coming. I didn't want the walls to go up.

I checked into a nice little hotel along Highway 400. The front hall was crowded with friendly people and the echo of children's voices as they romped in the pool. In my room I began to put my clothes away carefully, then suddenly realized that this was Karoline's routine. I took everything out of the drawers and folded them back into my suitcase.

I strolled out into the sunshine in search of food. I had a couple of hours before Elizabeth would be home from work. I was determined not to arrive at her place hungry. Fortunately, I found a big Chinese food buffet restaurant at the top of the hill, where I feasted on salads, shrimp, crab and a myriad of desserts while I contemplated the fish swimming in colorful array behind a huge glass tank.

The walk downhill was somewhat uncomfortable. I had eaten more in those few minutes than I had in months. When I got back to my room I lay down on the bed, undid my jean shorts and promptly fell asleep.

The sun was waning when I awoke. Instead of the grizzly feeling I usually had after a nap, I felt invigorated. I brushed my teeth and set out in my zippy little vehicle once more.

Elizabeth lives on the other side of the highway, just that much removed from the city and its environs. Her career as a surgical nurse is, from all accounts, satisfying and challenging. Right after her marriage at nineteen she had three children. All of them grew up adventurous despite their almost-country upbringing.

They are spread around the world now, collecting memories, doing good works, teaching in foreign countries or going to school in distant languages. I don't know them any better than I know my sister and her husband. When I infrequently think of my two nieces and my nephew, I imagine them as crusading heroes armed with an absolute certainty about who they are and where they are headed.

My brother-in-law, Samuel Cummings, is a tall handsome man who moves with confidence and sensuality. He's a far more outwardly affectionate and gregarious person than his wife. I like him. A computer software designer, his career has been somewhat of a rollercoaster. Though he appears to have hit his stride in his forties.

I turned off Duckworth St. onto the side road that led to the home Sam and Liz have inhabited for over twenty years. Tucked on a hill opposite the Barrie side of Little Lake, the house overlooks a pristine body of water that kisses the air with the promise of cool swims and shiny fish. The long steep driveway leads to a massive two-storey that must echo without children's scampering footsteps. It's a house that combines brick and siding gracefully. A wide porch runs all across the front and along the right side, offering stunning views of the lake.

Bracketed on both sides by forest, the neighbors a comfortable distance away, the Cummings residence has a rural aura, accentuated by the barn-like structure behind it. I say barn-like because it's far too flower-boxed and frilly to be taken seriously. On one visit long ago I'd glimpsed a hayloft, a play area for the kids and four snowmobiles stacked two-by-two inside. I think they even had a pony at one time.

As I pulled up in front of the garage I could see lights in the open windows that graced the living room, though no sign of a living being. It struck me, for the first time, that Elizabeth's house was so familiar not due to past visits, but because it resembled, almost twinned, the house in Bell Canyon. My sister chose a home and a career exactly like our mother's.

The apprehension flooded back. What if she wasn't home? What if she refused my request? By the time I had mounted the steps and pressed the bell, my mouth was dry.

I looked around at the tasteful decorations. Flowerpots lush with red and white and yellow. A clay chipmunk. A stark white sculpture of a small child with a bright orange, plaster butterfly on its hand. Our mom must have approved wholeheartedly.

The colorful wreath on the door announced gaily, "Welcome Friends". I wondered if that meant relatives, too.

I heard the clicking of her heels on the wooden floor before she yanked the door open, so I had time to brace myself. She stood utterly still, staring at me, her face unemotional, not even registering surprise.

Elizabeth is a lovely woman, though completely different from me. Her pigment is faint as though merely dusted by our black ancestry. Her hair forms a wild curly halo, cut fairly short these days I noted. Her eyes are a wide ordinary brown. A rounded face and pushed-up chin prevent her from being truly beautiful, but she always dresses to heighten her rather drab coloring. A splashy pastel scarf was tossed around her shoulders right now, highlighting the deep blue of her t-shirt, matching her snug jean shorts which showed off long, lean tanned legs.

"Hi, Liz," I said to break the silence. "I'm sorry I didn't call, but…"

Wordlessly she opened the door wide, gesturing with her hand as though I were a casual guest who often popped in for tea.

"Come right in, Anne, for heaven's sake. I was just so startled to see you there. Very unexpected."

She gave me a polite tentative hug, patting my back as she always did, like a baby being burped.

I stepped into the hallway, automatically removing my shoes, placing them on the carpet where others were lined up, just as we'd both been taught. Elizabeth walked ahead of me into the living room, where she perched on the sofa. I sat across from her on a hard-seated chair the shape of a giant half shell.

"Is everything all right with Mom and Dad?"

Elizabeth wasn't truly worried. I knew she had more than likely spoken to our parents that day. It was her version of what the hell are you doing here?

"Oh yes, they're fine. Absolutely fine. They still love it down there. They always have so much to do. And lots of friends. Mom sounds really happy and Dad, too. Whenever I see them, they seem…happy."

I was babbling, while Elizabeth sat straight and stiff, a slight smile on her lips. She knew very well I'd only been sporadically in touch with our parents in the last few years.

"I agree," she responded primly. "I do think they're happy. Would you like something to drink? Or eat?"

"Oh, I'd love something to drink. Not to eat though. I had a huge lunch, so..."

"Pop? I've got ginger ale, coke, root beer...or would you like wine or something?"

The way she spoke the word wine, I knew it was not the proper choice, so I said, "I'd love a red wine if you have it."

Elizabeth nodded and moved elegantly to a sideboard in the adjoining dining room. To my surprise, she poured two glasses, the scarlet liquid filling the bottoms of enormous bowls. Did she somehow intuit what I was going to ask her and needed fortification?

"You didn't bring Karoline," she said, a statement with the upward lift of a question.

"She's so busy with her work right now, doing a bunch of different things for her boss."

"I know what that feels like. I've just moved into this surgical team coordinator position so I haven't had much time off."

I took a sip of wine. "Do you like the new job?"

"Love it. Very intense, a little too busy, but...well, with the kids gone and Sam's new position..."

She didn't elaborate, so I asked and she answered, though I felt there was a tension in her voice when she said it.

"GilTech has him traveling now. He's their main salesperson and he's all over the world. He even got to drop in on the kids in their various locations. Meanwhile, I signed up for this job that keeps me..." As she waved her hand around the room I noticed her glass was empty. "...here."

Elizabeth got up and poured us more wine.

"That must be lonely for you, Lizzy," I said, deliberately using the baby sister moniker. "I mean, you're so used to a house that's full of people. I always thought of your house as warm and friendly and busy."

My sister sipped and stared as though I were a stranger whose face she was trying to memorize for future meetings. And perhaps I was.

"Let's go into the kitchen," she said, standing up and walking through the massive dining room into the equally enormous kitchen.

She situated herself on the counter side of the island so I perched on a stool on the other. She still hadn't asked me what I was doing there.

Elizabeth hauled out a plate of cheese and some pepperoni from the fridge, daintily spread out as though perpetually ready for guests. Artfully she arranged crackers in a basket and slid a plate with a flowered napkin in front of each of us.

"I know you said you're not hungry, but I really must eat, or..." She held up her glass and took a long swallow.

Obediently, despite my full stomach, I nibbled on one of the crackers.

"You look different somehow."

Her voice was suddenly tender. I didn't remember that tone coming from this distant woman, the person I called my sister but didn't really know. I considered Karoline more of a sister, partly because Elizabeth always seemed to regard me from a chasm of indifference, partly because of the gap in our ages. Now I looked into her steady gaze and met warmth and interest. My reaction was instant. A gathering of tears slid down my cheeks.

Suddenly I found myself telling her about Karoline, about the gulf that had opened between us. She nodded and nibbled, returning to her observer's mode, her face impassive, asking no questions. Her little sister a telecast of complaint.

In the wake of her silence at the end of my confession, I took the fancy flowered napkin and wiped my face, then reached down to fetch my purse. Before I could haul out my evidence Elizabeth began to laugh.

"Here I thought your life was so perfect," she said.

She refilled our glasses, went to the wine rack, selected a bottle, and expertly pulled out the cork. "I think we're going to need lots of this tonight, little sister."

She was still chuckling when she sat down again, so I shoved the paper across the island in fury. I wanted to see her face crumble. I wanted her to be upset. To take what was happening to Karoline seriously. I wanted her to cry in front of me, embarrass herself as I had just done.

With a tremor of shock I realized that her attitude mimicked my own. The Ice Queen, impervious and unmovable, refusing to be touched. For the first time, I had to admit that I was in danger of losing that ability. Along with that realization came a rush of fear. I was suddenly vulnerable, open to hurt. I was here without Karoline. The one that had been my leader, guide, boss, friend. The one who navigated me through tense situations by teaching me avoidance techniques and defensive moves.

All of these thoughts soared through me in a split second as I watched my sister scrutinize the papers before her. Had she developed an Ice Queen as a defense, too?

At that moment Elizabeth looked up, as though she had followed my thought train. Our eyes held one another's for a long moment. I saw flickers of anger and resentment, rapidly replaced by a blankness that made her dark eyes look bottomless and empty.

"I was wondering when you would find out," she breathed, her voice a sigh of satisfaction. "I told Mom and Dad that they should tell you. It was ridiculous to keep it a secret especially once you were a grown woman."

The nastiness threw itself out in spittle, spraying me with contempt as though I had deliberately grown up ignorant. She tossed the papers down on the island, tucked another full bottle of wine under her arm, and picked up the cheese and crackers.

"Grab those," she directed, nodding to our half-filled glasses and bottle before she flounced out of the kitchen.

She led me up the stairs into a large window-lit room, which I knew had once bedded one of her hero children. Nowadays it was a library. All three walls were lined with bookshelves, while the fourth gazed out onto the lake. Two comfortable reading chairs strewn with matching cushions, a small pot-bellied fireplace, two end tables whose dark wood reflected the grain in the shelves, a sleek coffee table with hand carved Inuit soap stones, and old-fashioned goose necked reading lamps completed a picture of relaxation and comfort.

Elizabeth produced placemats and coasters, snatched the glasses and bottle from my hand, and whipped everything into decorative stances with a practiced flare. She waved at the chair to her right, beside which sat a fat book of poetry. Sammy's chair. Appreciator of emotional words after spending all day with machines. As I sat, she reached for a large album at the bottom of one shelf.

I took a long sip from my glass, fortifying myself, then poured us each more of the rich dark liquid. Tonight this wine was comfort or condolence. I wasn't sure which. Maybe it was a key to the lock of a secret that had obviously eaten at my sister for a very long time.

"Who are my real parents, Liz?" I eventually asked.

Dear Diary,

Well, well, well. You won't believe what I found out about Her Royal Princess. Was everything that well hidden? Or is she just stupid, as I have come to suspect? Can't wait to see the shock on her dumb ass face when I tell her. Of course, I'll be terribly sweet about it.

CHAPTER 12

Three bottles of wine later, when the inhibitions were truly squelched, Elizabeth released the venom. But before that she recited in a clinical fashion the story of how I'd come to be her younger sister.

"Our mother has always hoarded her secrets," she said, upright in her chair, the large album flat and unopened on her knees. "I discovered purely by accident that I had several aunts and uncles living in squalor somewhere in eastern Ontario. To hear her tell it, you'd think she'd been an African or Indian Princess, maybe even both. Suddenly I learned that she'd escaped an entirely different kind of existence, one of poverty and alcohol and abuse."

I said nothing, feeling that if I interrupted the flow Elizabeth's speech would plow into silence. I wondered how long she'd practiced these words. She looked down at the album or into her glass, held it out often for a refill, but she never looked at me.

"She'd lived all the stereotypes, so she tried to rearrange the facts, create a new framework. Up to that point, I'd grown up believing that her heritage was a gift of far-reaching proportions. I was constantly reminded to be proud of my royal roots.

"Mom's sister telephoned our house one day. I happened to answer. I think the woman was drunk. She had no idea who I was. She cried and yelled in my ear. I could barely understand her, but I heard enough to know that this insane person was somehow related to us. I would never forget the terror I felt. Someone's mind was shattering, with a little girl as direct witness. When Mom saw my face, she grabbed the phone, did the classic I told you never to call me here response, then told me to go upstairs to my room. Of course I didn't. I hid on the other side of the kitchen wall and listened. That's how I discovered this raging lunatic was my aunt, my perfect mother's own sister. I wouldn't let Mom get away with not telling me everything. Besides, she had to tell me, because soon afterward she went and got you."

Elizabeth's words were beginning to slur. Though my head was spinning, I was lucid enough to identify the childishness in her tone. A young girl, daughter of a dreamy, flighty woman whose secrets created a kind of barrier between her and the rest of the world. Spoiled with things, with stories, with a highly developed sense of superiority. Just like me, or perhaps I was just like her. Both of us unschooled in how to love. Something missing in the way we viewed our fellow human beings. Into this dichotomy came a small demanding child.

"They were over the moon about you. You were so beautiful, so perfect in every fucking way. I don't think they even saw me anymore."

I could imagine Elizabeth the child, pulling back, fashioning herself into the distant, uppity person I'd always known. She hadn't been taught how to give and she wasn't taught how to share her parents with someone else.

"They were just trying their best," I said. "They thought they were doing us a favor by providing us with a huge ego, a sense of entitlement, so we could elevate ourselves into the status that our mother had literally dreamed about."

Elizabeth suddenly flung herself to her feet, spilling little square pictures all over the floor as the album upended onto the carpet. She leaned over my chair, regurgitating all the resentment she'd harbored since I'd entered her life.

"I saw where you came from, missy. So high and mighty all the time. With your fancy apartment in L.A. and your big deal job. Hobnobbing with the crème de la crème of the film industry. You were born in a broken down shack to a mother who was nothing more than a drunken prostitute. Your beauty must only be skin deep, literally. I can't wait 'til you see this filth for yourself."

Swaying slightly, she bent over and picked up the pictures one by one. Black and white darts landed on my lap. Blurred stick-like figures, mouths open in excess, leaning on each other for balance. Flashes of bottles, cans, a sagging porch. The detritus of careless consumption. A dirty-diapered baby squatted in the sand. Dirty-cheeked children unsmiling in the bright sun.

If Elizabeth hadn't told me about the poverty and abuse, they would have been pretty clear from these photographs. Every skin color appeared to be represented, a united nations of alcoholics.

My birth mother was, Elizabeth and the photos told me, the gorgeous long-legged mulatto with ringlets of curls piled high on her head, the girl with the biggest smile, the most number of antics for the camera, the least balanced look.

"She did the nasty with everyone. Her brothers, her uncles, the assholes next door or down the street. She fucked for fun or money or booze. She had twelve children to who knows how many fathers? She never knew, never married any of them. She was a pig."

I fought to hold onto one of the little squares in the whirlwind of Elizabeth's fury. Looking no more than twelve years old, the lithe young body openly sexually aware, prematurely experienced, my birth mother grinned back at me. Her beauty was apparent even in the graininess of the old picture. No wonder she'd never married, I thought. Imagine her view of men.

In the lull of one of Elizabeth's intakes of breath, I asked, "What was her name?"

When I received no answer, I looked up and nearly withdrew in fear. Elizabeth's face was mottled with anger. She flew at me, upending the armchair. We rolled, entangled, onto the floor, pulling at each other's shirts. Her slaps stung, her punches threw my muscles into reflex action. I punched and slapped, too, pinched and pulled, sobbing. Elizabeth grabbed my hair, yanking my head painfully backward. I kicked out and landed my foot hard against her shin. She yelped and cried, abruptly rolling away from me.

I sat up. "Elizabeth!" I shouted. "I was a child. I didn't mean to hurt you. I didn't choose this. It wasn't my fault!"

I was screaming, on my feet now. I leaned over her. Taking a huge breath, I straightened up, frightened by my loss of control. For a moment I stared at the ceiling. Focused on the carefully crafted beams, the immaculate paint job. Calmer.

Elizabeth was still on the floor, her back to me, fetus-like, clutching her leg. Her voice was raspy, but I heard her.

"Could you get me some ice?"

I went into the kitchen and reappeared with an ice pack wrapped in a clean dishtowel. Gently I held it against her shin, which had already purpled.

"I'm so sorry, Lizzy. I didn't mean to hurt you. Do you think it's broken?"

"Nah, I bruise easily."

She sat up, brought her knees to her chest and took the ice from me. She stared down at her leg.

"Besides, I started it."

I sat down beside her, staring into her red-rimmed eyes. Suddenly she began to laugh, but this time the sound was contagious, filled with self-mockery, wonder and release. I joined her until we were both crying once again, but this time wrapped in each other's arms.

"I am such a bitch," Elizabeth moaned when she could. "Of course you were innocent. You were a child. How could I not have just loved you?"

"You were a child, too. I don't think Mom and Dad meant to ignore you, especially Mom. But they didn't teach us to be very loving toward one another. Maybe it was the huge secret that clouded everything. Mom was so obsessed with being…"

"Royalty?"

I laughed again. "Yeah, something like that. She didn't want anyone to know who she really was. Somehow that created a wall around all of us, I think. We acted out our parts. We had no idea there was anything wrong with our family."

Elizabeth was silent for a moment.

"With Sammy and the kids, it was always different. But I never could put it into words. Sam is naturally loving and demonstrative. I think he was just born with a capacity to love. He taught me everything I knew about giving. But somehow it never translated over to you, or Mom and Dad for that matter."

"You were only nineteen, just starting out with your life, when Mom and Dad transplanted to the States. They took me and left you behind. No wonder you hated me. The secret just kept festering." I sighed. "I'm trying not to blame Mom, but I want to shake her. I want to let her know how much better things could've been if she'd only told me."

Elizabeth got up slowly, testing her foot. The purple had already faded and she was strong on her feet.

"See. I'm nearly healed again." She smiled and gestured to the fallen chair. "Help me, baby sis?"

We repositioned the chair. I poured more wine while Elizabeth foraged in the kitchen, emerging with a bowl of taco chips and her famous Mexicana dip. We sipped and munched in companionable silence for a while.

"Anne, I'm so sorry."

I wagged a cheese-meat-onion-sour cream finger at her.

"No. No more apologies. You're the only one in my entire life who had the courage to confront me with the truth."

Elizabeth smiled weakly, her mouth crammed with taco. "I guess I should've beaten you up a long time ago."

I grinned back. "Yeah, maybe back then you could've taken me."

"Are you really okay with knowing about your birth mother?"

"I'm not sure. Actually I'm not sure about a lot of things. I haven't really progressed from shock to reality yet. I haven't even tried to get my head around it. Why don't I remember anything from back then?"

"I'm not sure, but maybe it was an abusive situation and you've blocked it all out."

We were both silent for a moment. My head was beginning to ache.

"I realize that we have a lot to work out. I'm not naive enough to think this one night will take care of all the baggage. But, I'm glad you came to me. I'm happy Sammy wasn't home, to be honest, or I'd never have erupted that way."

I squeezed her hand. "I know, Lizzy. This eruption has been good for both of us. We can start over. We're still blood."

Elizabeth gave a short chuckle. "Cousins. Sisters. Who cares?"

"Friends maybe?"

She squeezed back. "Even better."

She hesitated. I could see by her frown that she was working something out, so I let the silence remain.

"I have to tell you, even though Mom will probably never forgive me. Your birth mother is still alive."

I digested that. For some reason, I had expected her to be dead. No longer a breathing entity but a shadow, a memory. Not someone I could meet, confront, love or hate. The letter Karoline had received and hidden, the one from the adoption agency, had mentioned nothing about my birth mother other than she was 'related to' the adoptive parents.

"Do you want to find her?" Elizabeth asked. "I'll help you if you do. We don't have to tell Mom if you don't want to. After all, she's withheld a few things from us."

"Yeah, that's for sure." I sipped and chewed, thinking. "I don't know how I feel. I'd assumed she was dead. I don't know why. Probably so she could stay in the background, not change my life much. Thanks, though, for telling me. Can I sleep on it?"

We spent the night together and two more nights after that, learning to be sisters and friends. I gathered my belongings from the motel, cooked Elizabeth some of my favorite Yankee recipes while she was at work. We confided, gossiped, debated, analyzed our parents and discussed what I should do.

We scrutinized the photographs, found the 'last known' address for my birth mother. Although no names were listed, there was a rural street and a number. We studied maps. We promised, hugged, watched television, shared our favorite memories, movies, music.

I told her about my difficulties with men. I told her more about Karoline, Glenn Simpson, Parris, my uncertainty about how to handle the changes in my friend. About her betrayal. Elizabeth described her love for Sam and her children, her fears that her life was evolving in ways she hadn't expected. So we also discussed what she should do. We compared the paths our lives had both taken, uncertain and changing.

Elizabeth and I planned for hours, for both of us. We called our parents to let them know we were together. Nothing more. It was an awkward conversation for me. So many secrets lay atop the words.

Mom was her cheerful, bright self. She expressed joy at our reunion, though I wondered if that was the way she really felt.

I tried to put my emotions into words for Elizabeth but I wasn't able to clearly articulate the myriad of thoughts competing for my judgment. Did I resent my parents? Was I angry? Could I understand their silence? I wasn't certain of anything. Except that I had to find her, the aunt-mother behind the wall.

In a fierce spring rainstorm I headed south toward the airport, feeling very alone. After the whirlwind of the days in my sister's company I was bereft of her voice, face and the dual exploration we'd experienced. Now I headed back to my home that was no longer a home. A friend who was no longer my friend but my betrayer. The certainty welled up inside. I had to confront Karoline.

The feeling of anger smoldered until I was back in L.A. When I stepped back into our place I didn't know what to do with the leftover rage. The apartment was warm, clean and refreshed. Every sign of Glenn Simpson was gone. Karoline had left me a note.

"Anne, I'm sorry things have been so messed up lately. I'm off on another art buying trip for Daniel. I'll be gone til Friday. When I get back, we'll talk, OK? Love you, K. PS I kicked Glenn out."

I still had questions. I still had a few days' vacation. I booked a flight for the following morning.

Dear Diary,

Their level of trust is not an indication of how deserving I am. Rather, it is a measure of their lack of intelligence and the desire to question. They accept everything at face value. See everything from the shallow pools of their catered lives. Like children—believing in fairy tales, in happily ever after. She is such a cruel bitch. Did she think I was going to allow her to get her nasty little hands on him so she could twist his heart into pieces all over again?

CHAPTER 13

M y route through Cleveland Ohio sprawled out on both sides along a steep hill. Once I'd rollercoastered from top to bottom to top again, I followed the directions I had cobbled out from my maps and took an exit into a leafy wooded neighborhood. This was clearly an older wealthier area. The houses were primarily red brick but all designed slightly differently, perhaps forty to fifty years old. Well-kept, with large yards and gardens, shrubbery, wide porches with swings or inviting chairs. Children's playthings suggested that a younger crowd had moved in.

The first street on the right was the one on the letters Giulio had sent. Here the houses were slightly smaller, perhaps a bit older. The kind built for families once the Second World War was over. I crawled along carefully, aware that children might be coming home for lunch. Until I saw number twenty.

A one-story clapboard house, it was surrounded by rose bushes. They blushed with the first hints of red and pink against the prim white walls. Along the short walkway lovely greenery marched in perfectly straight lines toward the entry. The front door was painted a deep rich red to match the roses. The cement porch was armed on two sides with black wrought iron. Lace curtains were pulled over the windows but there was a car in the driveway.

I could imagine Giulio here. His designer's touch, his love of dramatic color and flora, his regimented yet creative style. In my imagination I pictured him arriving home from his pharmaceutical research job where he bent over a microscope all day surveying dead cells. He would shed his white coat for shorts and t-shirt, his microscope for a trowel and spend time with insects and growth.

In my mind he was still lithe and athletic, his small dancer's body well coordinated and shapely. He'd probably have treats for the neighborhood kids and play kick ball with them. Winter would mean snowmen in the yard or hockey in the street. In my ears I heard his laughter, loud and delighted, unabashedly joyful and who cared if the people in the next block heard it?

I wondered what his neighbors thought of him. Were they open and accepting? Did they love him? Trust their kids with him? Play cards with him and Paolo? Or were they suspicious and critical of his nature, of his lifestyle?

I parked the car a short distance from the house, locked it and walked back. A lion's head knocker graced the door and suddenly a memory flooded back. Karoline, Giulio and I sitting in one of our living rooms watching Frankenstein with Gene Wilder. Over and over again we howl at the line, "Nice knockers". I almost laughed out loud again as I let the lion's head fall onto the brass plate.

A man did indeed open the door but he was certainly not Giulio. Nor was he Paolo. Even given that I'd only met Paolo once and that years had passed by, I still could not have mistaken him for a nearly six-foot tall man who clearly had Oriental roots.

"Hello," I said, stammering in surprise. "I was wondering if Giulio and Paolo Ricci still live here?"

Looking at me with the kind of appreciation most men threw at me, he looked puzzled for a moment, wordlessly telling me volumes. But he wasn't bewildered by the names.

"Are you a friend of theirs? I thought Paolo told all his friends…"

"I am a friend of his partner, Giulio. Paolo and I aren't..."

Aren't what? Little did this man know.

He opened the door wider.

"Come in. My name's Phil Kwan. My wife is here, too, just in case you don't want to enter a strange man's house."

He grinned and the lines around his eyes crinkled. He was used to smiling. Around thirty, he was a good-looking man with pleasant welcoming brown eyes and straight black hair cut short and fashionable. He was wearing a black t-shirt and track pants, comfortable attire for sitting around the house.

"Alison!" he yelled, turning his head toward the back of the house.

I stepped inside just as a short blond woman appeared in the living room. She was very pretty and very shapely. Dressed in tight shorts and a sleeveless fuchsia top, Alison looked healthy and friendly.

"Hi," she said, coming toward me and holding out her hand.

I shook it. "My name is Anne Williams. I'm a friend of Paolo's partner, Giulio Ricci."

"You are Anne?"

Phil Kwan's outburst froze our handshake into a clutch of astonishment. A silent exchange between husband and wife, the kind that only truly intimate people are capable of giving, silenced him. Alison dropped my hand and took the lead.

"We know who you are, but obviously, for some reason, you don't know who we are."

She gestured to a big, comfortable chair opposite the sofa on which husband and wife then sat, staring at me as curiously as I stared at them.

"Let me explain. Phil and I lived across the street from Giulio and Paolo for a number of years in an upstairs apartment, which we rented. We love this neighborhood. Everyone is friendly. We have street parties, lots of kids, barbeques in each other's yards, that sort of thing. Paolo and Giulio fit right in and we became very close. That's how we met Karoline."

"You met Karoline?"

"Of course. Every time she came to visit, we had barbeques and dinners or played cards," Phil answered.

"She came to visit? But the only times Karoline and I have been apart are for business trips."

I was beginning to sound stupid, but my brain had slowed to a sluggish, slack-jawed crawl.

Alison, unlike her husband, was patient and linear.

"She came to visit fairly regularly. Perhaps she was also in the area on business. That's why we know all about you. What's puzzling is that you don't know all about us. I mean, Giulio said that the two of you kept up a correspondence. We naturally assumed that he would've mentioned us or that Karoline would've shared her visits over the years."

As I shook my head tears began to slide down my cheeks. Alison got up and handed me a box of tissues. I said nothing.

She continued. "When Giulio got sick with cancer, Karoline was here right away, even though she couldn't stay long."

There was an implied criticism that only made me choke with more gulped sobs. You never came to visit him, even when he was sick.

"He was very brave, in and out of the hospital. Finally, Paolo nursed him here at home with our help and some of the other neighbors."

"Alison's a nurse," Phil said. "And I'm a paramedic. That's why we're home during the day. We both do night shifts. We were able to assist Paolo during the day and some of the neighbors took turns if he needed them during the night."

"Sounds like a loving community," I managed to say between swallowing hiccups of anguish.

"Giulio eventually seemed to get better. We knew it was just a remission, but it was wonderful to see. His color returned. He was planting in the gardens again. Then suddenly, he was gone. Paolo found the bottle of pills. He was absolutely devastated."

Giulio was gone. I was in danger of losing complete control here so I focused on the fact that Paolo had turned out to be a good guy. At least Giulio had experienced true love before he died. I was able to calm down somewhat, though I continued to require tissues for sopping up the grief.

Alison's eyes were full of tears by now, too, so this time I was the one to hand over some tissue.

"After Giulio died, Paolo sold their house to me and Alison. We loved this little place and he knew we'd keep their roses healthy and their garden going. He hadn't decided where he was going to go, so we kept the apartment even after the house became ours, to give him lots of time to decide. We were happy to have him stay here as long as he needed."

"One day, a huge rental car showed up on the street. I happened to be looking out of the window..."

"He's a self-proclaimed neighborhood watch," Alison inserted.

"...and saw a woman and two men at Paolo's door. He let them in after some gesturing and shouting in Italian. I waved at Paolo, but he waved back, signaled with 'a thumbs up' that he was okay. Eventually they went inside and several hours later, the car left. We never saw Paolo again."

My mind raced. I'd spilled my shock and sorrow, unclogged the dam so I could think again.

"Are you sure he wasn't kidnapped or something? I mean, why did he just disappear like that? Maybe it wasn't his family..."

"Karoline called Italy," Alison said. "She was able to talk to Paolo. Although she thought he sounded sad and somewhat strange, he was okay. Basically he had agreed with his mother and brothers to go back to Italy immediately. He said he'd send for anything he really wanted. Karoline did manage to get an address for him. We sent photo albums and some other things we felt were important, but he never replied."

Alison looked like she was still upset. A shade of anger flushed her cheeks.

"His family simply whisked him away, obviously ashamed of him, I suppose. It's been several months now, so..."

A long silence allowed me to digest the bizarre circumstances. Phil disappeared into the kitchen. He returned with a tray on which sat a large teapot, three mugs, the usual accompaniments and some banana bread. We sat for a long while munching and sipping. It felt like comfort.

"We haven't heard from Karoline since then, either," Alison finally said. "She told us she'd be in touch, but that she was moving and she'd send her new address, which she never did. We were a bit hurt, to tell the truth, because although we knew she was Paolo and Giulio's friend, we felt close to her too. We tried calling, but she never returned our calls."

"You don't have to tell us, obviously. But we're curious as hell about why you're here, why now, why not...then? And what about Karoline?"

I was becoming used to Phil's bluntness. I knew I couldn't supply all the facts or implications so I simply responded with the same candor.

"I...I don't know. Karoline's had a..."

I almost choked, stumbling on how to explain.

"She's had an emotional breakdown," I finally said. "She...she didn't even tell me about Giulio. I didn't know he was...gone. She's been...distant, different."

I knew that I sounded very odd. I was in shock, mind reeling, senses overloaded. When I initially found those letters I assumed I could reconcile with Giulio. Let him know the truth about Paolo and me. I assumed he would help me figure out why our friend had done this. I assumed that he would help me fix Karoline.

Alison and Phil clasped each other's hand. Clearly rocked by the news, they also looked uncertain as to whether or not they should believe me.

"Has she sought treatment?" Only a nurse would pose such a question.

I shook my head, my eyes on the floor.

"No," I managed to say. "She hasn't admitted anything. I haven't...been able to help her. No one has."

Then I cleared my throat. Ignoring their wide shell-shocked eyes I decided I had to tell some of the truth.

"She also lied to you about me. I didn't keep up a correspondence with Giulio. I didn't know he was here in the US until recently. She kept all of that a secret from me. She told him I never wanted to see him again, but that I'd answer his letters if he insisted. Then she didn't even tell me he'd died."

There was a deep silence in the room, a blanket of disbelief and suspicion. I could feel the air around my hosts change from curiosity to wariness. They exchanged that sideways look again, speaking without words.

"I don't blame you for not believing me," I said quickly before they could respond.

I reached into my purse and pulled out a few sheets of paper. "Maybe you'll understand when you see this."

Phil took the page from me and held it so that both he and Alison could read.

My dearest Anne, I am sorry that it has taken me so long to write. Many changes have happened since you left and I decided to stay. Paolo did not get married, as you know. We spent all the months talking.

Finally he admitted that his sex antics were all avoidance. He did not wish to admit that he is gay and in love with me. It is a very difficult thing for traditional Italian males. We have really been in love with each other our whole lives. So you see that something very good came from your moments with Paolo.

We have decided to move to Cleveland, where he has a job opportunity. I'm sure I will find something, too. Pharma gave me a very good reference and genetics is such a big, new field. So we won't be as far away from you once we return to the States.

My dear, knowing the way that you think, I imagine that you are asking my forgiveness just now. Instead I am asking for yours. For one instance of hurt, I was willing to trade years of love and friendship. I am very ashamed and I am begging you to forgive me. I am now happier than I have been in my whole life. I have always loved Paolo, which somewhat explains my behavior when I knew that you had been with him. But I do not want to end our relationship. I am hoping that you will see me in the future.

Alison finished first, then glanced up at me with a cool, appraising look.

"On top of one pile of letters there was a note from Paolo. It said that he was returning all of Giulio's letters as Karoline requested. See?"

I held it up for their scrutiny. Perhaps they recognized Paolo's writing because they both nodded.

Dear Karoline and Anne, Enclosed please find, as requested, your letters. Paolo

"Giulio always was a bit of a packrat, so they're all here. This one's an example. I did not, and would never, write something like this."

Dear Giulio, I never want to see you again. Your partnership with that man disgusts me. How can you possibly trust him, let alone love him?

"This was the last one he sent. At least, I assume it is, because there were no others in the packet."

Dear Anne, Karoline has at last told me about your continued affair with Paolo. Now I understand why you never came to visit. Now I see where Paolo went on all those business trips. I do not wish to confront him, for reasons that I do not care to share with you. I want you to know that when I leave, I wish you as much love and joy as I experienced with this wonderful man.

"And this is the horrid response."

Giulio, I'm sure you know that I am not interested in taking Paolo from you. I don't want him. He means nothing to me other than an occasional fuck. This works for him, too. Since he is obviously bisexual and does not want you to know, I am a safe choice. I would suggest pretending you don't know. Keep imagining that you mean everything to him.

"Karoline didn't move anywhere, either." It was childish to add this detail, but I was seething once more.

They were silent again. Phil's eyes remained on me, while Alison's focused on the papers.

"I loved Giulio," I said. "I would never have ignored his illness or turned away from him because of some paltry disagreement. I was led to believe that he never returned from Italy. I grieved for him. You have to believe me."

I never know whether it's my looks or my oratory skill that usually convinces people to agree with me, believe me or follow me. But it's a documented fact that good-looking people are more persuasive and win the job interviews. Whatever it was didn't matter at that moment. Phil and Alison Kwan decided I was genuine.

"I can't imagine that Giulio believed this final letter. Yes, Paolo went away on business quite often, but he always called and talked to Giulio for hours. Maybe he was feeling vulnerable or wasn't thinking straight because of his illness. For Karoline to do this when she knew how sick he was is—well, it's unforgivable."

"Clearly Karoline is mentally ill. The person we knew never demonstrated a mean bone in her body," Alison said. "If she ever does reach out, and wants to get better, as vacuous as this might sound, we would totally be there for her."

"I'm not sure I will be." Phil doesn't disappoint me in his bluntness. "This response is dated very close to his death. I wouldn't be surprised if it was the cause of his suicide."

I agreed thoroughly with Phil. I would never forgive Karoline. I wanted to go home and rip her face in half. The rage was massive. A startling, crippling fury that blurred my vision and made my head ache. She will pay. Mentally ill was just a nice word for psychopath in Karoline's case.

"Paolo must not have read these letters. At least, not that last one. He would have dealt with Karoline."

Ripped her face in half?

"Maybe it wasn't part of the bunch Karoline asked Paolo to return," I suggested. "Maybe she took the correspondence between Giulio and me when she came for the funeral. The fact that I found them all together in her closet doesn't really mean they were put there at the same time."

They were silent in the wake of my theory. Perhaps they were in shock, just as I was when I first read these letters. My horror was deepened now that I knew the result of Karoline's treachery. Giulio was dead.

"We have another little shock for you," Phil eventually said.

I smiled, a fairly weak spark amid my swollen eyes and tear tracks. "I'm ready. I think."

"Among Paolo's possessions...well, let me show you."

Once again, Phil disappeared. This time he returned with a beautiful deep blue urn, a bird in flight painted across the ceramic sky. I gasped.

"Paolo wanted to bury Giulio under the tree in the backyard. When the time came, he wanted to be placed beside him. Paolo's family has obviously thwarted that wish."

"We didn't know what to do," Alison confessed. "So we kept Giulio...the urn...hoping some day we'd get a message from Paolo or Karoline about what to do with the ashes."

I reached out and took the urn from Phil, cradling it as though I had after all been allowed to embrace Giulio in life.

"Thank you," I whispered. "You don't know how much this means to me. I loved Giulio very much."

I forced my thoughts away from the well of Karoline's deceit and those final words from Giulio's pen. Instead, I focused on the urn, the moment. This unexpected, exquisite gift.

"Are you still prepared to have Giulio's ashes in your backyard?"

"Of course...absolutely..." They answered at exactly the same moment, expressing the sentiment in different words but with the same eager posture.

"We really loved those guys," Phil said. "We are honored to have their house. We figure that, even if for some reason we have to leave here..."

"Or we never have kids or if we do, they don't want it..."

"...Giulio would still be here. Even though Paolo probably won't ever be buried beside him, if he comes back to visit, he'll see the tree they planted together. Seems perfect to us."

"We actually prepared the plot as soon as the ground warmed up, but we were still waiting."

"I know I'm just a substitute for Paolo, but I promise you, I loved Giulio. Would you allow me to witness the burial?"

Though I knew intuitively that they continued to be uncertain about me, they consented. They took a chance that I was telling the truth about not being the author of those letters. I think they did it for Giulio's sake. I was there. Hopefully I had been a friend. There was no one else.

The backyard was exquisite. Lined with evergreen bushes, dotted with flowers of all shapes and sizes, a neat plot of garden along the back fence. Over to one side stood a hearty little maple tree flourishing in the rich soil.

Alison and Phil allowed me to carry the urn as our little procession approached the tarp they'd thrown over the hole near the tree trunk.

Standing over the resting place, I clutched the beautiful vase that contained Giulio's ashes. I wasn't sure I could let him go.

Alison surprised me by pulling out a sheet of paper. The kind of diaphanous blue-tinted paper that had lain in a bundle in Karoline's closet. The flourishes of a creative hand were visible through the single leaf as she held it aloft in the sun.

"This is a poem that Giulio loved," she explained to me. "I thought he would've approved having it read at his burial."

Here with a little bread beneath the Bough,
A Flask of Wine, a Book of Verse—and Thou
Beside me singing in the Wilderness—
Oh, Wilderness were Paradise enow!

Really? I thought. *The Rubaiyat of Omar Khayyam?* Ice Queen Anne would have laughed out loud. I pushed her aside and bowed my head respectfully instead.

We stood hushed for a moment, the neighborhood devoid of human sounds on a workday so the songs of birds and the complaints of insects could be heard. Then the three of us knelt. Carefully opening the lid, I shook the urn's contents into the ground.

There were many things I liked about Alison and Phil Kwan. One of them was that they didn't attempt to extract empty promises about returning to Giulio's grave. I don't think they had entirely changed their minds about my claims or me.

Before my trip to Cleveland I was hurt, shocked and confused by Karoline's actions. Now I was furious. I allowed the anger to gather in my chest as I flew back to L.A. That night I entered our apartment in a seething rage.

"I decided I had to confront Karoline," is what I tell Ethan. "I rehearsed what I was going to say all the way home. But when I got here, she was…she was in such a state that I couldn't say anything. That was the night she died."

Ethan sits quietly holding my hand. I know from experience that he is thinking. He doesn't speak without planning ahead.

"I am so sorry this happened to you, my love," he finally says. "I don't know if I can make you understand that all of this was indicative of Karoline's mental health problems. She was clearly disturbed."

"I spent my whole life with her. I loved her." I say it as a lament, a sigh. A question. Who am I that I could live happily with someone who would do this to me?

"Maybe her mind began to break down slowly, just a few years ago. Maybe everything started out as a lark—let's see if I can sneak this one past Anne. Or maybe at first she thought she was protecting you. Then she didn't know how to untangle everything. We might never have all the answers. Sometimes people like Karoline are simply irrational. Their thought processes are skewed, so we can't really follow the patterns. Maybe there are no patterns."

I sit up straighter, try to show him that I am strong again. I am not Ice Queen Anne. I am not Crazy, Falling Apart Anne. I am someone altogether different.

"I know what I have to do, though, Ethan," I say. "I do have to follow Karoline's trail. I have to find my birth mother."

After a pause, he nods his head. "Yes, I know you do. I think you're ready to do this. And when you come back…"

He tilts my chin toward him so that his wide blue eyes, his wisdom and love, overflow into mine.

"…we'll talk about the word love and what it means."

Dear Diary,

Isn't it funny how one small thing can trigger all the madness? How one minute you can be sitting there talking and the next you are screaming at each other? What odd creatures people are. Especially the people in my life. They're weird, unnatural and foolish. I have no idea how I got stuck with them. Except they need me. I am the one who holds them all together.

CHAPTER 14

I make the preparations and tell Parris and my bosses. I want Parris to describe the flaws in my thinking. She offers a few bits of advice, but reluctantly acknowledges that this is something I have to do.

Her intense blue eyes search my face with affection and concern.

"Just don't have your expectations too high," she says. "This kind of journey can be transforming, but sometimes...well, it's simply disappointing instead."

I meet with Joseph and Vicki, talk about my future with Grace Productions. Speak of my slow recovery. They too agree that I am probably taking the right steps, though they still miss me. I get the sense that they want me back as my old self and are suspicious that I might already be someone different, but they are supportive nevertheless.

The night before I am to leave, Ethan takes me out to a new restaurant. Spago has just opened on the Sunset Strip. The area of West Hollywood is filled with clubs and bars and billboards. We love it because it's the center for introducing new bands. This section of Sunset Blvd is alive at night. Music permeates the air. People walk up and down talking loudly or humming to themselves. All dressed up. Wild and free and exotic.

We arrive in a limousine. I wear a turquoise dress that's very low cut and Ethan wears a dark blue suit that reflects his wonderful eyes. We grin at each other. Stepping out like this gives off a decadent and delicious feeling.

The chef who opened Spago is becoming well known. His reputation for creative food and superb service has spread rapidly through the young well-to-do crowd and the film stars. Ethan and I are led to a gorgeous half shell booth. We're immediately surrounded by waiters, busboys, the hostess, and of course Mr. Puck the owner and chef. I should have known that the Byrne name would be popular.

We cuddle up in the soft leather seat and take a long time to order and eat. As though we're not in the center of a bustling restaurant in the middle of a gigantic metropolis, but in a different dimension of no worry, no external influences, no ruined lives.

We wait for coffee and liqueurs to talk about my journey.

"I wish I could come with you," Ethan says, his voice thick with a mixture of apprehension and understanding. "But this case I'm on…"

Then he shakes his head, preventing me from having to say it.

"And I know, of course I know, that you have to do this on your own."

That night, our lovemaking is intense, tender and passionate, as though I am going off to war. In a sense, perhaps it is a war. A fight to know the real me. A struggle to the death in a sense. For would I be fatally wounded or would I return whole and strong?

I promise to call every night. I promise to tell him everything.

Despite the fear that courses through me, one moment I tell myself that I'll confess everything to him. Then uncertain I'll have the courage, I change my mind the next minute.

I close the door on that decision for now.

When I have packed my suitcase, I look around the apartment that has been my home for so many years. I have a feeling that I may never live here again. I close that door for now, too.

I fly from Los Angeles to Toronto, prevented the entire way from seeing the world I am leaving and the one I am about to enter by a huge persistent cloud cover. Perhaps that is just as well.

I drive away from the airport feeling odd. Dizzy, overwhelmed and uncertain. Suddenly I am completely alone. I don't have Ethan. I don't have Parris. I have only myself and I'm not even sure who that person is. My heart begins to hammer. After a while, I have difficulty breathing. I finally admit that I can't keep driving in this condition.

At the first decent-looking motel, I pull into the parking lot and pay for a room for the night. Though I feel like flopping down onto the bed into oblivion, I sit at the desk instead. I brought a notebook with me from home and now I feel the need to use it. The action reminds me of Karoline and her nightly scratching, but I ignore the thought.

I fill page after page as evening turns into night. Details, emotions, questions about Karoline that mostly begin with why. Questions for Mom/Vera and my birth mother whoever she might be. Accusations and longings. I put them all down in blue and white. I curse and apologize. I reflect on the person I am now, who I was before Ethan, who I could become. Ponderings that I probably should have considered in my teens the way most people did.

When I am finished, or at least too exhausted to continue, I wander out into the world and buy myself a huge submarine sandwich, filled with meat and veggies, with a side of potato chips and two donuts. Then I call Ethan.

As soon as I hear his voice, I don't even try to stop the sobs from erupting once more. How do I know this man, whom I met just a little more than a year ago, will understand? This isn't one of the questions I had to write down, because I have the answer. It echoes deep within me, a part of me that I only recently excavated but which I pray is real. For whatever reason I am suddenly blessed with love. And although I am a novice at it, I feel confident that I can grow into it with first-class honors under his non-judgmental devoted tutelage.

If I decide to finally tell him about the night that Karoline died, I am pretty certain that he will help me through the aftermath. But I haven't firmly decided that my conscience is developed well enough to feel the need to confess. For now, I vow to bask in our relationship. Grow stronger. Understand more deeply. I've never shed so many tears, but nor have I ever felt such all-consuming joy.

I tell Ethan about the mad scrawls in the hotel, my terrible calorie-laden dinner.

"How do you feel now?" His voice is tender and concerned.

I hesitate. Force the tears to come to an end. For now.

"I actually think I'm okay. I feel pretty tired, but I got a lot of shit out today. I might even be less angry."

"Are you sure you want to keep going? On this journey, I mean. I'm assuming you'll wait until tomorrow, but do you think it's too much to tackle? Or are you all right to go on to Vryheid?"

This time there is no hesitation.

"Yup, I'll wait 'til tomorrow, but I'm good to go. In fact, I think I'll be able to handle whatever comes much better now. If I feel overwhelmed, I know what to do. Pull over into a motel and start writing."

He laughs. "Sounds like a pretty healthy choice."

We talk about his parents, briefly about his case and what he did today. For a while, we make verbal love on the telephone, getting as close through words as it is possible to get. When we finally hang up, I give in to the exhaustion and sleep for twelve hours.

Dear Diary,

I read somewhere—I'm pretty sure it was Nietzsche—that "it is impossible to suffer without making someone pay for it; every complaint already contains revenge." Interesting, huh?

CHAPTER 15

On my map, Vryheid is a tiny dot perched on the Grand River next to the village of Burford. The nearest city is Brantford. Compared to the sprawl of L.A. it's a postage stamp. As I approach the area, nothing seems to match the lines on the map. I am submerged among trees and fencing. Surrounded by trucks and other cars, signs flying by too fast to read, I am suddenly frustrated and lost.

The berms in the middle and on each side of the highway are lush with wild grass and every kind of tree you can imagine. Pointed evergreens and fat spreading deciduous make every road look the same. When I take one exit, I get lost several times amongst sterile city streets, a boxy mall and circular overpasses.

Once I retrace my steps, discover the right exit, I am, as I should've been, surrounded by flat countryside. Yellow fields of hay and wheat whisper and sigh when I roll down my windows to the cooling breeze. It's a hot summer day, the kind that feels as though you've put your head into an oven. But I am tired of the air conditioning and I love the scents of the country. Acrid manure mingled with sweet pine and dampened dirt. A fragrance that can only be green and growth.

A little town with yawning verandas and multiple church steeples lazes in the sun. A few people sit with cold drinks in the shade while some, large hats as umbrellas from the heat, dig in their gardens. This is Burford, a place I'd like to visit if I had time. Instead, I drive past the town out into wilderness again, surrounded by the long hairy leaves of cornfields. Even the birds are silent in the heat, though the cicadas violin madly.

When I reach the outskirts, heralded by the pioneer cemetery, I know I have gone too far. Once again, frustrated and hot, I turn around. Vryheid should be tucked like a small pinky finger alongside the river, just north of Burford, but there is no hint of its existence whatsoever.

Half hidden among drooping cedar trees, their long spindly arms nearly reaching one another across the road, I suddenly spy the sign I hadn't noticed before. 'Vryheid' in white on green. 'Est. in 1784' written underneath. It's no surprise that I missed it. The sign is nearly covered by vines and leaves, not to mention the faded condition of the printing.

The road is perhaps a lane and a half wide, bracketed on both sides by old bushy trees, lined with wild grass and shiny white Queen Anne's Lace. A tunnel of hushed tones. Birds are encouraged by the cool shade to sing softly, while squirrels chat and click the branches when they jump. Grasshoppers and cicadas play their instruments. Since humans are nowhere to be seen, nature can be heard. Until I plow my car into their midst that is. I leave behind a wake of frightened silence and dust.

There is absolutely no sign of a town, a village, or even a crossroad. The growth on both sides obscures most of the view, but there are no laneways. No buildings peer through the forest.

It's obviously been a dry couple of weeks in hot sun, because the grasses are brittle and the roadway is scattered with sand. My wheels catch a couple of times as the pavement turns to dirt. The trees are even older and more bent over, their long needled limbs weighted with age and abundance. Then quite suddenly the tree line ends.

I burst out of the shady tunnel into yellow light and green fields. Broad-leafed little plants huddle together, resembling dark cabbages in a grocery store bin. I think these are ginseng. To my right, up a slight incline and across a low fence, I can see a paved road, which has clearly been built to skirt around this deserted area.

On my left, a little island of trees surrounds a lone farmhouse. Green and red maples, weeping willows, oak and evergreen, anything that provides a shield for the lonely home standing amidst a vast field. Sentinels against the wind that runs rampant across the flat land. A mailbox lurches drunkenly at the end of the long narrow driveway. The number from my crude map, #49857, is stamped on a spindly emergency flag atop a firm fat post. The house can only squint out from among the greenery.

Does Vryheid consist of one single farmhouse?

Although I drive slowly, the wheels churn up stones and bits of gravel, making my entry noisy and intrusive. I am astounded that the yard, once I torpedo through the clusters of branches, is still empty. How has no one heard my approach? Perhaps, despite the presence of a small red car, there's nobody home. Maybe they're out working in a field far from the house. I almost use this as an excuse to turn around. Faced with the reality of this place I am tempted to give in to cowardice. I force myself to put the car in park, turn off the engine and open my door.

The house is a squat structure that seems to have sprouted thick legs in every direction. It's not a typical farmhouse, although the original red cedar shingle exterior is common. Over the years someone has obviously added to the small cottage it once was, with no regard for outer beauty. Some of the additions are white cedar, some red siding, some natural stone. A hodgepodge that has even encroached upon the surrounding trees, forcing them to embrace the rooftops, it resembles a motel built by different owners. It doesn't look particularly poverty stricken or cheap, just ill planned.

This does explain why no one heard my car. If they are in a back room, they are probably shielded from any noise from the roadway.

The initial front entry remains. A huge porch all across the front looks new, relative to the rest of the house. Painted brown, it matches the window frames on the center cottage. Twin willows weep over the roof of the veranda, covering the entire front with cool dark shade. *See a weeping willow, crying on his pillow, maybe he's crying for me...*

Surrounded by giant purple clover, wild grass and geraniums, the effect is a lack of inhibition rather than carelessness. The thick oak door is firmly shut, shaded by a matching screen. Lace curtains frame the small shuttered windows at the front. The place looks deserted, calm and silent. An artificial cake baking in the sun.

My footsteps echo on the wood as I mount the steps. I am nervous, hot and thirsty and doubtful. It's all I can do to reach up and ring the bell. My hand trembles and I feel faint. When the door is yanked open a couple of minutes later, the only reason I stay on my feet is because I have recently experienced an even greater shock looking over my own balcony.

The woman standing in the dim hallway is my mirror image. She has my height, my coloring, my build—my face. We stare for a long universe of a moment. Then I stagger backward just as she pitches forward, so I almost miss catching her in my arms.

My purse tumbles to the porch, scattering papers and lipstick and coins, but I ignore it in favor of bringing us both gently to the surface of the wood, where I sit awkwardly, panting. She lays half on top of me. Her face turns upward. Her eyes roll back.

I hold her head up, wait for her breathing to settle. Study her face with a fascination that's unbecoming under the circumstance. But I can't help myself. The contours of her cheekbones, her lashes, her eyebrows, mouth, nose, neck...every part of her is identical to mine.

Her eyelids flutter and her chest heaves as she regains consciousness. When she does, she sits straight up, an arrow aimed in disbelief. Her eyes are wide with shock. She pushes herself around to face me and we end up in a kiss position.

"Who are you?" she demands.

Other than the rounded-vowel-accent that I lost long ago, even her voice is mine. For a moment, I think I won't know the answer, then I recover slightly.

"I'm Anne Williams."

"You are not Anne Williams, that's for sure."

We scramble awkwardly to our feet where I proceed to gather the contents of my purse, including my passport. She stands frowning at me, hands on her hips.

"You're my twin. Or my ghost. Or…what the hell is this?"

She spits the words at me, angrily, as though I committed the crime of stealing her face. Her skin is red with the blush of emotion, probably mimicking my own precisely.

I gulp and try to recover, but all I can say is, "Can I please have a drink of water? I think this time I might be the one to faint."

There's a bench running all around the porch, attached to its railings. I sit abruptly, grateful that the willows keep the sun off my head. Sweat pours from my hairline and I am parched. The Other Me says nothing, but disappears into the house. She returns quickly with a huge pitcher of ice water and two glasses. We both sit and pour the cold liquid down our throats. It has the earthy tinge of a spring well, full-bodied and delicious.

When my throat feels able, I start to tell her my story.

"I found some papers…" I don't bother to explain when or where "…which revealed that I was adopted. I didn't know before…" I pause, not sure which 'before' I am thinking of. "This address was listed as my birth mother's. So I came here…"

It sounds lame and stilted, but my brain isn't back to full capacity yet.

"You must be my twin. I mean really, you have to be. Were you…did you grow up here?"

She shakes her head, her lovely me head and puts her glass down.

"I was adopted, too. I found out two years ago."

She glances behind her, as though to indicate the entire household.

"Obviously I know about Dembi, but you…"

"Dembi?"

"He's our brother. Our triplet. We're triplets."

She says the word slowly, as though tasting it on her lips and tongue.

I don't know what I am feeling. I sit as though I haven't heard her. I breathe in the scent of clover and something else sweet. Listen to the birds flutter and chirp overhead. I am afraid that if I move, this will all be real. Or else it's a dream and I am going crazy again.

"What's your real name?"

I blink at her. "What's yours?" I snap back, in the same snooty tone.

"Miriam. Miriam Hunter, though our birth surname was Johnston, in case you didn't know. But I know you can't be Anne Williams."

Wordlessly, my hands shaking even more than they had previously, I hand my passport over to her.

Her own hands tremble now. Miriam looks it over carefully, then stares back at me.

"I don't understand. I just don't know how…"

We are interrupted by the sound of the front door. A tall young man bounces out onto the porch, his face alight with a huge grin. Except for the off-kilter set of his mouth, he is identical to Miriam and me. In fact he's even more beautiful. His skin is a slight shade darker, resulting in a face that's youthful and smooth. Though he is obviously thirty-three years old, he appears much younger. Angelic. His eyes are innocent. His hair is also slightly darker than his sisters', but perhaps the brush cut only makes it look that way.

His clothes are twisted as though he pulled them on in the dark. The t-shirt reflects a Disney character and the shorts are baggy on his gangly frame. His hands, curled and fluttery, seem to probe the air before he passes through it. When he finally becomes aware of the two-ness of us, he stops dead. The smile disappears. His eyes dart from me to Miriam and back again.

I feel as though he is scanning me, a machine-like brain tapping into my pores with a million antennae. He is clearly mentally handicapped, disabled, differently wired, whatever language I should be using. If I had not been shocked and uncomfortable before, I certainly am now. I have no idea how to respond. I realize that I have never, in my pampered and cosseted life, been this close to a handicapped person other than someone begging on the street.

I hear Karoline's voice, silent for so long, suddenly lecturing me should I make a move for my wallet. "He's probably got his Mercedes parked down the street. These people are usually frauds and if not, you don't want to get too close, they have lice."

This man is well dressed and clean, though. He's not on a street begging. Karoline's advice doesn't seem to apply and I flounder. I stay rooted to my spot. Miriam leaps to her feet to hold his hands until his gaze meets hers directly.

"Dembi, this is…our triplet."

She can't bring herself to say my name, unconvinced even by my official identification.

"You know what I mean by triplet?"

He nods his head eagerly, tears himself from Miriam's hold. Abruptly he's in my space before I can move or think. His soft hands unfurl and glide over my face, tickle my cheeks, feather my neck.

"Triplet is the same."

His words are thick as though his tongue is several times too big.

"She is Miriam and she is Dembi."

Miriam comes over to his side, gently taking his hands again. She can see the discomfort written in the expression of my eyes and mouth, snapshots of her own without the judgment.

"That's it, Dembi. We look exactly the same."

"Amazing," I manage to stammer. "Obviously you and I are identical twins. And he is our triplet. But he can't be identical. He still looks just like us. But he's mentally…"

I blather, saying the wrong things. Rude selfish Anne bubbles to the surface so easily. Aftershocks from yet another earthquake.

Miriam takes pity on me, though there is a flash of anger and disgust that she quickly abolishes in favor of sympathy.

"You're right. Obviously up until now I thought we were fraternal twins, not triplets. And yes, he's different. But you will be amazed by Dembi in so many ways. If you stay long enough to learn."

There's an accusation in her tone. An assumption that I am simply on a research mission to gather the bare facts but unwilling to live with what I discover. She is not entirely wrong. She's my twin and she can see through my façade, my fancy L.A. clothes, my ridiculous responses. But I am determined to prove that only Ice Queen Anne would have responded negatively. That I have evolved. I am loved. I have learned regret and humility and layers of emotion. I am no longer Surface Anne.

"I would like to stay long enough, Miriam."

I don't know how to describe my journey to her. Who I am. What I am. "I killed my best friend. I threw her away like a bag of unwanted clothing. Then I came looking for my family." Might not be a good way to introduce myself.

"I'd like to get to know you and Dembi. I'd like to meet our mother…"

Dembi clasps my hands. His own slightly unfurl in my palm as though he has relaxed in my presence. I feel somehow complimented.

"You stay with us. You are us."

Tears come unbidden, slipping down my cheeks. I am not used to handling these feelings that well inside me. I begin to sob. There are no controls, no handbook. No Karoline to help me through this part. No voices at all.

My siblings sit on either side of me as though we have done this all our lives. That circle of three re-created by blood and luck.

When I am calm once more, Miriam sits up straight and slides a distance away from me on the bench. Dembi remains glued to my side. He's so close that I can feel the heat from his body. Hear the beat of his heart. He hums a sad song in my ear, very softly, comforting himself and me.

"I can't do anything until you explain how two sisters can have the exact same name," Miriam says. "I realize that we were all adopted out, but to believe that two of you ended up being Anne Williams is ridiculous."

"I'm sorry, I don't know what you mean. What other Anne Williams?"

"The one who's been coming here for the last three years. The one who found our mother first, eventually contacted me, brought me here. The one who helped with our mother's illness and Dembi's needs. Our sister. Anne Williams. She lives in Los Angeles."

Suddenly I understand. How could I not? This is a repeat of what she did with Giulio and Paolo. I unfold my wallet, slide an old square out from the hidden pocket and hand it to Miriam. It's one of those photos from a fair. Karoline and I squished into a booth. Eyes widened by the flash. Mouths opened in unabashed fun. My twin stares at it for a century, silent and confused.

"She was my friend," I say, stumbling slightly on the last word. "Her name was Karoline."

Miriam's eyes fill with tears. I feel the reactions of dismay and disappointment at the betrayal as though they are my own, which indeed they are. For a moment I wish I could put my arm around her narrow shoulders but a wall of doubt prevents me from doing it. Old cold Anne struggles with the emotionally immature new one.

Dembi has no such qualms or conflicts. He goes to Miriam's side, puts his arm around her. His head on her shoulder, he stares down at the picture.

"Sister," he says.

Sister, friend, mentor, guide, colleague, genius. How many faces had Karoline presented? Clever, deceitful, unforgiven Karoline.

A couple of squirrels scream above our heads, leaping frantically across the branches. Just then a big grey and black tabby cat strolls onto the porch, heaving himself at Dembi's feet.

"Rolly," he says in delight.

He picks the big feline up like a toddler, cuddling him on his shoulder. The animal purrs and settles into Dembi's arms, an obviously frequent embrace. The squirrels are not so impressed by the presence of a cat.

Still there is silence from Miriam, though she smiles briefly at our brother and his pet. At last she turns to look into my eyes. It's a weird sensation having that face inches away, identical yet separate. Her thoughts her own, the vibrations and expressions so similar.

"Why would…Karoline…do this?"

Despite the fact that more tears are struggling to be released I keep my gaze on hers. I angrily push my sorrow back, tired of the emotional wreck I've become.

"I don't know. I just can't explain it, Miriam. She had a breakdown, a complete mental collapse."

My sister hasn't noticed that I use the past tense for Karoline, so I try to gentle my voice when I tell her.

"She committed suicide."

Miriam gasps but Dembi is too wrapped up in Rolly to take note. I'm not sure he would even understand the word.

"Oh my god, that's horrible. That's…" Miriam bursts into tears. "I was so angry with her for abandoning us. She just stopped all contact. No more visits, calls, just silence. And all along, she was…"

She lifts her tear-stained face to study my expression.

"How did you handle all that?"

"I had a severe bout of depression too when I found all of this hidden information about my own life. I still don't understand how she could betray me like this. I can't quite forgive her. Or myself for that matter."

"Yourself?"

I choke back the urge to tell her everything.

"I didn't do enough to save her. She broke down practically in front of me, but I kept thinking she'd come back to herself. Maybe I was just lazy or in denial, or whatever. In any event, she's gone."

Miriam weeps quietly. The tears track slowly down her cheeks. Her shoulders hunch over.

"I grew to love Anne," she says, then corrects herself. "Karoline, I mean. I don't understand either. Maybe now we never will. But she found me and led me to Memé and Dembi, so I can't quite be angry. Just very confused."

She turns around and puts her arms around me, drawing me close to her in a fierce hug. At first I am startled into my usual reaction, an instinct to pull away. Then I feel the heat from her skin, the dampness of her tears. Smell the light perfume that she wears. I respond to the energy flowing from her. I wrap my arms around her, too. I cling to this other version of me. My blood and my cells twinned in another human being who'd loved Karoline.

"And now I have you, too."

Miriam is so natural and gentle. She's already open to accepting me, giving her love to me. I know that I can learn a lot from her. We both cry for a while, soaking each other's shoulder, both with regret, though mine is a much different version from my sister's.

When we part I notice Dembi sitting at our feet. His arms encircle our legs, giving us unnoticed comfort. True anonymous charity.

Oblivious to the human drama, Rolly stretches out on the porch.

"Triplets," Dembi says.

Something about the forlorn sound of his voice makes both Miriam and me smile. We reach down at the same time and pull him into our circle.

I am nearly breathless from the strange emotions zinging through me. I feel as though I have my formidable trio back again.

Miriam lifts her head from the huddle.

"I hadn't heard from Anne…Karoline…for months. I called and there was never any answer."

I think of the deserted telephone in Karoline's room. We'd had separate lines for so many years that I hadn't even thought about it. She must have unplugged it that night. Had she anticipated what was going to happen?

"I assumed she couldn't handle Memé's condition."

I focus once again on Miriam.

"Who's Memé?"

Dembi heads excitedly for the front door, pulling me along. "Memé!"

"Wait, Dembi," Miriam says, her voice stern. "Let me tell Anne first."

"Anne?" He looks around, searching. I realize he expected Karoline to be standing there.

"I'm Anne, too," I tell him, pointing at myself. "Anne, too."

"Anne, too," he says, astounded. "Triplet Anne."

Miriam and I laugh together.

"Exactly," I say.

"Okay. See you."

He strides through the doorway with Rolly in his arms. The screen slams behind him. We hear him humming for a while as he traverses the hallway.

Miriam grasps my hand. She talks without looking at me. Facing the door, she lectures the facts. A distancing technique I recognize well.

"Our birth mother's name is Elizabeth Johnston."

Elizabeth. My adopted mother hadn't truly given up on her sister after all.

"She was a beautiful girl, known as Libby. She grew up on this farm. A free spirit, really, not very smart, always loose and running through the fields. I get the impression that her parents drank a great deal and didn't pay too much attention to their offspring. They were tobacco farmers and made a really good living, but they liked a good time a little too much. You can see they had money..."

She waves her hand over the landscape and the rambling house.

"But they pretty much drank it away. Anyhow, Libby became pregnant several times over the years, beginning at fourteen years of age. In all she birthed twelve children."

I gasp and she squeezes my hand.

"Some of the kids were a product of incest. Her brothers probably and an uncle or two apparently. Libby always told everyone that each time, she'd been raped. And maybe some of those times she was. Karoline was able to contact only two of our other nine siblings. Four of them are in institutions of one kind or another. Mentally deficient mostly, unable to care for themselves."

"That's awful. How could children's services let that happen?"

"I don't think they paid much attention to what was happening around Vryheid," Miriam says. "And there wasn't much they could do anyway. They did take her babies away, most of the time. We were her last. She kept Dembi. I assume Family Services took me...and you."

"No, our aunt raised me. Vera. Her daughter is Elizabeth, too. I thought they were my mother and sister until a few months ago. Elizabeth was the one who gave me this address. She showed me some early pictures, too, ones that our...her mother had stashed away. The Williamses never did tell me I was adopted."

Miriam shakes her head sorrowfully.

"And Karoline never..."

I change the subject.

"Where are the two siblings she contacted?"

"One, a brother, is in New York and the other, a sister, lives in British Columbia. Neither of them wants anything to do with their birth family. One more sister is dead. Karoline couldn't find the other two. We must've been spread far and wide."

"Why do you and Dembi call her Mémé?"

"I think it's a twist of grandmother and mother in French. That's what Dembi always called her. Mémé talks a lot about a French Canadian named Larue, asks for him every day. He's been dead for a few years now but sometimes she forgets that he's gone. When I first arrived and she was more lucid, she told me Larue was like a father to Dembi. Maybe he was our father. I'm still not sure on that point. Dembi doesn't seem to remember him, though, so he must have died pretty young."

"Is Mémé...mentally deficient?"

"Well, she was always slow, but this is what I wanted to tell you before you see her. She's dying of cancer. She was diagnosed nearly a year ago. Around the time Karoline stopped coming. Mémé was doing pretty well at first. Didn't seem to have much trouble with the radiation and even the chemo. Then about three months ago everything seemed to catch up to her. That's when I came to stay here full time. She needs round-the-clock care and she really can't afford it."

"My sister—our cousin Elizabeth, I should say—she was under the impression they were pretty well off and that the farm was still producing."

"It is. They very wisely switched to ginseng around here when tobacco started to be taboo. But most of this land no longer belongs to the Johnston family. Memé's parents sold it off bit by bit. All except this parcel where the house stands."

"Are you a nurse, Miriam?"

"No, I'm actually a massage therapist." She smiles in a self-deprecating way. "The Victorian Order of Nurses drops by three times a week and the local doctor comes once in a while. The rest of the time we've been coping."

Miriam leads me down the front steps, where she points in every direction.

"The fields on either side of us are leased to a couple of farmers who grow the ginseng. Other than that, it's all been sold off. The abandoned area behind the house used to be Vryheid…"

"Yes, I took the Vryheid road to get here."

Miriam laughs. "I'm amazed you found it."

I can barely see the laneway on which I'd driven. It quickly disappears into the clump of trees that form a tunnel over the road. The little forest actually hugs the sides of the ridge.

Miriam waves toward the road above us.

"You probably noticed all the homes they've built around the area. That road is the access for them, but you can get to the farmhouse, too. You have to go past it, then circle back for a bit on the dirt road."

I gaze around the small plot of land on which the house stands and remember the black and white pictures of drunken carelessness. We walk toward the back of the house. Off in the distance I can see where the land slopes downward toward a river.

"That's the Grand River," Miriam says.

It's a wide, tumultuous river that curves out of sight and is bounded on both sides by the short cliffs. I wonder how much erosion will be necessary before the farmhouse is threatened.

"Behind those trees on the other side of the river is Vryheid. It was a little settlement of black and native people. I have no idea who owns it now."

All I can see is a dense forest, deciduous and evergreens entwined with bushes and vines.

"Karoline did a lot of research on our family. Which of course she passed off as her own history. Our mother grew up here. Had her babies here. And now she's going to die here."

"I'm finding this story so bizarre, Miriam. Sad, weird...I just have no idea how to react."

Finally she looks at me.

"You and me both. When Anne first...when Karoline contacted me and I came out here I couldn't believe any of it. But there was Dembi, whom I obviously could not deny, though at first I did think he could be a doppelganger. Of course Memé greeted me with such love and enthusiasm I couldn't turn away. You are the icing on the cake."

I can't help myself, I laugh.

"No wonder you fainted. This is spectacularly odd. We'll have to write a book."

Then I realize I skipped over the part where our mother is dying.

"I'm sorry about Memé. No one deserves that."

"You're right. I have to admit that I wasn't sure I could ever love her as a mother—she's too childlike for that—but since I began taking care of her I've come to admire her strength and courage. Which is a kind of love."

"Definitely. Do you think it will be too much for her if she sees me?"

"No, I think it'll be okay. I'm surprised she didn't mention you. She's been telling me all kinds of things that I wonder about."

"Is it okay if I ask what things?"

Miriam pauses. "I'll tell you everything later. Let's go see Memé before Dembi wonders what's going on."

We head back to the farmhouse and Miriam opens the door into an enormous country kitchen. The house is as rambling on the inside as it appears from the outside. Several connecting hallways lead to more rooms, an old-fashioned parlor, another living area, lots of bedrooms and bathrooms. A hodgepodge of nooks and crannies, both large and small, appear everywhere.

It's as though our grandparents constructed a room for every whim. Company came and stayed. They built a bedroom. The well was deep and strong, another bathroom. A significant birthday approached, a large open space was called for.

I wonder how Miriam can live here. It's large and spooky, with dozens of doors that lead into open fields or wooded enclosures or forest.

I am reluctant to enter the room of a sick woman. I've never had the experience of seeing someone who is dying of cancer. What if I can't handle it?

Miriam, bless her kind soul, sees my hesitation and gives me a reassuring squeeze.

"It won't be easy, Anne, but you can do it. I'll be right there with you and if you have to leave quickly, that's okay. The first time is the shock, then you'll get used to it."

She's right about the first time being a shock. My initial reaction is to the smell. The air in the room is sour, musty, like wet blankets and sweaty clothing. Underlying that is an odor of decay. A pungent assault on my nostrils as though I am absorbing the dying cells of my birth mother. I only prevent gagging by putting my sleeve to my nose as I stand in the doorway. I stare around with bulging eyes, unable to dredge up any compassion. Instead I feel a visceral fear tingle along my spine, a terror of ever dying this way.

The bedroom is fairly large with a greasy window shuttered by a grey blind. No one has changed the wallpaper since the 1970's by the look of the faded flowers trailing up to the ceiling. There's no overhead light and, despite the sunshine outside, it's dim and dingy. An old four-poster bed stands in the middle of the room. *Oak*, I think. *Very old. Probably worth a fortune.*

Surely the thing that lies here cannot be human, or at least not alive. Her skeleton is visible through the opacity of skin that has shrunk to adhere directly to her bones. She is so tiny that she appears to be a grotesque doll. Even her breathing is so shallow and ragged that it emits a mechanical, inhuman sound. Her emaciated chest rises minutely every now and then.

Her eyes flutter behind closed lids, darting back and forth. Thoughts? Nightmares? Her lips are a bluish color despite the oxygen mask obscuring much of her face. Long skeletal fingers lie across her breast in a coffin pose.

The smell is fierce as Miriam leads me closer. I keep my arm across my nose, breathing in the cottony fragrance of my blouse.

Memé is uncovered. Her spindly legs poke through a flimsy nightgown, which is pulled up around her stomach to expose her diaper. Suddenly another smell mingles with the sourness of death. I have to bite down on my sleeve to keep from vomiting or crying out. This is awful.

Just as we shuffle alongside the bed, Miriam pulling me forward because I am glued to her arm, Memé opens her eyes.

Her reaction reminds me of that picture of a wide-open skeletal figure. The Scream, I think it's called. Except in this case, a ragged dry sound shudders from behind the mask. The mouth opens and closes. A fish gasping for water.

Miriam is clearly confused about what to do. I, on the other hand, do not hesitate. I turn and run out of the room.

Dear Diary,

Giulio always said she was a lot smarter than we gave her credit for. Somehow I doubt that. She might be as smart as a monkey, since she's always copying whatever I say or do.

CHAPTER 16

We walk along the river in a bright yellow sun that broils our heads whenever we saunter out from under the trees. Huge bushy oaks and maples spread their thick limbs toward the sky and over the water, casting shadows over weeds and waves.

Although the noise is different it's just as deafening as the traffic outside my Los Angeles office. The birds screech in rage, hundreds of them it seems, clinging to the branches yet poised for flight. Squirrels and chipmunks scatter as we tramp along, ranting messages of alarm. And above all, the sound of rapids roars in our ears.

The river is wide, dark and ferocious. It races past, knocks over displaced branches. Pries rocks loose from the bank. Just ahead the water splashes over a small concrete dam, tumbles once, twice, in two mini waterfalls. The sound of the stream smashing against the bottom is a rush of wind in my eardrums.

Dembi leads the way. He pokes through the fallen branches and weeds with his enormous shepherd's walking stick. He's as tall as I am, so his dark head is easily visible through the leaves as I follow confidently in his footsteps. He leads me from the farmhouse down a steep path to the riverside.

"The Grand," he says proudly, as though he discovered it.

Where the river narrows, just before it careens off in another direction, a sturdy little wooden bridge connects farmhouse land to the other side. We are on our way to the former village of Vryheid.

The night before, I gave in to Miriam's insistence that I stay with them overnight. Memé did settle down without a sedative. The disturbance of my presence hadn't lasted.

"You don't have to see her," Miriam said, "nor she you. I was wrong. Obviously seeing two of us was a shock. Maybe she'll get over it. But the house is big enough that you don't have to go near her. We have lots of bedrooms. I'll show you."

As much as the place makes me shiver I acquiesced to her desire to have me stay with them for a night or two. It's the only way to get to know one another, she said. And I suppose she is right.

Miriam chose a beautiful room for me that's obviously been redecorated in the last century. It's painted a light soothing green, adorned with white crown molding and baseboards. Devoid of any wall hangings it is nevertheless well furnished. A canopy bed, an ornate dresser with brass knobs, an old-fashioned washstand with an original bowl and pitcher still sitting in the sink. Situated in the L of the wing closest to the kitchen, my room is surrounded by huge windows that have not been updated. They slide open and shut without a creak, and, to my relief, the latches still work.

There are two thick wooden doors with enormous brass knobs. One door leads out to a private little courtyard surrounded by walls but softened with greenery, bushes and little evergreens. The other appears to be an outlet into the side yard. There is a clump of trees very close by. The locks on the doors work, too. There are no deadbolts or sliding chain door locks. I'd have felt much better with chains. But there *is* that ensuite bathroom and the huge closet beside it. Pretty much makes up for the isolation, I suppose.

Before she went to bed Miriam directed me to the telephone in the parlor room. The instrument was an outdated style, thick and black, but it was located beside a chair big enough to curl up in. The rest of the room was filled with antiques. Furniture, heavy old statues of religious figures and musty books. I can't help but wonder what all of these pieces are worth.

Poor Ethan didn't get much airtime because of my torrent of words in his ear. Maybe it was the talk with my lover, or the fresh air, silky sheets, feathery comforter, or just plain exhaustion from the emotional roller coasters, but I slept like a baby afterward. Despite the strange bed and the yawning openness to the countryside I didn't awaken once.

By the time I washed, dressed and wound my way along the hall to the kitchen that morning, Miriam and Dembi had made breakfast.

"I guess I shouldn't be surprised," I said to them, smiling at the faces-from-the-mirror, the me's-but-not-me's who turned to grin at me. "You cooked up all my favorites. Pancakes, bacon…"

"And real maple syrup," Dembi chirped. "It's Other Anne's favorite, too. She is from the United States. They don't have it there."

Miriam filled my plate and poured me a coffee. "I tried to correct him, but it hasn't registered," she said so quietly and directly that I almost had to lip read.

Triplet Anne tried to keep the smile genuine. I sat in the chair opposite my siblings, wondering if Karoline sat here, too.

I have almost gotten used to feeling strange. Nothing is the same. Once again I am on stage before rehearsing my lines.

As we ate breakfast, Dembi astonished me with his continued chatter. Though he speaks slowly, with odd blips and slurs, he really is quite articulate. His vocabulary is fairly simple, but the thoughts that drive the words are not. When he relates the history of Vryheid he sounds like an encyclopedia written for children.

"Vryheid was founded in 1784," he said formally this morning. "You can still see the cornerstone at the church, but you can't read the names any more. Other Anne said the writing had been worn away by time."

Karoline had been privy to my ancestry before I was, I thought with a flash of anger and jealousy. I wanted Dembi's revelations to be mine alone. On the other hand, the history of Vryheid was probably public knowledge. Something I could look up in the library. I tuned into his recitations once more.

"The black people didn't want to go with Chief Brant to the other city. They decided to move here and he let them even though they were his slaves."

"Joseph Brant had slaves?"

I couldn't help myself. The Six Nations Chief is a hero to my mother, my adopted mother that is. Surely Brant was not someone who kept human beings to do his bidding. Vera, particularly in her Native phase, spent hours lecturing about his life, waxing eloquent about his accomplishments. Like her, Joseph Brant had straddled two homelands, though only Upper and Lower Canada officially existed then. In my California classrooms the famous Chief was a citizen of the northern United States of America. In Brantford and Burlington, Ontario, he was Canadian. Revered and admired. Surely not a common slave owner.

Miriam smiled over at both of us. Dembi stopped speaking in the middle of a sentence, clearly derailed by my outburst.

"Dembi's right. It's part of recorded history. The only debate is whether or not Chief Brant brought the blacks to Canada to protect them or use them. From some accounts, they were pretty free. Even married into Brant's own family. A couple of eye witness statements, however, claim that they were treated as servants, if not strictly as slaves."

The button on Dembi's recorded history was immediately reset.

"Slaves were people who were owned by other people. They didn't even have last names. They used their master's name. They changed all the names like Dembi to other ones. Like they might have called me Donald."

Miriam and I smiled at each other.

"Vryheid means free. When Chief Joseph Brant went to settle in the city of Burlington, he let the black people come up here. They built their own village. He made them free. They even got last names. They made their own school."

"Where did the black children go to school before that, Dembi?" Miriam asked as if she were testing him.

"They didn't go to school before that. They just had to work, even though they were children. But in Vryheid they could learn about other things. I will show you today, Triplet Anne. I am the keeper of the secrets."

"Dembi's one of very few people who has shown an interest in Vryheid," Miriam said to me, a touch of pride in her tone. "Recently a couple of historians came around. Dembi has uncovered the history from the headstones and cornerstones of the village. He and the new Burford museum curator have begun to connect the threads. It's very exciting. The curator thinks they could end up with a new history book. If we get someone to write it, that is."

Dembi nodded his head. "Mrs. West said that I have turned up some very interesting facts that other people might like. But she doesn't know the secret of the gold. Just Other Anne and Miriam and me. And now Triplet Anne."

"Mrs. West? Gold?"

Miriam laughed. "Mary Lou West is the curator of the new museum in Burford. She's young but very knowledgeable. She's really encouraged Dembi. As for the gold there's a legend that Chief Brant sent some with the group who were given this land. The theory is that he wanted the funds as insurance against warmongers. He continually warned that there were roving bands of Americans determined to take over Upper Canada and the Grand River tracts. But apparently he was notorious for encouraging or even spreading rumors, so the story about the gold is a little suspect to say the least."

Dembi reacted to Miriam's speech by continuously shaking his head in disagreement.

"I know where the gold is," he said.

Miriam gave me the kind of indulgent smile that parents might when their child says something cute but clearly erroneous. I smiled back.

"I will show you, Triplet Anne. Let's go on a field trip."

Thus I find myself traipsing through the bush a couple of hours later. Miriam stayed behind just in case Memé needed her. I wonder how she can do it. The thought of that emaciated half-dead creature and that dark fusty room makes my skin crawl. My sister is a saint.

For the hundredth time, I nearly trip on a twisted clump of grass and weed under my feet. Vryheid must have been buried for a long time. I recall what Miriam said about our birth mother's life of abuse and neglect. No one paid much attention to what happened in Vryheid. Prejudice, I wonder? Or simply years of isolation and separation? Maybe both.

I am beginning to be interested in my roots at last. Won't Vera be proud? I feel a rush of anger toward my parents. At thirty-three years old, I ought to have known about my background. I should've had the right to visit my birth mother, especially now that she is dying. Does my mother/aunt know that her sister is on her deathbed? Has she enjoyed updates from Karoline? Am I the only one kept entirely in the dark? I trip again, this time nearly stumbling to my knees. I have to pay attention. I spend the rest of our walk with my head down, watching my feet.

A few minutes later Dembi indicates a small footbridge. A relatively newer structure, it was constructed over a section of the river that narrows to only about ten feet across. Possibly built by Johnstons in the 50's or perhaps by Larue. The way my brother bounces over it, the little overpass was obviously very well built.

We follow the Grand on the other side for what feels like hours before I see the first indication of past human habitation. Rocks that are no longer haphazard appear alongside the roots and weeds that have grown up and around them. These stones are hand squared and placed, the foundations of a home or church or even a fortress wall.

Dembi stops and points back across the river. In the distance I see the rambling rooftops of his home. The farmhouse is very close to Vryheid, just over the river. It only feels like miles away without a bridge at this point to traverse the rapids and the wide expanse of water. We had to go quite a long way to reach the narrows and then back again.

We step out from the curtain of maples and evergreens to a comparatively clear space. Now I see the shape of the former village. A small center street forms a circle with several pathways leading out from it, like the spokes of a bicycle wheel. The ruins are mostly indistinct. Piles of rubble, brick, rock and rotted wood that nature is using for planters.

As we trudge along in the heat I notice the rustle of other feet frightened by our advance. Small animals have taken over where humans left off.

When I finally look up, released from the tentacles of untended land and tree trunks, I don't know how I could have missed the structure. It's almost as much a shock as the library in Ephesus when Karoline and I traveled to Turkey. Perched on one of the pathways that rises slightly into a small hillock, the building would once have been quite imposing as it looked down upon the village.

The pointed spire is still erect, although a great number of stones are missing. The old church was built with local rock, sculpted and evened, cemented together with some kind of mortar. Grey, white, black, even reddish stones give the walls an artistic appearance. Although the sizes of the rudimentary bricks are not precisely the same every time, the lines of larger to smaller follow the building upward in neat little rows.

Small wooden wheelbarrows would have gathered rock from every path of ground hereabouts. I imagine the hands picking out the right size, scraping and shaping them to fit, layering the church higher and higher. How had they completed the steeple, I wonder? With ropes and scaffolds and ladders? It's impressive even in its ruination. A former beauty queen with the last vestiges of her glorious stature still visible.

I never could understand why people spend their precious time and resources on churches. Here in the wilderness it seems even more ludicrous. All the little huts and structures that housed, protected and provided for the people were trampled underfoot, while this place clung emptily to a deserted hillside. It's ironic, I think.

There had once been a door to the church. Pieces of thick wood still cling to the framework, oak I guess, fragmented in shards. Possibly done in by rain and wind, or hacked away by human hands. It might've kept someone's fireplace going. If there had been any pews, they likely disappeared for the same purpose. The inside is empty. Our footsteps echo on the stone floor, the sound reverberating back to us from the high ceiling.

The building has an eerie feel to it. It's cool and musty. Birds perform a constant cacophony of sound from the cupola. Now that we have intruded, the sound escalates. They flutter up into the empty spiral complaining all the way. Rudimentary stained glass windows filter the sunlight, casting patches of red and purple over the floor. A white stone altar stands in the center of the room, a bit grayish with age, but the rock from which it was carved is still smooth and stunning. I cannot at all imagine how they hauled this enormous piece into the church where it could be shaped into a table of worship. Maybe it was the reverse and the church had been formed around the boulder.

It's amazing how the structure has survived. I wonder when it was constructed.

"This church was built in 1837," Dembi recites as though reading my mind. "The same year as the school. Look."

He leads me to a wide flat stone in the front corner of the church. This is obviously the cornerstone he mentioned. As Dembi told me before, the only writings left are the four numbers etched deeply into the rock. A faint outline of some other dedication has faded into the stone. Invisible ink.

"This is fascinating, Dembi," I say and he grins.

He is pleased to show off his knowledge. I am glad that I've earned his trust so quickly. Must have something to do with looking exactly alike.

We turn around to a spot in the middle of the building, tucked under the obese legs of the altar. It would have been very difficult to see on my own. Here in the floor is a flat square stone. Set into the cement, it's carved all around the edges into a slight recess. A tripping hazard if it weren't surrounded by the altar. With its handle-like dip in the rock it looks exactly like a lid, which, as it turns out, is almost correct.

Dembi expertly puts his hand under the small lip and shoves. Though it appears to be quite heavy the stone moves easily. My brother is obviously accustomed to its weight. He pushes it sideways. The lid disappears halfway into the rock with a screeching sound as it scrapes across the ancient ridge. A giant cigar box carved from stone.

I see nothing but black inside. Dembi reaches down and reverently pulls out a leather book. It's a large square, barely fitting inside the hole. Jammed with papers, parchments, notes and other pieces that might, at one time, have been tiny pictures. My brother opens the first page. He proudly displays the title written by hand in ink. Fancy letters speak of the days when cursive writing was an art.

"The History of Vryheid," it proclaims, "as recorded by the Johnston Family on behalf of the Church of Freedom and the residents herein."

Dembi smiles at me. Holding on to the book tightly, he allows me to see its contents, dappled in the afternoon sun as it slants through crannies and openings in the walls.

"Mrs. West doesn't know about my book," he says. "Only Memé, Miriam, Other Anne and Triplet Anne. Memé showed it to me. She said not to show anyone but family, so I won't."

"Good for you. Can we look at it together?"

"Yes." He is solemn and reverent as he closes the book once more.

"Let's sit over here with our snacks."

Miriam packed peanut butter on crackers, soda (they call it pop), and cookies for our trip. I'd thought I couldn't eat another thing after that enormous breakfast. However, once we sit on a flat edge of the altar I discover that I am hungry. I can't remember the last time I had peanut butter or crackers but the salt is tasty on my tongue.

The diet soda is thirst quenching but makes us both burp. Dembi laughs until tears roll down his cheeks and I join him. The next burps are even louder, until the cans are empty. The sounds echo and re-echo through the deserted church.

Dembi immediately becomes the serious historian once more. "This is called the introduction." He points to a long paragraph that follows the title page.

"This book will be kept as a record of our journey in freedom," I read. "On August 10, 1799, a group of fifteen slaves founded the village of Vryheid. Chief Joseph Brant, who brought us from slavery to Brantford in 1781, has granted us our freedom from this day forward. We are no longer slaves. We work the land for John Morey. In exchange we have been granted this territory whereupon we may build our homes and gardens."

Dembi gently turns the page for me. The paper is thin and delicate. Under a less careful touch it might have crumpled like a dried leaf.

"Look, last names." Dembi turns the page, as engrossed in the list of inhabitants as though he's never seen them before. "Slaves did not have their own names. But when they were freed by Chief Brant, he let them pick a name."

There are fifteen owners neatly printed in a straight column, along with their laneway or location and how much land they occupied. Surnames and first initial only. No listing of wives or children, so there may have been quite a few more actual residents. Many of the monikers were obviously chosen to reflect the chosen (or given) professions, such as Miller, Butler, Cotter, Smith. One of the landowners is C. Johnston. He had a parcel of forty acres and a laneway named after him. Our forebear must have been someone of prominence, as he owned one of the largest tracts. Plus his family was responsible for keeping the records.

The next part of the journal is entitled 'Our Life Before Vryheid'. A Johnston who was taught to read and write must have copied down the accounts of any resident who wished to participate, which appear to be most of them. Some quotes are a mere sentence long, while others fill a paragraph. The writer was well educated, for the spelling and grammar, although reflective of simpler English, are correct. He has also added some observations of his own beside the quotes.

"I was a slave to Chief Brant and his wives. I worked in the kitchen. Most of them were quite mean and gave cruel punishments. They hit me with spoons or knives if they did not like my cooking. I have scars here to prove it."—("Note: This writer concurs that there are indeed scars on the woman's forehead and upper arms.")

"I was kidnapped by the Indians from my master's plantation. They put me and some others in the hold of their ship and took us up the river to Brantford. My life was much better. I worked hard but I was treated fine."

"My wife is Indian. We met when the Chief brought me from the United States of America to Upper Canada. Brant was happy when a Negro and an Indian joined in marriage. He threw us a feast. I have always worked on his land. We have a family and good food. Now we have our own land and freedom."

The accounts go on and on. Stories of kidnapping. Disgusting conditions of slave ships cutting the work force in half. Bodies thrown into the sea like garbage. Working on the plantations from dawn until dusk, fed only with cornmeal. Very little clothing. Descriptions of children running naked in the searing sun. The huts they lived in are described as tiny mud hovels where adults and young ones alike slept in cramped corners.

The journal makes me sick. I shiver. A couple of centuries between my actual birth year and these poor souls' made all the difference. I don't want to know this history. I don't care to picture the animal existence, horrific abuse and tragedy of my ancestors' lives. What purpose does dredging up all this stuff serve?

I have no idea how much Dembi understands. His fascination is clear. That aside, does he really understand what horror he is witnessing? And if he does, is this really any good for him?

I am rapidly losing interest when my brother suddenly becomes even more animated. He turns to a page on which a diagram is sketched in fine blue pen. As I peer more closely I can see that it's a map.

"Gold." Dembi looks up at me with bright, excited eyes and begins to read. "We the residents of Vryheid hereby promise to safeguard the future with the burial of our treasure within our boundaries."

First, I am astounded at how well Dembi can read, albeit very slowly. Often lingering over the syllables of a larger word. Or has he memorized the passage? Maybe he switches to another part of his brain, an undamaged area that can mimic another's words. Second, I am amused, excited and intrigued by the mystery of this treasure. Buried within the boundaries of Vryheid. What if we can find it? What if it really is Chief Brant's gold?

I look through the open door onto the little patch of village that I see from here. I am astonished that I am actually sitting here in this old church, birds muttering above us. I feel as though I am a little girl, back in Bell Canyon, racing through the trails with Karoline and Giulio. I feel free and alert, light and happy.

Dembi calls my attention back to the book by tapping insistently on my arm. I smile at him and decide to indulge him. After all, I can be as much fun as Karoline.

The trouble is, this map is virtually useless. The lines it forms bear no relationship to the tangled, tree-choked area before us. If the gold was already discovered a century or so ago, or even more recently, the finder would have been wise to keep that quiet. Its discovery wouldn't necessarily be common knowledge. On the other hand, Dembi said only he, Memé, Miriam and Other Anne knew about the book. Maybe this map to its whereabouts had been just as lost as the gold itself.

"We can find the treasure." Dembi grasps my hand as he leaps to his feet. Carefully replacing the book in its alcove, he races out the door.

I figure, what the hell, it's an adventure, and follow him as quickly as I dare.

The first place Dembi takes me on the treasure hunt is deep into a clump of trees that's as dense and overgrown as anything I have ever seen. The vegetation is so different from the places I've lived in California. These trees and bushes have arms that wrap around each other to keep strangers out. At least that's the way I feel, as we push our way through to…well, I'm not sure, until my brother bursts into a clearing.

The trees surround a hill of rock. Their trunks have grown so tall that the mound, which is about twenty feet high, is hidden from sight. The only way you could see this little enclave would be from the air. The hillock resembles an upside-down bowl. Although not very high, it's at least thirty feet in diameter. Maybe it's the top of a mountain that has sunk. Or it fell from an alien ship.

Dembi leads me through an opening that has either been carved into the earth or is a natural gap. Inside, the cave is fairly light. Tree roots have burrowed through the walls to allow in some of the sunshine. It's cool in here, though, a welcome respite from the relentless sun.

"This is like a castle!" I say to Dembi and he beams.

Covered with a red blanket and a pillow, a single bed stands against one rock face. The table and two chairs look as though they might've been here since the 1800's when Vryheid was alive. Etched into their softening wood are initials and symbols that I can't decipher in the gloom. A rocking chair, outlined with gold embossing, sits in one corner. I approach it cautiously, wondering if it will hold my weight. It does, so I rock and observe.

Dembi has decorated in his own fashion. Newspaper clippings, mostly about historical events, especially concerning Chief Joseph Brant, are stuck to the cave walls. A Canadian flag hangs from a stick poked through the dirt floor. A picture of Miriam and Memé. The latter appears frail but certainly strong enough to be seated in a chair. The picture of Karoline and Dembi makes me stop in my rocker tracks. In this one she is smiling, standing next to her 'brother', clearly on the front porch of the Johnston farmhouse. She almost looks attractive.

I smile at Dembi, but I want to rip it down and tear it into pieces. Now that I have found my siblings, I feel irrationally jealous of Karoline.

Irrational because there is no possibility of her stealing them away from me again. I'm shocked by the ferocity of my anger.

"Where did you get all your furniture, Dembi?"

"Miriam and Other Anne helped me." He fusses with the blanket, straightens a clipping or two.

"Why?"

Puzzlement and concern on his face, he gapes at me.

"Why do you need this place? You have your own room at home, don't you?"

He nods. "This is for resting when I am looking for the treasure," he answers in a tone that says, 'stupid' right after. As if to prove my lack of intelligence, he lifts a gardener's tool bag from underneath the bed and hands me a trowel.

Off we trod through the woods. Dembi finds a spot and instructs me on how to dig. Half-heartedly, compared to his frenetic actions, I do so. As we work I watch his beautiful face, red with exertion and excitement. Will this be the trio who never betrays you? Ice Queen Anne whispers.

Once Dembi decides we've looked enough for this day, we replace the gardening bag and make our way back to the church to pick up our picnic things. It's deathly still in the duskiness of the old building.

"Where are the birds?" I whisper to Dembi.

"They sleep in the loft," he answers in the same whisper. "Look."

I gaze upward, following his outstretched finger, and notice the choir loft that runs along the upper edges of the roofline, just before the spire shoots straight upwards. Quite large, at least in comparison to the tiny church, it follows the upper wall on three sides, facing the congregation, above the stone altar. The birds line up along the railings, their heads tucked under their wings, looking like a choir who's become very bored with their own music.

"There's some big cupboards up there," Dembi says. "I found some old paper in there, too. Other Anne said they're choir stuff."

"You were up there, Dembi? It doesn't look very sturdy."

We are still whispering so as not to disturb the napping choir.

"Oh, it's really safe. See the steps? It's really a ladder but it's OK."

I stare at what looks like a fairly new ladder up against a corner of the church. I shiver. I don't think I'd ever want to make that climb. Leave the singing for the birds.

When we return to the farmhouse it's almost dark. Dembi and I are covered in dirt. Mud is smudged on our noses and ground into our hair. Miriam is angry, I can tell, but she doesn't express it. She simply stands and stares at us from the front porch, one hand on her hips. A frown furrows her lovely brow.

"I'm so sorry, Miriam," I say immediately as we mount the steps. "I know we were gone a very long time. Dembi and I got carried away searching for gold."

"Gold!" Dembi says. His grin is mischievous and hints of secrets.

"I guess we look a fright."

"You do indeed. Dembi, go inside and have a shower. And make sure you wash your hair. And brush your teeth, too."

Dembi hands over the picnic basket and skips inside. We hear him whistling all the way down the corridor.

"I really am sorry. I know I was the adult in charge. I shouldn't have gotten so carried away. It was just so much fun."

She sits down on one of the benches.

"To be honest, I don't think I would've been so worried, but…I guess the shock of Karoline is finally sinking in. I feel so betrayed. I was anxious suddenly that you and she had cooked up some kind of swindle. I mean, maybe you came to see if the gold deposit was real. Maybe you had taken off with Dembi…"

"My car's still here. Not to mention my purse and my passport."

She has the grace to laugh along with me.

"Yes, okay, I was being melodramatic." She sighs and I sit down beside her. "Memé is so bad today. She's been yelling and muttering, tries to get out of the bed. It's getting me down."

I'm shocked by what comes out of my mouth next. "Listen, I've got some money. Please let me hire someone to help Memé. There must be a recently retired nurse around here who wouldn't mind the extra cash."

At first she shakes her head.

"Please. I haven't been here for you or Dembi or Memé. I know that wasn't really my fault but I'd still like to make up for it. I can afford it. Honestly."

We stare at each other for a long minute, each of us still trying to come to terms with the fact of our existence. Although we are clearly different in many ways, it's difficult to look at the mirror image of your face without imagining that the emotions and reasoning are identical too.

"We can spend more time together. You agreed that we should get to know each other. As long as you don't mind my staying longer, I would like to do just that. But you can't be tied to Memé every minute."

That's when she relents. I know she is persuaded by the opportunity to be with me, know me, but Miriam's shoulders also demonstrate the burden of responsibility that has weighed on them for too long. She suddenly sits up straighter, looks lighter, when she says yes.

"Do you know of an agency we can call?"

"Yes. When the community care people came around, they gave me a card. I just never called."

"Do that now, Triplet Miriam."

We grin at each other and, as we stand, she embraces me.

Afterward I wind my way to my room and shower. The water is soft and the pressure strong. Once I am clean and change my dirty clothes, I feel magnificent. A surge of love for my siblings races through me, warming my cells just as the shower heated my skin. I make my way back to the kitchen.

Dembi, too, is fresh and clean, his short hair still damp and sticking straight up from his head. He looks like a cat who's swallowed a mouse. Although I have misgivings about going on this merry treasure hunt with him, encouraging him, I can't help but bask in his delight. After all, Karoline went with him. I high-five him as I walk in and he grins even wider. He sits at a small table in the corner, where a thousand-piece jigsaw puzzle is slowly taking the shape of a full picture. He goes right back to work.

Miriam has a pad of paper in front of her along with the agency's card. She looks up at me in relief.

"It looks like you were right. The agency said they could probably send someone in the next day or two."

"Excellent!"

We sit at the kitchen table and talk while Dembi does his puzzle. As the sun completely disappears, we work side by side in the bright kitchen light while we prepare dinner. Miriam dashes off once in a while to check on Memé, who is at last sleeping soundly.

We talk about everything. Lovers, friends, jobs, aspirations. Our adoptive families. My twin was raised in Ottawa, Ontario, by a fairly elderly couple—both light skinned blacks like us—who doted on her. Despite finding out later that they weren't her biological parents, she says she feels lucky that she was a part of their lives. They died too soon, one after the other, which devastated her. Her experience of family and her roots are decidedly different from mine. Perhaps because she wasn't straddling two races all her life, despite the lightness of her skin.

Miriam is particularly interested in my parents. These are her aunt and uncle, Elizabeth her cousin.

"There is a bible with a bit of a family tree. It stops at Memé and her siblings. We should look at it later."

"I brought some of the pictures Elizabeth showed me, too. Maybe we can match up with the names."

Memé's screams interrupt dinner several times. When Miriam scurries off, Dembi and I sing a song or tell a funny story. Anything to keep us from hearing the guttural sounds from the bedroom. The last time Miriam returns, her eyes are puffy and shadowed.

"I don't know what she's saying half the time." She pushes her curls off her perspiring forehead. "She won't settle down and I hate to give her too much sedative."

We are enjoying our dessert before the screams start again. I stand up.

"Miriam, let's switch blouses. This time, I'll go. You've had enough for one day."

My sister reluctantly agrees. We step into the next room, peel off our tops, and trade.

"If this doesn't work, I'll call you," I promise her.

I tiptoe into the hallway. Follow the hoarse screeches as much as the memory of where Memé's room is located. When I reach the doorway I see the skeletal body of our mother, scrunched up in the sheets, twisting and writhing on the mattress. Her nightgown is, mercifully, pulled all the way down this time. In fact she appears to be trying to crawl inside it. Even her toes disappear into the cotton. Her knees are doubled and she attempts to shove her arms in as well.

Silently I approach the bedside. I am very close to her before her rheumy eyes focus on me. At first, I can tell Memé thinks I am Miriam. When the reality hits, her face contorts with fear. She gapes, opens and shuts her mouth continually. Spit drips down her chin. She's unable to emit any sound, however.

I hunch down to hover just at her ear and whisper.

She struggles to get away from me, but I hold onto one wrist as I tell her what she needs to hear. Finally she lies very still, as though her last breath has already rattled through her. I mix a dose of her medication and she obediently swallows. I am not afraid to give a little extra sedative so she'll stay asleep tonight. If anyone asks, I am simply being kind. She's had a shock today.

Just as I turn my back to leave, she hisses.

"Diable," my mother says very clearly.

I smile at her and join my trio. The one I lost and found, the one I was cheated of for far too long. The one I substituted with poor choices, people who ultimately betrayed me. It isn't going to happen this time.

Dembi and Miriam cleared the dishes while I was gone and are happily washing and drying. I take Miriam's place. She knows where the dishes go and I don't, I say.

"It worked," I tell her. "I don't think Memé realized I wasn't you. She's asleep again."

"You're a miracle worker. Thank you."

We have fun doing this simple but satisfying chore. I can't help but recall my breakdown, the hours I spent washing every dish. Purifying, perhaps. Tonight, the task is pure pleasure. We laugh at Dembi's antics and his silly, funny stories.

Miriam checks on Memé, but she is sound asleep. We settle in the room that I called a parlor, with tea, cookies, the Bible and the pictures I brought. Dembi is as interested as we are.

I look more closely at all the antiques. An old gramophone, its reddish wood polished and mostly unscratched, stands in the corner. It still works, Miriam tells me. She demonstrates with an old record by a singer from the forties whose voice is warbled and soft.

The chairs are of the Louis XIV variety, stiff and uncomfortable for long sits, but beautifully covered and carved. Several brass or iron statues look at me with disapproving frowns. They are so heavy I can barely lift them. Judging by the dust, nothing has been moved in here for quite some time.

I try very hard not to think about how much all of this is worth.

The three of us sit together on a fairly new sofa, new at least in comparison to the rest of the furniture. Miriam is in the middle, the family Bible on her lap, while I hold the pictures, ready to be disseminated. Dembi is alert and excited. This is history, his favorite subject. His obsession.

The Bible is enormous, leather bound and filled with brightly colored pictures, most of them depicting horrific scenes. Bodies spread out at the feet of a serpent with a variety of death grimaces etched on their faces. People are punished in so many different ways, drowned, speared, killed by toppled towers, that we stop looking very quickly and focus on the pages at the front.

They are designed to fill in your family tree, with a spot for birth and death dates. As Miriam mentioned, the names at the top are those of our mother and her siblings. We start there and go down the tree backwards.

Elizabeth May Johnston, born May 31, 1926. It's a shock to realize that Memé is only 56 years old. She looks thirty years beyond that, the way her body has shriveled and caved in. I shiver.

Vera June Johnston, born June 4, 1924.

I can't help but laugh. "My mother—our aunt, that is—told me and Elizabeth that she doesn't have a middle name. No wonder! Looks like they just picked the month the girls were born in. Not too creative."

"The boys didn't get a second name at all," Miriam says.

William Johnston, born February 11, 1923. Died August 3, 1928.

"Wow, just a little boy when he died. I wonder what happened to him."

"Memé would only have been two at the time. I wonder if her parents ever told her how he died."

"Maybe he drowned in the river," Dembi says.

"Why would you think that, honey?"

He shrugs his shoulders, but he has that furtive look around his mouth. I wonder if he found some information that he's withholding. Dembi isn't exactly good at hiding his thoughts.

"At least he couldn't be our father," I say and instantly regret the gaffe, my siblings' faces reflect such shock. I must remember that Canadian sensibility. "Sorry. It just slipped out." Which is the truth.

David: October 9, 1921. No death date listed.

Philip: September 7, 1920. Died April 11, 1954.

John: July 15, 1919. Died April 11, 1954.

Cornwall: July 23, 1918. No date of death listed.

"Two of the brothers died the same day," Miriam says. "I wonder if it was a farm accident or something. Maybe we could look it up in the local paper archives."

I think of the C. Johnston listing in the Vryheid history book. Was it Cornwall back then, too? Did its origin have an exotic counterpart or had the enslaved ancestor taken a location for his name? Why does Cornwall Johnston sound so familiar?

"Somebody kept this Bible up to date until 1954. I wonder if it was Larue. He's not listed here anywhere."

"None of the other spouses are listed, either. He could've been Memé's lover or even her husband and still not be here," I say. "Maybe you're right. Maybe Larue was our father. Memé would have been twenty-three when she had us. I would think she'd have made her own choice of lover or husband by then."

"True. Perhaps Larue and Memé were married. You're right, there are no marriages listed for anyone of her generation. David and Cornwall might still be alive. They'd only be in their sixties. And all of them would have been old enough to marry before 1954. I wonder why nothing's recorded about their marriages."

"Maybe they had all left the area by then. In the case of Vera, she ran away and never looked back. She pretended that she had no siblings. Instead she built an entire legend for herself. Indian princess intermarried with black slaves who were undoubtedly descendants of African kings."

Dembi smiles at me. "Joseph Brant's slaves married his family."

I laugh. "Yes, I guess Vera's story is almost true, Dembi. She just left out the part of her dysfunctional family and poor Memé. Not to mention the fact of my real birth and the two of you."

"They thought they were protecting you," Miriam says.

"I know. But I still think it was wrong. I'm angry with Vera and Ian Williams, I must say. Your parents never told you either, did they?"

"No. They didn't. And I have to admit I was angry, too, once Anne—sheesh, I mean Karoline—found me. But don't you think it's odd that Karoline discovered us and we didn't?"

"We weren't looking. We didn't know we had anything to discover."

"Other Anne looked in the book," Dembi says, startling us both.

"What book?" we ask in unison.

"The book of Vryheid."

Miriam and I look at one another.

"How on earth did she get here in the first place, though?" Miriam asks.

Dembi shrugs, as though the question is moot. Other Anne simply appeared and that was good enough for him. Same with Triplet Anne.

Our grandparents are listed as Cornwall Johnston and Margaret Fredricks, married in 1904, born in Vryheid. Cornwall had five brothers, all carefully noted, with birth, marriage and death dates. Every single one of them had been born in Vryheid and every single one was deceased.

I wonder which of these uncles were among poor Memé's rapists. Curiously, no offspring are mentioned for any of Cornwall Senior's brothers. Perhaps this Bible belonged solely to Cornwall Junior and Margaret. Maybe Grandma planned to keep better records, but got sidetracked by booze and shame.

The tree ended, or began, I should say, with our great-grandparents. Once again he is called Cornwall. I wonder where the name originated and how many Cornwalls there had been. Was the name handed down over generations or is this some anglicized version of an African name? Like Dembi to Donald. Maybe the slave's owner hailed from Cornwall, England. I want to know more about the Cornwalls, especially Junior Junior.

Now I place Elizabeth's pictures down one at a time. We are able to discern Grandpa Cornwall and Grandma Margaret as young parents, the wide expanse of the farmland behind them. My sister is as shocked at the images as I had been. This house, which now looks so quaint and well preserved, is strewn with garbage and discarded bottles. The porch, half the size of the one now out front, leans dangerously.

The young ones are barefoot. Tangled hair erupts over their heads. Tiny faces are unscrubbed and dirty. Babies appear in diapers scrabbling in the dirt. Every year a new face. Their expressions don't reflect the normal carefree nature of children their ages. In most of the pictures the adults laugh, drink, list with drunkenness, while the kids hang around at their feet or in the background. There are lots of adults, mostly men, presumably Cornwall's brothers. Strong farmer bodies designed to hold a lot of food and booze. Did they still work the fields in those insane days?

We debate, at least Miriam and I do, the origins of our mother and her siblings. The older generation suffered through the depression, despite the fact that they were farmers. Perhaps they hadn't gone hungry, but had they been damaged in other ways? Did their drinking and carousing reflect a desire to drown their previous sorrows? From what Miriam had been told, they had slowly sold off all the land. Every time they needed a new room in the house for another child or an uncle, whenever the booze ran dry, the crops failed or the jobs were scarce, they sold an acre.

As we leaf through the photos, we discover the dazzling images of our mother as a long legged youthful beauty. She has the same coffee-with-cream complexion as we triplets, wavy luxurious hair, thick lips and come-hither smile. Her eyes are wide and guileless. The countenance of a naïve innocent unable to think deep thoughts. No wonder the poor child was abused so easily. She must have melted into any male's arms, searching for attention and love. Unable to tell the difference between that and sex.

Is this the origin of my disrespect for men who tried to woo me? I suddenly remember one suitor's excuse for stalking me. "No man can resist you, such is the power of your beauty." He mistakenly thought I would consider his statement poetic and flattering. Instead I had spurned him with even greater alacrity. Was beauty and its allure the excuse my mother's family used for incest and rape?

Gazing at these photos and comparing her to the skeletal shape in the bed, I can scarcely believe this is the same person. The one whose face launched a thousand sins.

Despite the tragic reality of her background I refuse to forgive Memé. She split my trio. The one I was meant to have at my side all my life. Instead I unconsciously substituted the disappointing Giulio-Karoline combination, which had not exactly worked out well.

My brother and sister ooh and ah. Lament our mother's loss of beauty. Mutter sweet responses. Even Dembi recognizes her from her youth and appears to understand that she is gravely ill with a disease that has robbed her of any real life. He has easily transferred his affection to his sisters. Perhaps he suffers from the same mental affliction as our mother and many of our other siblings. They are merely simple creatures formed from too many duplicate genes. Maybe they don't have very complex emotions.

"I wonder why there are no picture albums here in the house," Miriam says. "You'd think there would be lots, especially since Margaret seems to have been somewhat of a record keeper."

"That is weird. Seems like Vera was the only one who had any photos. And she hid them at my sister's so I'd never see them."

I know I sound bitter, but as the days go on, anger builds inside me for the deceptions Vera perpetrated. Memé, Vera, Ian, my sister/cousin Elizabeth, Karoline, Giulio. Were they all complicit, all guilty, of hiding the truth from me? And if so, why?

Once Dembi, Miriam and our mother are tucked into bed, I call Ethan. My conversation doesn't exactly feel intimate, since the only telephone in the house is located in this parlor room, but for some reason I trust that my siblings respect my privacy. Again I jabber on about the day and my discoveries.

"I wish I were there with you," Ethan says when I take a breath.

The longing in his voice makes me feel both guilty and happy. I haven't felt as lonely as he. My day has been filled up with two new people. Yet I'm glad to my core that he misses me.

"I wish you were, too," I respond and I mean it. How amazing it would be to share this adventure with him. "I'm so sorry we're apart. But I have a feeling that I have to do this on my own. Especially now that I've discovered Miriam and Dembi. And Memé, of course, though I'm still so…I have to admit that I'm angry with a dying woman. That's really horrible of me, isn't it?"

"No, I'd say it's really human of you. What would be horrible is if you acted on the anger."

I flush with the thought of my hateful whisper in her ear. Ethan's right. My actions will make the difference between the new me and the person I used to be. I am suddenly ashamed and vow to clean up my behavior.

"You're so wise," I say out loud. "I'm still a bitch learning to be nice."

He laughs and the sound sends shock-waves to my toes.

"If you could see me at work these days, you wouldn't think I'm wise. Honey, I do understand that you have to do this journey on your own. I would just be in the way of your new relationships. Anyway, even if you were here I'd barely see you. I've been working on this damn case twelve hours a day."

"Oh, Ethan, you must be exhausted."

"Trust me, I am. But we're close, so close. We'll be rounding up the perps any day."

"I'm picturing you on a white horse riding down Ventura," I say, just so I can hear that laugh again.

As I walk down the quiet hallways to my room, I hear the shifting of the trees in a night wind. Little mouse feet scratch behind a wall. A squirrel or a raccoon tramps across the roof tiles. It's so quiet in the country that the background noise of other inhabitants sounds like drum beats in an empty tavern.

Suddenly, I am almost certain I can hear Memé whisper 'Diable' in my ear. I race back to my bedroom, shut the door and lock it, then bury myself under the covers. I'm not sure I like my new life. It's frightening and haunted. It takes a long time to finally reach unconsciousness.

Dear Diary,

I may sound bitter. But I'm really not. I exacted my revenge and I'm content. It's too bad I didn't see her face when she realized what I'd done, though.

Chapter 17

The next morning Dembi and I resume our gold-seeking adventure. We are even better prepared than last time. Drinks, snacks, as well as lunch are packed in the picnic basket. Insect repellant, sun lotion, hats and trowels in a backpack. Shovels in our hands and rubber boots on our feet.

"You look like real explorers," Miriam says.

Dembi holds up his shovel. "Gold diggers!"

We don't dare laugh in the face of his seriousness, but we smile indulgently at one another. Miriam stays back with Memé. Hopefully, she'll receive some word from the agency about a caregiver.

The low cloudy ceiling keeps the insects buzzing around our faces as we plunge into the forest once more. I'm glad we sprayed repellant, but I still find the helicopter-ing by my head annoying. Once seated on the rock in the cool dry church, birds complaining above, I feel far more relaxed. Dembi lets me hold the Book of Vryheid on my lap.

What a curious inheritance we have! Descended from one of fifteen very brave families who left their comfortable, though sometimes abusive, situations. It must have taken a great deal of courage for the lot of them to break away from the relative safety of Brant's protection to strike out on their own. How ironic that our branch tumbled down over the decades to become drunkards and half-wits.

I flip quickly through the pages from the early 1800's. More angst, crop failures, deaths, disappointments. The handwriting of those who kept the records changes constantly, getting steadily less flamboyant and neat. In 1954, the records stop altogether. Over two hundred years of history abandoned in a hole under a church altar.

Each of the fifteen original families have several pages devoted to their trees, as long as anyone cared to fill it in over the years. Some are meticulous and detailed, while others are pretty sparse. But every one of them ends on April 11, 1954. I don't bother dwelling on that date. I am here as a treasure hunter for my brother's happiness.

Dembi and I search, dig and talk for a couple of hours. We eat our lunch under the noisy canopy of birds inside the abandoned church. The flat section of the altar rock is becoming very comfortable indeed.

My brother turns out to be really good company. His knowledge of the history of slavery in Canada is astounding. My mother Vera always led me to believe that her birth country is a haven for all people, devoid of racism or hatred. Naturally, that isn't true. Human beings are simply not perfect, wherever they may live. And of course, Vera is certainly capable of embellishing. A polite way of saying that she's a liar.

Dembi loves delicately searching through the Book of Vryheid. Some of the stories are tales told by visitors to the area. Perhaps people who are traveling further up river in search of nirvana. There are mentions of flights through 'de underground railway, on de Abolition line', up the Grand River from Buffalo and Niagara Falls, often landing in nearby Paris, Ontario, where there was a 'safe house'. They used the Quaker Quilts, in which secret directions were sewn, to guide them.

I wonder if some of the quilts at Memé's could possibly date from that period. Maybe the original farmhouse was a beacon of safety, too. They'd be very valuable if they were.

The descriptions from these fugitives portray far more difficult and treacherous lives than the slaves of Joseph Brant experienced. Perhaps old Joe was a hero, after all. Perhaps this is one thing that Vera got right.

There are many pages of sketching done by a very talented artist. One picture depicts a long dress with lace at the neck and sleeves. It's all in pencil, with no color, but I imagine a lovely mauve. A penciled pail hangs on a hook over an old fireplace. A kettle and frying pan huddle on the shelf. An old weigh scale.

The drawings are fascinating. Their placement in the book, plus the objects themselves, suggest they were drawn in the early 1900's. So far we have traced one hundred years forward in little Vryheid's history. Over the years, some of the families left and several fugitives from slavery took their places. The population, however, remained fairly small. Most people likely went to the larger centers for work or land.

The Millers moved to Burford to open a grocery store in 1856. The Cotters relocated to work as 'skilled laborers'. Nowadays, Burford feels like a stone's throw away but that's by car. On foot or horseback would've been a very different trip.

The city of Brantford must have seemed like another world. Some enterprising soul had recorded a few noteworthy news items from the 'big city', such as the execution of two ex-slaves. Perhaps the writer was trying to deter any more Vryheid inhabitants from moving out of the safe little enclave.

Whenever I get bored and antsy reading the book, which is often, Dembi and I scamper out to dig for gold. I have never experienced such exhilaration. Though I don't have much faith in really uncovering a treasure, I enjoy the physicality of the adventure and the fresh air. The activity constantly reminds me of Bell Canyon, out on the trails with my other trio, the sky filled with birds and the air with the scent of flowers.

We discover a small cemetery at the rear of the church, mostly overgrown with weeds. Stone monuments have crumbled back into the earth. Grave markings are now indistinguishable. We spend a long time in the graveyard, wondering if this was a good place to bury gold.

When we return to the church for our afternoon snack, driven inside by the intense sun, we look at some of the parchments and pictures that are jammed inside the book. A few of the scrolls have crumbled into tiny pieces, an aged ash left behind. One has been preserved in a kind of leather sleeve. It's a deed bequeathing the land upon which the actual village of Vryheid stood to Cornwall Johnston, dated 1920, and 'in perpetuity'. I sharply suck in my breath. Obviously Vryheid was not sold off along with the rest of the parcels. Does Memé now own everything?

I wonder what happened to the other residents. Had the village been abandoned in 1920? But no, here are further news reports. Life in the early 1900's described in detail by various authors. No more mention of slavery by then, thank goodness. Canada had had her birth. Wars had been fought. Vryheid had struggled on. Had it ever been incorporated as a village, or had it merely been a gathering of clans? Eventually to be owned by only one of them. No wonder the historian in Burford was interested. And she hadn't even seen the Book of Vryheid.

In 1918, there is a list of men who'd gone off to war and beside them, whether or not they returned. This battle really decimated the male population. It's difficult to tell how many people would have been left in the village, especially since the tradition of mentioning only the males continued. Maybe the dearth of males was the reason Vryheid had been purchased by or given to the Johnstons?

If the entrenched tradition of male ownership continued into the 1920's, how had Memé inherited everything? Or had she? Was she living on the land through her missing brother's charity?

The tiny squares I spied before indeed turn out to be pictures. Delicate little pieces of black and white history. Dozens of them, mostly of indistinct faces, men with arms crossed or pitchforks or shovels in hand. Others of wooden houses that surrounded the stone church. Some of the church itself in all its newly constructed glory.

Despite the lack of success in the gold department, Dembi and I are in a great mood as we trek back home. We are tired and hot, covered with dirt. Grass-stained but happy. We stand for a long while above the gushing river, basking in the breeze that trails through the little valley shaded by the chestnuts and oaks that lean over the water. When we finally turn up the lane toward the farmhouse, the sun streaks over the trees toward the west.

"Hey, Dembi, let's see if Miriam got a helper for Memé," I say. "If she did, then next time Miriam can come gold digging with us."

"Yippee!" He claps his hands. "Let's go see Miriam and Memé. Maybe Other Anne will come back."

He obviously hasn't absorbed the fact of Karoline's death.

When we enter the cool dark house we are met with silence. Dembi skips along the hallway calling out for Miriam. I don't hear her answer but she must have, for my brother whistles his way toward Memé's bedroom. I don't plan to go anywhere near there. I stop in the kitchen to deposit our picnic paraphernalia. I am washing my hands at the sink when I hear Miriam walk through the door behind me.

"Did you get a response to your helper request?" I ask without turning around.

My sister says nothing, so I continue to dry my hands and swing around to face her. She is stiff and silent, her face pinched and furrowed.

"They finally got one candidate who will come out here," she says, as though she has spent days on the project, slogging uphill to no avail.

"That's good," I say, as though it's a question.

"No one else would come out here. We won't have much choice."

"What do you mean?"

"I mean I was told by the supervisor that most of their casual staff are too afraid to come out to our place."

I sit down, clutching the towel, and stare up at her lovely troubled face. Her eyes are clouded by something. Mistrust? Fear? I'm not sure.

"I don't understand."

She sits down across from me. "They believe the place is haunted."

"That's ridiculous. It's the 1980's, not the 1880's."

"Most of the casual workers are older women who have lived here a long time. Some of them are retired nurses or assistant nurses. They're native to Burford. They have only one person who will agree to take on the job."

"Did you ask what they meant by haunted?"

Miriam nods. She still looks odd.

"They say a witch burned down Vryheid in 1954. April 11. And two people died. After that, everyone deserted the village and the farm except our mother."

I almost laugh but choke on it instead. Miriam's look is too fierce to brook any levity. I haven't even had a chance to tell her about Vryheid and the fact that it's attached to the farm property.

"But that's ridiculous," I repeat. "How can people these days believe in witches? Even in 1954, it seems…"

I suddenly recall the death dates of our uncles, Philip and John. April 11, 1954. I stop talking. The silence is weighty.

"Do we at least have the opportunity to interview this single candidate?"

"She'll be here in a few minutes, as a matter of fact."

"Good. Maybe she'll be able to tell us something. Miriam, what is it? What aren't you telling me?"

"I'm just freaked out. I didn't tell you this before, but there have been weird things happening. Doors slightly ajar to the outside. Little things missing, like an ornament that I could have sworn was there the day before…stuff like that. I'm spooked, to be honest."

Uncertain about how to react, I pat her hand. "It's probably Dembi. He wanders a bit, as you know. Plus even though I've only been here two nights, this place is pretty spooky in itself. Memé has been behaving strangely, then hearing this crap about a witch…" I stand up and replace the hand towel on its rack near the stove. That's when I notice the slow cooker is bubbling, a rich gravy underneath its glass lid.

"Miriam, you're not alone now. You have me. We're in this together." I put my arms around her in an awkward hug, but I feel her relax a little.

"You made dinner, too, I see. You are so thoughtful, you know that? Do you think we have time to eat before the candidate comes?"

Miriam glances at her watch. "Not really. But we should feed Dembi. Can you wait 'til after?"

"Absolutely. I'll just go and change."

"I'll set him up in the television room. He'll be thrilled that he can break the rule of not watching TV while eating. Then we can do the interview in peace."

At last, she smiles.

In my room I change into clean shorts and a golf shirt, one that has a Grace Productions Crew stitched into the pocket. Nervously I check the outside door and the windows, but they are locked tight. I am beginning to get spooked too, which is, I repeat to myself, ridiculous. I do not believe in witches and I do not think the ghost of one is prowling through the house. Another thing to research besides gold and slavery. Where did this witch story come from? How was the Vryheid fire started?

Back in the front hallway Miriam introduces me to a large black woman dressed in a flowered smock. She has a round, motherly face and eyes that shine with mirth. Her soft enormous hand encircles mine firmly. Her hair is a ball of tight dark curls that harkens back to the sixties. She's the kind of woman that everyone must instantly like.

"This is Melody Fischer," Miriam says. "She's a retired registered nurse. Melody, this is my sister Anne."

"Retired?" I ask. "You must be older than you look."

Her face is unlined, a smooth dark chocolate complexion that makes her appear to be in her forties.

"I'm sixty-eight. Fat is a great wrinkle filler."

She gives a deep-voiced chuckle, a pleasant sound that makes me want to laugh along with her. Miriam and I just smile.

"You two must be the missing Johnston twins," she continues. "I'll never be able to tell you apart."

"I never wear green," Miriam quips, pointing to my t-shirt.

This time we all chuckle.

"Come on into the kitchen, Melody," Miriam says. "We can have tea while we talk. Or coffee if you'd rather."

"Tea is perfect. And please call me Dee. I hate to sound like a song or something. Thanks to my parents for being whimsical, but I never did like my name."

"Oh, I love it," Miriam says. "Imagine being named after a figure in the Bible, like I was. So boring."

"At least she was one of the more exotic Biblical characters, though. Lots more interesting than Anne. Now that name is boring. I always wanted to be a Melody or a Christina or something."

We continue the idle chatter until all three of us are gathered around the table with tea things.

Miriam and I have not discussed the interview, but though I have been through hundreds of them with scriptwriters, directors or even actors, I know this is closer to Miriam's field. She immediately senses that I want her to take the lead.

"You know a lot about us, Dee."

I think it's a brilliant prompt.

"I do know some, yes. I've met Libby and Dembi, along with Larue many years ago. I just learned about the two of you recently."

It's an odd feeling, realizing that not only is she our one and only candidate, but that Dee also knows more about us than we do. Certainly more than we know about her. Once again Miriam is brilliant as well as a mind reader.

"Tell us a little about yourself, then, Dee."

"I was born in Nova Scotia, so I'm not considered native to Burford, even though I've been here forty years. That's a small town for you."

Again, that throaty laugh makes us grin at her. "I met my husband in Toronto when we were both at a medical conference. He's a doctor. He swept this big body off its feet and I followed him to Burford without a question. I have a happy marriage, three grown children and five grandchildren. I had a great career. I nursed mostly in Brantford, but worked in my husband's office in Burford for many years, too. When I decided to retire I thought I'd spend most of the time visiting the kids and grandkids, but they have their own lives. So I started to get bored. Tommy—my husband—is supposed to be retired, too, but recently he took a job with the local jail and he's been there constantly. So I joined the agency. I can pick and choose my jobs."

"You're a doctor's wife and you need to work?" Once again, my mouth runs away from me, inserting snobbish L.A. stereotypes into rural Burford.

Melody is unabashed. "I don't need to work, dear. I'm bored and I want to work. As I said, I have control over what I do and how often. I picked this one, to be perfectly honest, even though it's full time, because I care about Libby and have an historical interest in Vryheid."

I can't help myself. I get off track right away. This version of Anne is not very patient or prudent. Or perhaps it's Old Anne making it all about her.

"So you were in the area when Vryheid burned down? Why weren't you afraid to come out here?"

Miriam glares at me and so she should, but Dee laughs.

"Indeed I was here when it happened. I do not believe in witches nor do I believe in haunting. This area is filled with very superstitious people, but I wasn't born here, so I think that's why I'm different. I don't listen to gossip nor do I spread it. And because I was the town doctor's wife, most people respected that and didn't try to change my mind."

"Would you tell us what you know about that fire? Miriam and I are kind of freaked out about it. The agency told us no one but you would come out here."

Now I am not only rudely asking her to break her rules and gossip, but I have also told her she's the only candidate. This time, however, Miriam doesn't look angry. She's as thirsty for information as I am.

Dee sips her tea and leans back a little in the chair. The woman already looks at home. I immediately envision her as the perfect nursemaid for Memé. I can imagine her handling Memé's outbursts, settling the poor thing down, soothing her mean spirit. Being truthful with her rather than too soft, as Miriam is. As the stew bubbles and the television blares from the family room, we listen to an odd tale that occasionally shoots embers of familiarity and fear along my skin. It's a horror story I've been told and then forgotten.

"The Johnston family, and I apologize for saying this because I know they are kin, were alcoholics. With that addiction came irresponsibility, carelessness, even violence. They straddled two sides of this community, being a mix of black and native, but they were eventually shunned by both. They grew up during the Depression, poor and ignored, especially in Vryheid. Seems most of the world passed this little area by, worried about its own troubles. Didn't pay a lick of attention to us blacks and natives.

"The only people who came out here by the end of the '70's were losers and boozers. Sometimes the cops were called in, sometimes the Children's Aid. The poor kids who were born here—your mama being one of them—were frequently abused. I think Elizabeth—everyone called her Libby—from what I've heard she got the worst of it. She was a great beauty. Obviously, she passed that on to the three of you. But the men couldn't keep their hands off her.

"I didn't see much of her until Larue came along in the late 40's. He was a very nice man. Libby had apparently given away all of her children, or was forced to when she was younger. Once Larue got here, some of the kinder talk was that she was really loved for the first time. Others, of course, made fun of him because he was French and not terribly smart. But he worked hard around this place, fixed it up, built that big porch out front, for instance. The mean gossip was that he was a cousin. That Libby's family just couldn't leave her alone. I don't know where any of the information about Larue came from, since he never talked about himself that I know of."

For someone who professes not to listen to or spread gossip, you certainly have a lot of inside knowledge, Melo-dee dear, Uncharitable Anne thinks.

"When Libby got pregnant, she was once again the talk of the town. You'd think people had nothing else to do. I was privy to some information, since Tommy was her doctor. She wanted to deliver at home, with a midwife. Maybe because lots of her babies had been taken directly from the hospital with her parents' consent, not hers, and she was afraid the same thing would happen.

"In the middle of the night of February 21, 1950, Tommy got an emergency call from the midwife. It had snowed the previous day so it took him a long time to get out here. The roads were so treacherous. By the time he arrived, you two girls had been delivered. Poor Dembi was tangled in the umbilical cord and had already turned blue. Tommy was able to save him, but just barely. The rumor mill always claims he's slow because his parents were cousins, but I know the truth.

"Something happened to Libby that night. She was never the same afterward. She had to be hospitalized, lost a lot of blood, and underwent surgery to remove her uterus. Dembi was kept in hospital with his mother because he needed a lot of care, but you girls stayed home with Larue. I don't know exactly what happened, but very soon, there was only one daughter left."

I look over at Miriam, surprised to see tears rolling down her cheeks.

"My mom and dad—the ones who adopted me—said I was three weeks old when they got me."

"Sounds about right." Dee pats and squeezes Miriam's hand in a motherly, comforting way. I get her a tissue.

"No one seemed to know why he gave you away. Maybe Larue couldn't handle two babies. Maybe someone suggested that three would be too many once Libby got home."

Miriam cries quietly. I imagine what she is thinking. Why her? Why did they give her away? Why not me? Why not place Dembi in a home or an institution and keep the two of us? Of course, Miriam is too nice to think of that last one; that thought is all mine.

"Did your adoptive parents tell you that they visited here quite often?"

Miriam almost snorts, so surprised is she in the midst of her tears. "Really?"

Dee nods. "Yup. For about four years. They usually brought you over to see Tommy while they were here. I think they were real cousins of Libby's. Personally, I'm surprised that Larue let you go. But the way Libby was after she got home with Dembi, I suppose it was the right decision."

"I had a wonderful upbringing," Miriam concedes. "I do have some memories, very, very faint ones. No wonder this farm felt so comfortable when I arrived. The front of the house, the kitchen—they both felt eerily familiar. I have impressions of little friends that I'd loved to play with. Now I think those friends were Anne and Dembi. I always figured I was odd. Not quite whole. I know everyone goes through that, but I seemed to have it worse than others. Now I know why."

Miriam looks at me and smiles. Her eyes are tender.

I want to screech, what about me? When did they give me away? Why can't I remember any of this? Why does this farm feel anything but comfortable to me? Is Miriam's melodramatic 'not quite whole' the same as my apparent quest for a trio? Why don't I have any faint memories at all?

In my head I show up as the daughter of Vera and Ian, sister to Elizabeth, fully formed. Talking, remembering. Vera even had baby pictures of me. Did she steal them from Memé?

Fortunately our brother interrupts my inner turmoil when he comes into the kitchen to ask for more stew. Wiping her eyes, Miriam immediately spoons some into a bowl for him. Dembi looks at her closely, noticing her distress. The television must be fascinating, for he simply pats her arm, grabs his meal and disappears again.

Dee continues as though there has been no interruption. "Then came the fire and that changed everything around here. It was April 11, 1954, and conditions were fairly good around here. Tobacco farming was reaching its peak. The public didn't yet know that smoking was hazardous to our health, even though the medical community had suspected for some time. Tobacco farmers were getting rich, including the Johnstons. They added to the farmhouse, spruced up Vryhcid, and..."

"They spruced up Vryheid?" Miriam interrupts.

I remember with a jolt that I haven't shared the deed with my sister.

Dee, however, has all that information, too. "Oh yes, dear, didn't you know? The acres around and including Vryheid were bequeathed to the Johnston family around the time of Joseph Brant. They sold off a lot of it, during the thirties and forties, but my understanding is that everything belongs to—well, to Libby now, I suppose."

Miriam squeaks.

"But the fire..." I prompt. We can get into the deed later. Get to the damn fire.

"The fire burned down the entire village. A couple of the Johnston boys died. I have a feeling there was some kind of still there, because from one small match there was a huge blast. Before any fire trucks could arrive, all the old wooden homes were just sticks. And it seemed that before the smoke even died away, the rumors about the witch were flying everywhere."

Dear Diary,

Do you think evil is the opposite of good? Or the absence of good? Do you think it's a conscious and deliberate wrongdoing? Or do you think people are just born without a conscience and do bad things because the devil makes them do it? It's a very interesting debate. Too bad you can't talk.

CHAPTER 18

"This is all so strange," Miriam says. "I can't take it all in."

"Why on earth would they think a witch was responsible?" I ask, trying to keep everyone on track.

Dee pours us more tea, completely at home now. In her element. Memé hasn't interrupted once. Dembi is obviously absorbed in the television. Miriam is spellbound and I am antsy.

"Well, I think it goes back to the native legends and our own black history. We were a superstitious lot to begin with. Add the native stories and you have a hodgepodge of beliefs and tales and exaggerations and outright lies. Most of the legends were designed to be warnings. You know the sort of thing; don't step on a crack, you'll break your mother's back. The Johnston family, because of their isolation, the exotic history of Vryheid and its connection to Joseph Brant...well, they were ripe for not only gossip but legendary status, too."

As though she has read my mind, Memé starts a loud wail from the bedroom. Miriam asks Dee if she'd like to see her potential patient.

"The agency told me you and your husband used to visit fairly often, but I gather you haven't seen our mother for a few weeks. I'm afraid you'll see a terrible change."

Dee squeezes my sister's hand. "I'm used to what this horrid disease can do."

"I'll check on Dembi," I offer. I can't face Memé right now.

Dembi is perched on the edge of the sofa. Rolly is tucked in beside my brother and raises his sleepy head to yawn at me. Dembi, however, doesn't look at me. His eyes are glued to a program that looks like a western. At first I don't notice that the cowboys are vampires or zombies or something until they begin to rip off heads and toss the bodies in the air.

"Dembi." I force a gentle tone. Avoid admonishment. "Don't you think this is a bit scary? It might give you nightmares."

Dembi turns his clear, gorgeous eyes to stare at me. He has no guile, no depth, in those eyes. His thoughts are transparent. It's refreshing to be in the presence of someone with no hidden agenda. I sit beside him and impulsively, tenderly, take his hand. Rolly gives a grumpy mew at having to move over.

"It's okay, Anne," Dembi says, patting my hand in response, soothing me. "It's not real. It's all on TV." He points as though to prove his assertion that the zombie-vampire-cowboys are not here in the room with us, but locked up in a moving box.

I smile back at him. Let him know I'm relieved. "Okay. But if you get scared…"

"I won't." He slips his hand from under mine, mesmerized once again by flying objects and headless walking dead.

Miriam and Dee are gone a long time. I have time to clean up the kitchen, where I find a very expensive bottle of scotch under the cupboard near the stove. I pour myself a hefty helping. Stir the stew, munch on a hunk of soft yet crunchy bread heaped with butter, and think. I want to call Ethan desperately but don't want an interruption in our talk. I have so much to tell him.

Once again I am traversing unknown territory. My heart is hammering. I reach too often to sip the warm golden liquid in my hand. Inside my head the voices of those different Annes are arguing. Pain streaks across my brow and for a moment, I teeter. Driftwood in an angry wind. I grasp the edge of the table until it passes.

By the time Miriam and Dee return I can tell that their relationship has changed. They have bonded over their patient's torturous dying. I am left out, though my sister grasps my arm and pulls me close. I watch myself behave with appropriate responses.

"You must be starving, Anne," she says. "I know I am. Dee, can you stay for dinner?"

I want to say "Yes, yes, please, I need more information," but the woman is suddenly panicked at the idea of being here so long.

"Oh, dear, we're having the neighbors over for dinner and I'm late! Tommy will not be happy." She grins, as though the idea of Tommy being annoyed with her is actually ludicrous. "But I will see you tomorrow. And think about next Saturday."

Tomorrow, I understand, she will start working for us. "Next Saturday?" I ask.

"I'll tell you all about that," Miriam says. "Goodnight, Dee. Thank you for everything."

Suddenly the big motherly presence is gone in a flurry of waves and smiles. Miriam turns to the stove, stirs a bit and piles a heap of stew into our bowls. Wordlessly I cut the rest of the bread, pour some white wine for my twin and more scotch for me. We sit at the table facing one another. It's still odd, perhaps always will be, that I am looking at my mirror image. A moving, warm, breathing one.

"Dee has invited us to a powwow next Saturday," Miriam says between mouthfuls.

I have noticed that she eats like I do—voraciously.

The stew is spicy, filled with summer vegetables. Incongruous on such a hot night, but comfort food is what we need. We both slurp and speak with our mouths full.

"What's a powwow?"

"It's a celebration, usually native, but this time it's different. They're honoring the anniversary of Vryheid's founding. Dee says they've been working on this event for several years. The native councils and the black organizations and the town councils—everyone is helping. They're advertising it as the biggest community of races in North America. Vryheid meant freedom for natives and blacks, but they intermingled with whites, too, so they want it to be an example of what can happen when people forget about color and creed and try to get along."

Miriam sounds like a walking advertisement herself. All I need is a reminder that I am not simply half and half. I have roots in a third that up until now I've been able to ignore or discount.

"Lofty goals," I respond. "What do they do at a powwow?"

"Dance, play music, parade their traditional costumes. That's about it, I think."

"And Dee has invited us?"

"Yes. She thinks she could get Memé a wheelchair and it's supposed to be a gorgeous day. She believes in sunshine as an anecdote for pain. But she'll be able to assess her more closely over the rest of this week and next."

I say nothing. Concentrate on the food and my amber liquid, unable to clear the fog in my head to articulate any response. I ponder the stuffy death-scented room in which our mother lies. I am inclined to agree with Dee. Surely fresh air and sun couldn't hurt at any rate. But how will she cope with the fact of two daughters? Will she remember what I said to her? Will she somehow convey her abhorrence of me to Miriam, Dembi and Dee? To the hordes at this powwow extravaganza? I shiver in the hot night.

Dembi comes bustling into the room with Rolly in his arms. He places the cat on the floor in front of its food dish and sits down beside us.

"Is there dessert?" he asks, eying our empty plates.

Miriam laughs. "There is dessert, Dembi! Look, I made a pie from the blueberries we picked the other day."

My sister is a marvel. As we chomp on the fluffy pastry and sweet fruit, Miriam tells Dembi about our new helper, Dee.

"Now I can come treasure hunting with you."

Both my brother and I are thrilled.

I have trouble sleeping tonight. Perhaps it was the late dinner. The scotch? The sound of the rather fierce wind trying to slip through the tree barrier, rustling pine needles, rattling loose bits of the old house? Maybe it's because I couldn't talk to Ethan for more than several seconds. He's deeply involved in that case. It's about to come to a potentially violent conclusion, nothing really unusual for L.A. Maybe I am transferring my fear for Ethan into a general nightmare.

I get up several times to check the locks on my doors and my window. Does anyone do this for the rest of the house, I wonder? There are so many openings to the darkness. A darkness far deeper than I experience in L.A. Even deeper than Bell Canyon. There are no streetlights. Only the moon and stars cast a very faint sliver of illumination across the lawn and through the trees. Goosebumps prickle my skin despite the warm night. At least my head isn't aching.

Gathering my courage, I clasp my small travel flashlight, throw on some socks, and prowl through the dark hallways. This house is a maze and I haven't even explored most of it. I keep reminding myself that I have only been here three days, but I feel as though I arrived years ago. In a way, I suppose I did.

The inside door to my room leads directly into a long wide hallway that eventually opens to the kitchen. A closet and a pantry line the opposite wall. An empty bedroom and the parlor are straight ahead. I turn right. On my left is the living room with the big old television. I turn right again. The halls are narrow, the floors creaky. I have no idea which areas formed the original house and which are newer. Four bedrooms occupy this wing on both sides. Memé's bedroom sits across from Miriam's and next door to Dembi's.

I slowly open the door and listen to Memé's ragged breathing. Our mother sleeps all night, thanks to some wonder drug and the oxygen canopy. A rush of body odor streams out at me. I shut the door, unwilling to allow the scent of death to follow me up the hall. An empty smaller bedroom and a huge bathroom complete this wing.

I retrace my steps and find two living spaces on the other side of the house. They are filled with enormous sofas, coffee tables, lamps, bookshelves and footstools. There seems to be little room for people. They are all hulking shadows layered with dust. Remnants of a house that used to be filled with loud, rambunctious, talkative sorts who loved to party.

When I walk back toward the parlor, where we'd sat and pored over our family Bible, a breeze tickles my ankles. It's sliding in through an open door at the end of the black hallway. I tiptoe along in the dark. My little flashlight sends a tiny spot of light ahead of me, picking up shadows and cobwebs. My heartbeats echo in my head, filling the silence with the pulse of sound. I am terrified but I must shut that door.

Suddenly a shape appears at the doorstop. I take in a shuddering pre-scream breath before I feel Rolly brush past. *Fucking cat*, I think. Then I recall Dembi's arms curled around the animal's furry body and I have to smile. Once the door is shut and the lock is in place, I feel better.

As I stand in the darkness I can feel the house around me. Its slight musty odor invades my nostrils, my pores. The drafts scuttle along like cockroaches, under the doors, through the aging seals on the windows. Boards sigh, the creaking joints of an old person. I have a sudden flash of my little girl self. I stand on tiptoes, gazing out the window at a field of tall green stalks. Someone strides toward me. I am terrified.

I slip-slide frantically back to my room, my feet skating along the hardwood. Chased by an enormous, breathing, grunting fear. It's as though a giant whispers nasty, threatening words in my ear. I am not myself. I am little and weak and incapable of fighting back. When I reach my room I close the door and lean on it, panting. I slide the lock into place.

There are no other sounds. Nothing moves. I want to run and jump into bed with Miriam. I want Dembi to grin up at me. When my breathing slows, I crawl under the duvet and shiver. I sob into the sheets. I have experienced a memory and the grief wells up from there. I was little in this house. And I was vulnerable.

Dear Diary,

Do you believe in capital punishment? I mean, the death penalty for say, committing a murder? Some states still use it and lots of countries around the world, too. People used to go and watch hangings. Sometimes I wish they still had that.

CHAPTER 19

In the morning, I am red-eyed and groggy. I dress in my treasure hunting jean shorts and a light blue top and stumble to the kitchen. Miriam gets up from the table when she sees me and puts her arms around me. I let myself collapse into them. Encircle her. Feel her warmth, the beat of her heart. The tears flow again. Dembi jumps up too and we are trio-d in comfort again. I am a mess once more. I can't seem to stop feeling marshmallowy, soft and sad. This is not me.
 I think.
 Miriam has been up early, tending to Memé. She's made breakfast and now she tends to me. Her face is mine but her eyes reflect love and certainty. She knows who she is and she knows how to love.
 We have waffles and strawberries and maple syrup and pecans. I devour them as happily as my siblings do. As we are finishing coffee, Melody appears at the kitchen door. She is laden with several bags including a leather one that resembles a doctor's kit.
 All three of us help her into the house where she fills the kitchen with her big voice and her laughter. She has several things for Memé, sent by Tommy. Contraptions to stretch muscles, stimulate movement and assist with breathing. Other paraphernalia I am too overwhelmed to contemplate, adult diapers among them. Once Dee is unpacked, she and Dembi deliver the items to Memé's room while Miriam and I clean the kitchen. We wordlessly start on the picnic lunch, pulling out bread and meat and apples.

Dembi appears in the doorway with a white package. "Look what Dee brought for us." His slow, slurry speech is sped up by excitement. "Cookies for our treasure hunt!"

Holy crap, she bakes too, I think, wondering how on earth she had time to prepare this incredible-smelling mixture of chocolate, peanut butter and coconut.

Miriam claps her hands. "Wonderful! Anne and I are getting the picnic ready. Do you want to help, Dembi?"

He wags his head happily as though she has asked him to a party. It turns out to be fun, actually, as we pile up sandwiches, goodies and drinks. We are nearly finished when Dee comes back. She's not smiling this time.

"Libby is in worse shape than I thought," she says bluntly. "If I can't see any progress today, I might call Tommy and see if we should take her to the hospital."

"I knew I should have acted sooner," Miriam says, immediately taking on the burden. "She was so much better up until a few days ago and any mention of the hospital sent her into..."

Dee puts her large, beefy hand on my sister's shoulder. "Do not blame yourself, Miriam. This horrible disease can turn in a few hours, let alone days. She could even have worsened overnight. Let me see what I can do for her. Then we'll all make the decision together."

"Should we go on our treasure hunt or should I stay home?"

"No, no, you go on your treasure hunt," Dee answers, looking at Dembi's sagging expression at the thought of canceling. "Be back by around 3. That'll give me enough time to make an assessment and, if need be, have Tommy swing by for a visit."

Melody is precise, decisive and kind. Exactly what we need. The three of us finish our preparations. Then off we go as though we've received permission from our mother to retreat into an innocent childlike adventure.

Although it's still early, it's very hot. The sky is cerulean, cloudless, and the sun is a blazing heat lamp. We all don our hats. Slather on a bit of sun lotion and spray insect repellant. Down the hill we go, through bushes filled with buzzing insects and pincers from angry leaves.

Dembi hacks our way through, heedless of the flowers and weeds alike that we trample underfoot. He sings in a high-pitched, sloppy voice, *A-hunting we will go*. After a moment of giggling, Miriam and I join the singing.

In a shallow part of the river we walk into the stream with our arms straight out for balance, pausing a bit to let the refreshing water splash our sweaty skin. We hang over the bridge for a few moments watching the ripples and waves as they course away from us.

Our voices continue to drown out the cicadas' symphony, the bees' dance, the scampering of mice and squirrels and chipmunks as we invade their territory. We holler camp songs that have crossed borders and time. We attempt a few songs from the radio.

Dembi sings louder than we do.

"See that girl, watch her scream, playing the tambourine."

Miriam and I have to put our hands over our mouths to avoid laughing out loud.

"Nobody knows what it's like to be Batman."

Better than the bad man, I suppose.

"There's a bathroom on the right" instead of "There's a bad moon on the rise" puts us over the edge. We have to stop. Bend over and choke with laughter. Dembi joins in though he looks puzzled by our merriment.

By the time we reach the old church we are covered in perspiration, breathless and sporting Cheshire cat grins. All three of us sit side by side on the rock altar, swill a bottle of water each in one gulp and munch on Dee's cookies. Dembi holds the Vryheid book reverently on his lap. Gradually I ensure that Miriam sees the deed. The land we are sitting upon probably does belong to Memé. Her eyes widen. She's silent for a long time. Dembi and I turn the pages carefully while our sister contemplates.

I am mesmerized by the drawings as we progress through the years. Although throughout the decades different hands have made the sketches, there are similarities, as though the artists were related. Perhaps they were. The book was handed down by one family whose interest in recording Vryheid's history continued through generations. Namely, the Johnstons.

As we flip into the 1940's the artistic renderings are breathtaking. Mostly done in pencil, the pictures reflect the era both in the dress of the people depicted and the appearance of the village. They are distinctive, too. Where there is color, it's stunning despite the fading of time. The figures are so realistic, utterly arresting, especially the eyes. I feel as though I am gazing into someone's face. I'm not an art critic but I did learn something from Karoline's expeditions for Daniel's collections. These pictures, although meant to simply accompany the diary entries, are magnificent. This artist was highly talented.

Dark faces gaze back at us from the pages. From lined skin to youthful smiles, from short and hefty women in printed dresses to young slender girls carrying buckets of water, the portraits are mesmerizing. The combination of black and native is highlighted in the cheekbones, straight black hair, thick lips and flattened noses. The people are not all beautiful, but they are interesting characters. The landscape is so realistic that the houses of Vryheid live again, surrounded by colorful flowers, vegetable gardens, bushes and the paraphernalia of a rustic life.

Miriam leans over and stares at them, too. "They're lovely," she breathes.

"They look familiar to me," I say slowly, trying to remember something that has slipped into the fog of my recent tumult. "I feel as though I've seen something like these before."

"I know. I do too. Dembi, did Mrs. West see this book?"

He shakes his head. Emphatic, possessive. "No. No. Memé said to keep everything secret. Only the family. Memé, Miriam, Other Anne, Triplet Anne. Dembi."

Miriam and I look at each other. The topic obviously upsets Dembi. He regresses into his childish manners, closes the book, hugs it and rocks back and forth.

Miriam touches his shoulder gently. "That's all right, Dembi. We're not going to show it to anyone. Let's put it back and go on our treasure hunt."

He smiles now, carefully replaces the book and jumps to his feet. For the next couple of hours we prance through the woods, across the fields, in and out of Dembi's cave. We laugh. Hide and seek. Dig. Listen. We watch a hawk circle and dive. It lurches back into the sky with a dangled prey. We stand very still as a pair of young deer, upwind, munch on berries and leaves. Their beautiful brown faces turn in our direction when I snap a twig, but none of us moves. Eventually they meander away.

When we settle in for lunch we're happy to be out of the sun in the cool dry cave, tucked away under trees and rock. I sit in the rocker once more while Miriam and our brother perch on the wobbly chairs. Dembi is quiet, but his eyes are more alive than I have seen them. The perspiration has settled on his forehead and cheeks, making his dark skin glow. His shirt is inside out, I notice, but right at this moment, his unkempt look seems endearing.

Miriam laughs as she hauls the goodies out of the backpacks and distributes sandwiches and cookies and fruit and more water. Her face is dusky, kissed by the sun. Her eyes shine with merriment. The pink shirt hugs her curves and highlights her color. She's indescribably beautiful.

I am overwhelmed with a rush of love. The feeling leaves me gasping for breath, almost tearful. I'm uncertain about this new emotion. Not sure how to handle it. I wonder if I've ever felt this kind of pure love before. It's very different from what I feel for Ethan. Nothing like I ever felt for Karoline, Giulio or Parris. Even Elizabeth and my parents.

I am utterly connected to these two people. I shared a womb with them. They have my smile, my eyes, my skin. It's a strange astonishing sensation. Even Ice Queen Anne is silent in wonderment.

As I gaze around Dembi's cave I notice a stack of wood and paper shoved under his bed that I hadn't seen before. He must be in the mood to redecorate. I still have a flash of rage each time my eye rests on the picture of him and Karoline but the feeling is fading the longer I am here. Maybe he'll take that down when he changes things around. Maybe I can suggest it...

We chat and laugh. I rock and eat and drink in the sight of these lovely people. My true trio.

After lunch we pore over the rough copy of Dembi's map again. It's nearly impossible to make out the depicted village from the overgrown bushes and trees in our way. We spend about an hour digging and hunting, really to satisfy Dembi. But it's far too hot and the insects have come out to hunt. We head back to the farmhouse early, singing as we go. We slurp on water to keep our energy high.

Melody is in the kitchen. She's singing, too, in a deep throaty voice that sounds like someone in a jazz cellar. She sparkles with confidence and good news. It's infectious, an oxygenated air that pumps all of us, even Dembi. He scoots off to "see Memé and tell her about the hunt" while Miriam and I clean up the picnic gear and visit with Dee.

"I am so happy to tell you, girls," she says, as she assists us with the bags and tins and bottles. "Libby is resting very peacefully. Tommy did come by and, although of course she's terminal, he thinks he can make her remaining days much more comfortable and lucid. He's switched some of the meds and increased the oxygen intake. Plus, I opened her windows, even though at first she was terrified for some reason. She's already more alert with the better air. She'll enjoy Dembi's stories!"

I think of two things. The stale putrid air in Memé's room and the gaping door the evening before. Despite the heat in the kitchen I shiver. When we're finished cleaning, Miriam puts her hand on my arm.

"I'm going to visit with Memé, too," she says. "Do you want to try the two of us again?"

I know she means well. She wants Memé to accept me, along with my brother and sister. Unlike Miriam I am aware of the underlying tension. The fear that emanates from our mother when she looks at me. I'm still not certain of the reasons, but I am determined to find out. Memé will remember what I said to her when I first arrived. She will tell me, eventually, why she separated my trio.

My breath quickens as rapidly as the thoughts jet through my brain. I try to calm myself to answer but Miriam notices immediately.

"It's okay. We'll give it more time."

She dashes off down the hallway. Dee smiles at me with an understanding that seems deeper than it should be.

"Do you know why our mother rejected me?" My breath gives out and the 'me' is almost a whisper.

The woman sits in a kitchen chair and subtly signals for me to sit, too. I obey in puppet fashion, collapsing at the table. I am terrified. A sudden rush of grey memories clouds my eyes. Fire. Running feet. A dark shape in the hallway. The groan of springs as a monster sits on my bed.

Dee's soft big hand covers mine, a motherly gesture that I don't remember ever experiencing. I recall Vera's distance, her bustling, businesslike attitude. Her habit of patting my back perfunctorily as though that constituted a hug.

I feel Ethan's warmth as he wraps me in his arms. I stop shivering. Ice Queen Anne does not appear. Although I know I am going to be hurt, I leave myself open and soft, albeit breathless and afraid.

"I told you about the huge fire that destroyed Vryheid."

I nod as flames pass my vision. I smell the acrid, overwhelming smoke and almost cough.

"You must try to understand that people around here were backward and isolated in the 50's. They were a culture unto themselves, pretty much ignored by the rest of society for decades. A native and black mix who didn't know what to believe. They straddled two sets of histories and philosophies. They had very few tools for dealing with the encroachment of the town and its laws and so on. Over their history they were often incestuous, too, since few of them moved out to get married or mate. So they passed on some very weak genes in a lot of cases. I'm not sure of the original evolution of Vryheid, but it had something to do with Joseph Brant. If you get time, you should talk to Mary Lou West. She's the curator in the new Burford museum and has worked very hard on the archives."

I nod, my breath normal again as Dee drones on. She's probably rambling on purpose, gently leading me to the real nuggets of information that I need. I am calmer so her method works.

"I'm setting the background to try and get you to understand the atmosphere in 1954. Everything was changing rapidly. The towns were forcing change on Vryheid. The ownership of the land was in question. The Johnstons had evolved into drunkards and troublemakers. No one policed them very carefully. Brawls were so commonplace that someone had to be hospitalized before the law took any interest. But with the amalgamations of some counties and enforcement agencies, that hands-off policy was changing.

"In the village itself the people were poor, miserable, discontent and superstitious. They refused help from outside agencies, distrusted anyone outside, but didn't like each other much either. Around them the towns were booming with post-war affluence. The Vryheid residents were starting to talk about selling out to a subdivision development, while the Johnstons fought to keep the status quo. There was a rumor that all the land belonged to them anyway, but that wasn't substantiated until much later."

I flash to the Vryheid book and the wealth of information it holds.

"Anyone who wasn't related to the Johnstons hated them with a passion. And some who were related, too, I suppose. Stories went around about how they believed in voodoo and witchcraft. Strange rituals were supposedly carried out in the compound. None of this was ever proven. There was never any evidence of such goings-on. But the fear was wild. When the fire burned the village to the ground, the death of the Johnston men drove everyone away. The incident was blamed on witchcraft."

I conjure up the vine-choked, tree-hidden paths of the old village. The beautiful drawings in the book. The penciled outlines of Dembi's treasure map. The stone church still perched on the hillock. Safe from the hell fire. Now a bird sanctuary. A keeper of secrets. An orange glow lights up the darkness of my memory. I see my own face reflected in the pops and flashes as the fire eats its prey. I am smiling.

"And I was the witch," I say.

Dee leans closer to me. I can feel the heat of her body, the warm motherly quality that oozes from her naturally. Her eyes are kind and wise.

"Yes. Someone reported that they saw you with a torch of some kind, similar to a smudging stick. You walked around and lit piles of straw and paper. Supposedly you tipped over a couple of gasoline cans and lit them up, too. Personally, I adhere to the theory that there was an illegal distillery.

"Regardless, the village was a tinderbox, everything made of wood, everything crudely put together. It went up in seconds. No one contacted the fire department for hours. By then all the houses and much of the forest had burnt to the ground.

"But, Anne, you were a little girl. You were four years old. How could you have done that? I have never believed it and you shouldn't either. There were plenty of people who hated the Johnstons and had reasons for getting rid of them. It's also pretty suspicious that they were the only ones who died."

"I think Memé believed I did it. That's why she sent me away. Probably so did my adoptive mother."

Perhaps this explains Vera's wariness, her distance. I am a being to be feared.

Dee pushes her chair closer to me. I almost flinch when her arm drapes over my shoulder, pulling me to her. Instead, I allow the heat of her sympathy to drift over my skin. I'm not sure what I will do if she doesn't hold me upright.

"Remember that Libby was, and still is, limited in her understanding. She was the product—and the victim—of incest. Despite her beauty and gentleness she was not very smart. She couldn't help but believe in the superstitions and tales of witchcraft."

"So she called her sister to come and get me."

"Yes, I think so. Of course I wasn't here, so I don't know for certain. No one but Libby and Larue would know."

"And Vera."

Dee takes in a large breath and cuddles me closer. I don't resist. I can't sit up.

"Maybe. You will have to ask her some day, poor child. The important thing for you to remember is that you were little more than a baby back then. It's extremely doubtful that you could have done such a thing of your own accord."

I think of the pampered, oblivious, selfish, icy Anne. The 'me' who walked through life with her haughty self-aggrandized attitude. Could that person have lit a fire that killed two people? I believe she could and would. She murdered her best friend. She could easily eliminate those abusive uncles from her life.

And who am I now? Can a monster of such epic rage transform into a loving, beloved creature?

"But what if I did do it?" I ask Dee, my voice tremulous against her breast as she holds me.

She grasps my chin and forces me to look straight at her. "You were four. A little girl in a terrible situation. Most of Libby's brothers were cruel drunks. Who knows what they did to you or to Dembi? Maybe you had reasons to burn down that cesspool."

On some level, she too thinks I did it. She believes I was justified. But wonderful, generous, kind-hearted Dee will never know what it's like to feel responsible for the death of three people. To experience a rage so deep and uncontrollable that it turns you into a raving maniac. To not know who you are. She is a wife, a mom, a caregiver. Who is Anne? Which Anne can I trust?

I am suddenly too tired to think. A blanket of exhaustion washes over me. Slowly I extricate myself from Dee's embrace and sit up.

"I have to lie down, Dee. I can't even think."

"You rest, love. We'll talk again soon."

The big woman lifts herself gracefully from the chair and leans over a cupboard. She pours something into a small glass.

"I found some very nice Scotch in the cupboard just now," she says with a smile. "This will calm your nerves."

I smile back, remembering my binge the other day and take a satisfying sip. "Thanks, Dee."

"I'll see you in the morning, dear."

I traipse a little further into the hallway, past the route to my room, and listen near Memé's door. I can hear the soft voices of my siblings though I can't tell what they're saying. The cadence is excited and joyful, held quiet out of respect alone. The puff, puff of the oxygen machine is our mother's only reply. I take a sip of the scotch and feel a burning sensation in my stomach that has nothing to do with the alcohol.

Guilt churns its way through my intestines. I am, for the first time, truly sorry. I'm sorry for telling you I hate you, Memé. I'm not sorry for the feeling, only for the selfish act of saying it out loud.

I slip quickly past the doorway to the parlor where I curl up in a chair and dial Ethan's number.

He sounds sleepy when he says "Hello."

"Are you okay?" I ask, and suddenly he's awake.

"Anne," he breathes, as though he has just discovered me.

I picture him falling asleep in his chair, hair sticking straight on end, big eyes blinking without the glasses to focus them.

"I'm okay. Just bushed. That case kicked the shit out of me. I'm glad you can't read the L.A. papers."

I listen to his voice for a while as he outlines his harrowing experiences. Try hard not to imagine how dangerous it must have been. In mid sip, he suddenly asks me how I am doing. I swallow quickly and a hiccup bursts into the receiver, which makes him laugh. I love the sound of his laugh, so I giggle, too. I decide to leave out a few details of my own narrative, keep the conversation light.

"I assume you're imbibing again this evening, milady."

"Yes. I'm becoming quite the lush, kind sir. I shall return to LA LA Land with several new habits."

He laughs again. "You'll fit right in. But seriously, how's it going? I can't imagine how strange all of this must be."

"I'm okay, really." I feel the reverberations of truth. "I can't believe how easily Miriam and Dembi and I have bonded. They're so…good, Ethan. Easy to love. I can't wait for you to meet them."

"You say the word, my sweet, and I will be on the next plane. I'm getting sick of the smog and the crime. L.A. and I are not on good terms right now."

"Wow, I don't think I've ever heard you so down about the job. Don't tell your parents."

He laughs again, even heartier than before. "They would be thrilled if they knew how I was feeling. But I think L.A. is just missing a spark or something. Or maybe a beautiful body snuggled up to mine. Something like that, anyway."

"Aha! You're not depressed, you're just horny."

Now we both laugh and it feels great.

"I mean it, though. If you want me up there, I have weeks of vacation coming to me. And if that doesn't work, we can take a trip when you come home."

"A trip sounds wonderful. As for coming up here, I think not just yet."

I struggle to put it into words for him.

"We've hired a nurse for Memé and she's terrific. Dembi and Miriam and I hung out together all day. Ethan, I think I'll be here longer. I want to see how Memé progresses with the new help."

How can I tell him that the real reason I don't want him here is because I haven't yet discovered whether or not I am a monster? That I cannot trust myself, as a friend, sister or lover?

"And we've been invited to a huge powwow near Vryheid next Saturday," is what I do say.

"What's a powwow?"

I explain the celebration in general terms, the way Miriam told it to me. At first Ethan sounds intrigued but a yawn soon betrays him.

"I'll let you go, babe. You sound so tired."

"I hate to admit it but I can barely stay awake. At least things are back to normal around here, if there is such a thing as normal in L.A. My hours won't be so long. We can talk more often."

We say good night. I am left with an unsatisfactory, empty feeling. Despite the scotch I am no longer relaxed.

Out in the hallway I hear my sister and brother laugh as they prance toward the family room next door. I join them in front of the television. We watch a movie that I've never even heard of. Something Canadian I think. I mostly watch Miriam and Dembi. They think it's hilarious, can repeat some of the lines and love tossing popcorn at one another.

I try very hard to loosen up but I am tense and uncomfortable. Ice Queen Anne rears her ugly head and wants to comment haughtily on the poor quality of the hick film. I override her voice with a hearty guffaw. I feel apart from my siblings right now. The newbie. Removed from some of the quirks they have learned about one another. I have not been given this gift of knowing through time. Both Memé and Karoline robbed me of that. Ice Queen Anne laughs at me.

Miriam stretches and yawns as she reaches over to grab my stockinged toes. Next she pats Dembi's arm. I am enthralled with the way she does this so naturally. She touches us constantly. Her love is reassuring and physical.

"I'm sorry, guys, I'm so tired. I'm going to bed to read and fall asleep forever."

Dembi frowns at her. "If you fall asleep forever, you die," he says, his voice serious and worried.

"Sorry, Dembi, I was just exaggerating. I think hunting all day has made me very, very tired. But don't worry, I will wake up tomorrow."

"Okay." He nods, walks over and turns off the television.

"Did you want to keep watching, Anne?" Miriam asks.

I stand up. "Nope, I'm right behind you. Even though I've hunted for a couple of days, I am still not in shape. Not like you, Dembi. You are so strong."

He curls himself into me. His tall frame c-shapes the way a very large dog would try to sit on its owner's lap. I instinctively reach around and pull him close. His head lolls on my shoulder. We stand side by side, child-man and childish woman, neither of us quite fit for this world.

Miriam joins us. Wraps us in her firm, responsible, generous embrace. For a moment there is no sound but Dembi's contented sigh, until Rolly begins a loud purr at our feet. My brother automatically breaks the huddle, reaches down and sets the cat on his shoulder. We all toddle off toward our rooms.

Dear Diary,

I had some friends who were Catholic and I think they have the right attitude. Sin, sin, sin all week, then off you go to confession and get forgiven. I like that.

CHAPTER 20

From Friday to Wednesday, our days become something of a routine, though not in any usual sense. We arise, have breakfast and go hunting for gold. On hot days we swim in an inlet of the river that's deep and cold and protected from the rapids. Every afternoon we're back at the farmhouse.

Melody comes to work every single day, including the weekend. Her husband, she informs us, is off on a course. Her own children have gone on vacation with the grandkids in tow. She insists that she's bored and lonely, that Libby needs her.

We certainly don't object.

Dembi and Miriam visit Memé to bring her up to date on the treasure adventures. By the fourth day, I stand in the doorway watching, but I am still reluctant to enter. Although our mother is clearly dying, her color has improved. She is able to speak a few intelligible words. She doesn't react badly to my presence, though I'm not sure she really sees me.

I send a post card to Parris and call her once. She's supportive and kind. I realize that I haven't really been gone that long. Yet it feels as though I have been away forever. I am not the person who left L.A. such a short time ago. Despite the occasional resurgence of the Ice Queen, I am different. It's reassuring to know that the separation hasn't altered my friendship with Parris or my love for Ethan.

I used to be terrified that everything would change once I left. That I would lose what I'd gained. Now I am cautiously satisfied that those who really care about me will not abandon me in my absence. I must be on the right track. I hope.

On three separate occasions we venture out into Brantford to shop, consciously avoiding Burford. We decide that it's too small to provide the groceries and toiletries we need. But I know we're really postponing the three-ness of us and the inevitable scrutiny. The powwow becomes our target for the unveiling, though surely by now Dee has spread the word about my presence.

In the evening we play board games, watch television or work on Dembi's puzzle. Rolly curls around at our feet or hops onto the table to mess up a few checker pieces or roll a marble off the edge. I begin to feel quite fond of the little scamp.

Miriam and I talk every night about everything. She becomes closer to me than Karoline or Parris ever did or could. Gently she encourages me to be honest about my struggles with who I am. Ice Queen Anne slowly splinters, only rearing her ugly head now and then. Miriam teaches me that there are good and bad sides to everyone, though I'm aware that her definition of bad doesn't cover at least two of my sins.

"Miriam, I was so self-absorbed and entitled. You wouldn't believe it. I was the kind of person who took her own olives to the bar, so I'd have the right blend for my martini."

My sister gives me the laughter I was aiming for. I can tell her about my superficiality, my snobbishness, my shameful treatment of the men and women who lived on the periphery of my life. I can tell her about Giulio and try to figure out the why of Karoline's treacherous letters. I am able to speak of my breakdown after Karoline's death. I can talk about Ethan and how his love has helped transform me.

I cannot tell her about the night Karoline died. Or about the memories that began to surface when I set foot in this house.

Miriam speaks of her failed relationships. She too has been stalked, stared at, mistreated, but somehow she never saw her beauty as a handicap. One man broke her heart three years ago and she's been unable to reach out to anyone since. Of course much of her time lately has been taken up with family history and Dembi and Memé.

She talks about Karoline, too. I try hard to listen. We both continue to feel a depth of betrayal that may never disappear. I tell Miriam something about Karoline's disintegration. I confess my inaction and the consequent guilt. I attempt to follow Karoline's trail backwards, but I haven't got all the information. I vow to solve the puzzle of her actions eventually, but right now I am focused on the present. On the developing relationships, not the past disappointments.

We become almost as obsessed with our family history as Dembi is. We call Elizabeth. She and Miriam talk for a long time. I avoid Vera and Ian for now. I tell myself that I'm already dealing with too much.

We decide that we have to make an appointment with the Burford museum curator. Thus far we have avoided the village and the inevitable scrutiny. We shopped in Brantford or Miriam went alone. Even in the larger town we've been objects of interest, but who could blame them? Three identical beauties stroll through the mall in the middle of the day. I am used to the attention. However, it's far better when it's shared.

Our curiosity eventually overcomes the fear of gossip. Miriam makes an appointment with Mary Lou West. We don't even attempt to convince Dembi that we should show her the Vryheid book. We plan to soak in information, not provide it.

I also talk to Ethan every night. Although I am tempted to ask him to come up here, I resist. I am a little more self-assured but there are still so many questions. How can I say, "I love you", when I can't say that to myself? When I'm not sure if the deep-seated rage has disappeared or is simply hiding? When I can't forgive myself?

On Wednesday, a blistering sultry day that feels as though we are walking through a hot shower, Miriam, Dembi and I visit the Burford Museum.

Dembi is in a strange mood. He's fidgety and doesn't eat much. Although he says he's feeling all right and wants to come to the museum, he looks tired and cross. He brightens a little as we near the museum. His beloved history beckons.

Dear Diary,

Do you find nice people boring? I know I do. I like edgy, mean characters with some intelligence. I love that comedian, Rodney Dangerfield. "My psychiatrist told me I was crazy and I said I want a second opinion. He said okay, you're ugly, too." Honestly, that's hilarious. Especially if you say it to someone who's really crazy.

CHAPTER 21

"Hi, Dembi, hi, Miriam," the curator says as she gazes with unabashed curiosity at the three of us.

"This is Anne, our missing third," Miriam tells her.

Mary Lou West is a young, slim woman dressed in a professional blue skirt and jacket that look incongruous with the earring in her nose. Her straight black hair, deep brown eyes and dark skin hint at a heritage similar to ours. She is friendly, enthusiastic. Her handshake is cool and firm. Though a look of bewilderment crosses her face, she doesn't miss a beat in her greeting.

The museum is located in an old red-bricked, two-story house with a wide porch painted grey and a welcoming green door. I don't generally like old houses, but this one doesn't have that customary moldy scent. Its rooms have been opened up and are lined with display cases and bookshelves. In the middle, tables are piled with papers, books, and files. They look orderly, however. Mary Lou leads us to the chairs around one of them.

"I've pulled some files for you," she says. "Our collection is the result of several years of hard work and grants. Plus, there are volunteers like yourselves who have brought us a lot of information. Especially you, Dembi."

He grins, flaps his hands happily and returns her hello in an overly loud voice. He looks funny in a red shirt suspiciously spotted with something yellow. I wanted to help Dembi with his outfits but Miriam reminded me that this is a harmless way of honoring his independence. So I try not to be embarrassed.

"We're very proud of our museum and I'm thrilled that you've come. The history of Vryheid doesn't have much documentation, so Dembi's interest and insights have been invaluable."

You have no idea just how detailed the documentation is, I wish to say.

Mary Lou can't wait to give us her historical lecture. She uses some of the papers and books to prove her points.

"As you know, Joseph Brant lived in this area in the 1780's and he brought slaves with him from the United States. We think they came voluntarily and were more like employees than slaves."

The Book of Vryheid is certainly split on that theory.

"Lots of runaway slaves came up through the underground railway during those years. Some of them joined the native bands, married into the families and settled in this area. Others travelled to more distant parts of Ontario."

"They used the Grand River," Dembi says.

"Yes." Mary Lou smiles at him. She's not at all condescending. Her fondness for Dembi is obvious. "Most travelers used the river to move around. And that's where most of the native settlements were built. All up the river, so they could fish and hunt and travel."

"Joseph Brant had a lot of land."

"He certainly did, Dembi. But he used it so our native inhabitants could live and work there. He gave a lot of it away and sold some of it, too. Though he had to fight for permission to make those sales."

"Didn't he *own* it?" I ask.

"Sure, but not in the way the white man did. Indians had to get permission from the government to lease or sell the land. In fact, it's still much the same today on the reservations."

Miriam and I look at each other, stunned.

"That's what Chief Brant fought with the government about. Finally, in 1798 he received permission to sell off a number of tracts. We think this is around the time that he negotiated the Vryheid acreage. There is a theory that the gift was attached to the land he sold to John Morey, who was reportedly a runaway slave himself but who had married into the Brant clan."

That theory is correct I want to say, thinking back to the passage at the beginning of the Book of Vryheid.

"Why would Brant sell off all his land?" I ask instead.

"He wanted an income for the people," Mary Lou responds. "Land had become a great commodity and source of wealth, similar to the present. He thought it was unfair that natives did not have complete control over their own land. The Chief must be rolling in his grave these days."

I ignore her political declarations because I have no idea how to respond. I'm not well informed and I'm not sure I want to be. Even Miriam, a self-confessed left-winger, is silent.

"To whom was the Vryheid land given?" I ask.

"We think it was given to a group...sort of an ancient condo corporation."

Mary Lou pauses. In the silence, Dembi begins to fidget. I can see the struggle in the young woman's face. Should she say this out loud or not? With a feeling of dread, I am pretty sure I know what's coming.

"You're wondering why two sisters have the name Anne."

She flushes with embarrassment, caught having a non-objective thought.

"Well, yes. Plus I'm wondering why she hasn't told you about the research she's already done."

Miriam takes over, her desire for privacy flaring up.

"Many of us were adopted out. So ending up with the same name was a huge possibility." My sister doesn't quite lie. "I had no idea that the other Anne spent time here, too."

"She spent lots of hours here about two years ago. Sometimes with Dembi. I haven't seen her in quite a while, however."

"Our other Anne unfortunately passed away recently."

"Oh I'm so sorry." Mary Lou's voice displays genuine shock and sympathy. "She was a very nice person."

"Other Anne," Dembi says, mournfully placing his head on Miriam's shoulder.

"I'm sorry for your loss, Dembi. She helped us a lot with the history, didn't she?"

Oddly, since this is his obsession, our brother looks bored and restless. He closes his eyes as though he's napping and doesn't respond. Miriam and I exchange worried looks. Has our interest in the history usurped his feeling of importance? Or dredged up too many memories of Karoline? Perhaps he's merely got a stomachache.

Mary Lou converts back into the curator, the one in the professional suit.

"I hadn't the time to trace the Vryheid ownership, but Anne did. On one of her visits, she went to the country offices and looked up the deeds. She gave the copies to me for posterity."

Posterior is more like it, I think.

The documents are sharp, so we're able to read every word, though we mostly skim. In 1920, as we already knew from the deed tucked into the Book of Vryheid, Cornwall Johnston was officially listed as owner of the land. How he'd achieved that proprietary coup was not mentioned or has not been traced. In any case, I don't think it matters.

By December of 1954, the deed had been signed over to Elizabeth Johnston. Memé owns everything.

Cornwall Junior Junior disappeared.

Dear Diary,

Whenever I disappeared for an hour or a day—or more, no one really asked me any questions. They totally, thoroughly, accepted my version of events. They never checked the details. As I often say, they were not only too trusting but brainless, as well.

CHAPTER 22

My hallway leads along the kitchen to a wing at the side of the house where my suite takes up most of the space. That night, the little courtyard outside my windows is black, hidden from the moon and stars by a wall on one side and a fence on the other.

I flick on the light, check the sliding glass doors, and pull the heavy drapes across the windows. On the other side of the bed I check the locks on all the windows and the door.

In the yard I can see the fierce tree line. Every bump in the bark looks like a totem face. Every branch is a skeletal arm pointing my way, pencil thin against the vast black sky. There is no light, no moon or stars this night. I cover everything with the curtains.

I check the bathroom. It's empty. I gaze inside the closet, with its sliding door into a hidden shelving unit. I am reassured that no one is concealed in the blank recess, although they'd have to be very tiny to be able to do so. I wonder what on earth they used it for. To hide bottles of scotch?

Under the duvet, I shiver for a long while, both from the cool of the sheets and the depths of my imagination. I wish for that first night again, before the house crept into me. When I felt safe and warm in this lovely bed. When I didn't know this place—or had forgotten its menace.

The wind has returned with unusual fury, blowing in a cold that feels damp and distressed. I listen to it rattle at the frames, tug on the shingles, skirt around the fence. I haven't paid any attention to the weather, only subliminally aware that the day was hot and humid. Now I wonder about tornadoes. Do they have a lot of those here? Is this like mid-west US, with its tantrum-prone climate?

I toss, turn, wiggle, and punch the pillow into submissiveness. I read the book that Miriam has lent me. I stare at the line of the curtain where the night peers in at me. At last I am on the edge of sleep when I hear the noise. It's at the end of my hallway, past the long country kitchen, past the stiff parlor with its biblical secrets. That same door yawns out into the cool dark night, gateway for hellish things to come in after us.

Ice Queen Anne calls me a fool and forces me to put my toes on the drafty floor. The wind has pushed the door open again, idiot, she says. The damn retard probably left it ajar. Don't call him that, I say, but I shove my feet into slippers. Once again, my little flashlight illuminates the long hallway a foot or two in front of me.

The air shoves its way down the corridor seeking more space. Tinged with rain, it dampens my face with wet fingers. I am astonished at its strength and have to push myself forward. I hope two things: that Rolly is still wrapped safely in Dembi's arms and that this is not a tornado. With my shoulder against the wood, I am able to brace my legs and push the door shut. The big lock slides into place and it's quiet in the hall once again. I tiptoe across the wet floor. Flashlight helps me find the pantry. All I can hear now is the swish of the mop head on the linoleum as I force it to slurp water.

A slight dizziness floods through my eyes. He is there behind me, his breath foul and hot on my neck. His hands are huge as they encircle my waist.

"Come here, cutie-pie, and sit on yer old Uncle's lap." His voice is grizzly, loud in my ear.

I straighten up, whirl around with the mop as a weapon, but there is no one here. Only the wind as it searches each room. Seeps back outside under the doorways with a moan or a whistle.

Trembling from inside to out, I replace the mop. Quietly I slide up the hallway toward the back of the house. Past the pantry and the parlor, along the other wing, up to Miriam's door. It slides open without a whisper of sound. Perhaps she is nervous too, for Miriam is asleep with a small bedside lamp still on. It casts a soft light over her milk chocolate skin, her long lashes closed gently against her cheeks. One arm is tucked under her head. The other is flung out beside her as though she clutches an invisible lover. I want to wake her, climb in beside her, but I don't. She doesn't deserve to be dragged into my nightmare.

Across the hall is Memé's room. I haven't been inside since I hissed my vitriol in her ear. If she sees me, will she scream? Or are her nighttime drugs enough to keep her silent? Once the door is open I am suddenly aware of an odd sound emanating from the room. I slowly advance toward her, holding my breath. My heart flutters. Memé thrashes on the bed.

When I am beside her, I realize that the oxygen tent has been pulled away. It no longer covers her shoulders nor her head. In fact, the apparatus, with its normally vociferous tubes and machine, is silent. I am unsure how to fix it, but I quickly follow the lines, discover the on switch, and have everything going in a few seconds. The struggle occurs when I try to reassemble the tent over her. She gags for air. Her body twists with the effort of trying to breathe. Once it's in place, Memé gulps and gasps until the oxygen fills her lungs once more.

I sit on the edge of the bed. Hold her thin cold hand as she settles. It might have been kinder to let her go, Ice Queen Anne says, but I'm not sure if she's being sarcastic or serious. At that moment, Memé's eyes open and she stares at me.

I am terrified that she will scream again. That her horror will spill over once more when she sees the one she calls Diable. The child Memé gave away after raising her for four years. How much hatred must such an act contain?

She doesn't scream, though. She blinks at me. Somehow she knows that I just saved her. I can see the gratitude from inside her as her breath slowly becomes steady. I begin to rise, but Memé clutches my hand. Shakes her head very slightly. Don't go.

I stand anyway, but signal that I am going to the other side of the bed that's clear of the accouterments of dying. Some instinct leads me to lie down beside her. I draw up a spare blanket and cuddle along her emaciated body. Feel my warmth flow to her ice-cold skin.

Memé sighs, a long shudder. The expelling of air sounds like relief. Feels like acceptance. Her hand flaps in the air, seeking me, so I wrap myself around her.

Her lips move and my name whistles from her mouth. The withered brown teeth allow her tongue to lash her chin.

"Anne," she says, the word drawn from some tortured area of her mind. Not Diable, not the devil, this Anne is different.

"I'm so sorry," I whisper. "I shouldn't have been nasty to you. I hated you for giving me away."

A single tear drifts down her sunken cheek. "Baby." She draws out the word, an endearment, and pats my hand.

I remember Miriam and Dee's descriptions of Memé. A woman destined to always be a little girl, innocent and sunny. A beautiful simplicity taken and used. They twisted her innate search for love into selfish grunts of physical pleasure. When superstition, cruelty and fear drove her inside herself, how could I blame her for sending me away? Maybe she thought her sister would be kind and loving. Perhaps, in her own way or in the beginning, Vera did have the best intentions. Perhaps my own little fearful self pushed her away instead of the reverse.

I squirm a little closer. Listen to the rhythm of my mother's breath. Wonder how the oxygen turned off. Imagine Memé's terror as the life-saving tent became a death trap.

I think of the brief memories that have floated up in the last day or two. The man, my 'old Uncle'. Was I about to take my mother's path when Memé lifted me out of danger? Had she sent Miriam away for the same reason? We were baby girls. Perhaps Dembi was safe because of his gender. Maybe the question is why she waited so long to give me away.

Suddenly I feel a shudder worm its way through my body. It's a frisson of understanding. I consider how earthquakes change the landscape. How Los Angeles could, at any moment, become sea where land and concrete stood before. I listen to my mother's sighs, the puff of her breath as she exhales, and I am transformed.

Her thin cool fingers are soft on mine. A rush of memory soars through my body as I recognize this hand. Reach for it in laughter or tears. Feel its strong comfort on my cheek. I see my mother's face, her eyes guileless and joyful, grinning down at me. She laughs as we play. Whirls me around until I am dizzy.

Mama, I say, and she picks me up in her arms.

Mama, I cry, wet and confused with fever, and her hand cools my forehead.

Mama, I'm afraid, and her arms encircle me with safety.

I open a gift of warmth and surprise and Ice Queen melts. My mother loved me. She loves me. I was, I am, lovable.

I fall into a deep, reassured sleep, exhausted by the storm of emotions, curled at my mother's side.

First I hear the drumming then I feel a heavy hand on my shoulder. I twitch and raise my head too rapidly for my eyes to catch up. The figure dances across my vision. Her face is round, her eyes soft. A slight smile on her thick lips.

"Dee," I finally manage.

I am sweaty and crunchy. My bones creak as I untangle myself from Memé's side. My mother continues to breathe in sleep, her eyes shut in the dimness of the room.

I recognize the drumming at last. Rain pounds on the roof, shatters against the windows. Thunder booms above the rafters. Once in a while a flash lights up the grey air.

Melody helps me sit up. I swing my legs to awaken them.

"What are you doing in here?" Curiosity tinges her question.

"The oxygen shut down last night. I heard Memé thrashing around. I reattached everything and then...I just stayed."

The woman thunders to the other side of the bed. "That's impossible." She fiddles with some of the gadgets, rearranges unnecessarily.

"Well obviously it's not impossible," I say, more than a little irritated.

I feel as though I have slept for a week. Or been on a huge bender. If I didn't know better I'd think I was still drunk.

Unsteadily I walk over to Dee's side. She fusses with Memé's blanket. That's when I notice that Memé has opened her eyes.

"Good morning," the caregiver says cheerfully to her patient. "I hear you had an adventure last night. I'll call the home oxygen company and find out what on earth could have caused a shut down."

Memé looks up and gives a crooked smile that makes her face look twisted. But her eyes are lit up.

"She's so much better," Dee says to me. "I can't believe it's the same woman."

I sit down beside Memé and give her a brief hug.

"Anne," she sighs.

"You are amazing, Dee. You've made such a difference in Memé in only a week. You don't know what a gift you've given me. I don't care how long or short it lasts. I just…thank you."

As I stand, Dee wraps me in a bear hug. "I'm very happy for you. I think this reconciliation has done her more good than I have. Now, out you get while I change Memé and get her freshened up for some breakfast. Miriam and Dembi are in the kitchen."

Their twin heads look up at me as I stumble to a chair. They both grin and Miriam hands me a coffee. I feel a stream of love in my chest, nourishing me. I smile back.

"Triplet Anne is up early," Dembi comments.

Miriam and I laugh.

"I am up early. Memé's oxygen shut down last night. Fortunately I couldn't sleep, so I heard her."

Once again, Miriam takes the responsibility. "Oh, shit, I didn't even hear her! We need an alarm or something."

"You swore, Miriam," Dembi says.

"An alarm is a good idea," I say.

"You swore, Miriam. Say sorry."

"Sorry," Miriam responds, distracted and worried.

"Dee is going to investigate with the home oxygen company and find out how the machines could have shut down. She's less than impressed." I sip the hot, rich coffee.

"How was Memé with…?"

I know what she means and this time, tears that fill my eyes unprompted accompany my smile.

"I think she knew I saved her. I slept beside her all night."

Miriam immediately connects. She is instantly a part of the longing, the answer to a primal question. I realize that of course she has been through this, too. Her reunion was, presumably, not quite the rocky path that mine has been, but no less difficult. Her hand on my arm transmits joy, understanding and excitement.

"I remember some things, too," I tell her, placing my hand on hers. "I still haven't worked out everything, but Dee told me a lot. Maybe visiting Mary Lou West unlocked some stuff."

"Mrs. West likes my history," Dembi says as he reaches for another slice of toast to mop up the egg on his plate. "She's coming to the powwow."

"Maybe we can have some more time with her," Miriam says, eagerness in her voice.

There must be gaps in my sister's memories, too. So much has changed for her. A birth mother replaced the two people she thought were her parents. A farmhouse that she occasionally visited turned out to be her birthplace. A brother and mother who desperately need her suddenly became her responsibility. A duplicate self, strange, angry, clingy in turns, replaced the generous, gregarious and loving 'sister' she thought she knew.

Spontaneously, I kiss her hand.

"Miriam, I know these few days have been filled with turmoil. I've been going through so much that I forgot what it's been like for you. I'm sorry. I've been used to a selfish life."

Miriam squeezed me back. Her eyes brim with tears now, too.

"It's okay. I did have more time than you did to adjust to a lot of this. We'll get through the rest together."

Dembi gets up and encircles both of us, arms over shoulders. We touch our heads together. If only we could resolve everything the way our brother does.

All the rainy morning we play games in the parlor, clean the house and sing. After lunch finds us in Memé's room. Dee is off somewhere else, giving us private time. We laugh. Read. Feed our mother with both the sound of our voices and the occasional bite of something nutritious.

Dembi is still not himself. He continues to look tired. He's agitated and nervous as his enhanced flapping and humming indicate. Miriam and I try to placate him with games and joyful stories. He touches Memé continually. Lolls his head against us whenever we sit. If I didn't know any better, I'd think he was afraid.

Against the fingers of rain drumming in time with our fun, a crash and a knock announce that the home oxygen company has arrived.

Two hefty white men with enormous boxes of equipment appear at the front door. Along the hallway they seem determined to knock everything over. Miriam and Dembi return to the kitchen to wash cups while Dee and I crowd into Memé's room with the two giants.

At first Memé is frightened, but I sit on my side of the bed again and draw her to me while they work. She breathes from a small hand-held apparatus that the men hook up to a portable tank.

"We want to keep that, too," I say, pointing at the portable carrier. "You should give it to us for free in exchange for the trouble we had last night."

One of the men looks over at me with a frown. His pasty round face flushes an unhealthy pink. He is big and has piggy eyes that are pillowed by fat.

"This equipment is designed not to fail," he says.

"My mother almost died because it did fail." Ice Queen tone has not disappeared, though the anger I feel seems reasonable, manageable. "When I came in here last night, the machine was turned off."

His eyes flash malice at me, but he checks the device carefully. The second man, only slightly smaller in girth, adjusts the new tank. He turns it toward me so I can see the on/off button. He flicks it to OFF.

"Was it in this position?"

"Yes."

"The only way that can happen is with a human hand," he pronounces.

"No one in this household would be careless enough to do that," I fling back at him, biting down on every word.

Just then Dembi bounces back into the room. Flapping nervously he twists his mouth into a lopsided, anxious grimace. He hums and probes the air. His gait is sloppy, regressed by fear. He huddles at my feet. Pats Memé's legs obsessively. Our mother probes back with her own hand until they connect. Dembi rocks slightly on the bed.

The oxygen man gives me a meaningful look. Of course I know that he's thinking there is one person who could be careless enough—stupid enough—to turn the machine off. I wonder if he can be right.

Did Dembi think the noise would bother Memé? Does that explain his odd behavior this morning? But Dembi has lived with the oxygen for quite a while now. He is aware of its connection to Memé's life.

"But you can keep the portable machine," the man says as though he's being overly generous. "No charge."

Number Two asks Melody and me to double check the replaced equipment. We follow his instructions carefully. I decide that I will teach Dembi when they are gone. I walk them through the kitchen out the front door. Miriam is in mid chop of a bunch of green celery when I return to lean on the counter. I briefly tell her about the machine and the fellow's theory.

"Dembi would never do that. He knows how important the oxygen is."

"Does he know how to turn it on and off?"

She nods her head, her beautiful waves bouncing thoughtfully. "Yes, but..."

I chomp on a piece of celery. "It's probably a malfunction and they won't admit it. They think we'll sue. We do it all the time in L.A. But we have a replacement now and Dee gave it a seal of approval. I still think we should get an alarm, though."

"Absolutely. Dee probably knows a company we can call."

"I'll take care of it. By the way, they gave us a portable machine. We can take Memé to the powwow if Dee thinks she's up to it."

"And if the weather improves."

We both glance out at the deluge of water against the window above the sink.

When we all return to Memé's room, Dembi seems to have shaken his mood and is chatty and happy again. Dee fusses around us. Memé makes small sounds of joy.

As I watch our brother whirling and doing tricks for us, I wonder if Dembi did turn off the machine by mistake. Luckily Memé is all right. Judging by his reaction, he would never do that again.

By late afternoon the sky clears. Memé's room fills with sunshine. We slide open the curtains and prop the windows open a bit. The hot and cold fronts have finished their war, leaving a clean warm feeling in their wake. The air is freshly laundered, clear and pleasant. On an azure ocean of sky, the sun cheekily grins from behind white waves of friendly cloud.

With Dee's help we lift Memé into her wheelchair and take her out onto the porch. Before the cancer felled her she'd buzzed around on her own two feet. I wonder how she feels, having to be so dependent. Not to mention that the portable tank and mask look like an appendage from a dinosaur.

But Memé is altered by the sunshine. She sips from the after-shower, oxygen-rich day and smiles. Her wizened brown face seems less shrunken. A glimmer of the former beauty makes its way through her skin.

Miriam and I are so busy with thoughts about wheelchairs, oxygen, bodily fluids and long-lost relatives that we have no time to discuss any further questions about our history. After Melody leaves for the night, we barbeque burgers for dinner and eat off paper plates around Memé's bed. None of us feels like leaving her side. Once she is asleep, we curl up in front of the television and eat ice cream. We don't talk much. There's a new contentment between Miriam and me, though it doesn't seem to have spread to Dembi. Before bed, he's distant and restless once more.

I have a long exploratory conversation with Ethan. We discuss all the new developments. I tell him about my emotional transformations. Confide that I am still uncertain about everything. A fawn on newborn shaky legs. He's okay with all of this turmoil. He is far more confident of Anne than I have ever been. Me, reborn. Who knew it was possible?

Once again I sleep at Memé's side. I am too nervous to trust the new machinery. I cuddle beside her as she breathes. The chug of the oxygen is comforting and strong. Dreams and memories flit through my mind all night. Faces, voices, feelings. I awaken several times, afraid, then feel Memé's slight but reassuring frame next to mine.

Before dawn I am in the kitchen drinking coffee. I make French toast and bacon. Wash raspberries and sweeten them with real maple syrup. Around eight I step out onto the porch, mug in hand.

The day is trying to decide what to do. Dark clouds ring the horizon. The sun is fiercely hot once again. It dances from shadow to shadow and broils the wind. It feels as though the storms are not through with us.

Miriam and Dembi enter the kitchen at almost the same time. They are delighted with my paltry effort at cooking for them. Once he has eaten, though, Dembi announces that he's going to hunt on his own.

I give my sister a worried look.

"He's done it hundreds of times on his own. Don't forget, he grew up here."

"Make sure you use the bridge to cross the river, Dembi."

I almost laugh out loud. I can't ever remember issuing such a motherly command.

Our brother nods. He's distracted again. Flaps his hands and hops from foot to foot.

"It will be a short time," he tells me. "I am strong and careful."

"Yes, you are, Dembi," I respond. "I trust you."

To my surprise he gives me a scowl and disappears.

After Melody arrives we return to fuss over Memé. Elizabeth Johnston emerges bit by bit over the next few hours. She looks more comfortable in the wheelchair. Though wispy, her hair is clean. Her wide eyes blink at us over the oxygen mask but they are far more alert than I've seen them since my arrival here.

Miriam and I learn to maneuver the chair. How to replace the portable oxygen tank. Not that we should need to do this, Dee instructs. The tank will last for the number of hours we plan to stay.

We talk about the powwow. The ground may be difficult to traverse after the rain. Especially if the storm returns today. Dee says they usually put boards along the pathways. The ceremony takes place in the fairgrounds just outside Burford. There are bleachers for seats. Flagpoles for the traditional raising.

This year is particularly exciting because of the participation of the Canadian Black Heritage groups, some of whose members are descendants of the original Vryheid residents. Just like us.

Dembi comes home well before lunch. Miriam and I, caught up with Memé, ask him simply if he had fun. He nods yes and wolfs down a sandwich. No tales of history, the Book, or the gold map. I am too preoccupied to wonder.

The storm circles around again by afternoon. This time it's madder than ever. The old house literally shudders in fear. Thunder cracks right overhead, shakes the roof and rattles the walls. Lightning pitchforks the fields and dashes from cloud to cloud.

We huddle inside, keeping the atmosphere as bright as we can with song and stories and busy-ness. Melody goes home early during a lull in the torrential rain.

Miriam offers to stay with Memé tonight. At first I am tempted to say, are you crazy? I'm not sleeping alone in this storm... and then I see the need in her eyes.

As Miriam and Dembi turn toward their hallway later, my sister says cheerfully, "After Dee gets here in the morning I'm going grocery shopping. Want to come?"

Dembi shakes his head, so I respond that I'll stay home, too.

"Okay. If it stops raining we can go hunting after that if you want. Or we can stay home and play some games."

But Dembi has already disappeared down the hall. Miriam gives an indulgent smile and we hug quickly. I saunter off to the parlor and curl up in my telephone chair.

I give Ethan my customary rundown of the day. He's quieter than usual, lonely, he says, wondering when I will be coming home.

"I promise it won't be much longer. What do you think about coming up here for a few days?"

"When?"

I laugh. "I take that as a yes. I don't suppose you could get here by Saturday for the powwow?"

It's his turn to laugh. "That gives me a whole day. I doubt it, babe, but maybe Sunday? I can let you know tomorrow."

"Perfect! I can't wait for you to meet my family."

There is a slight pause. I consider what I have just said and what I want to say. My logical man is probably thinking about travel arrangements when I interrupt.

"Ethan, I'm learning that love's a lot more than a word. But it's all I have right now. I love you," I whisper into the receiver.

It may be all I will ever have but I said it anyway.

His intake of breath, shaky and joyful, hisses through the wire. "I love you, too, Anne. For always."

We both give a shy giggle. I say goodnight instead of goodbye and hang up. My hand rests on the instrument for a moment, unwilling to completely disconnect.

The storm does not abate all night. My body never gives in to complete rest. I toss, turn, awaken, get up and check my locks obsessively. My dreams are indistinct mists of menace.

When I enter the kitchen, Dembi and Miriam are already there. Cereal boxes and fruit line the counter. I grasp a cup of coffee like a lifeline. Unrelentingly gray and wet, the rain has not stopped, though the wind seems to have disappeared. No thunder roars and no lightning flashes. This is a straight-to-the ground shower.

"I'm going shopping early to get it over with. We can't go treasure hunting in this weather and I have a list of things we need. Dee's here already. She's with Memé. Do you two want to come with me after all?"

"No," Dembi says and straightens up.

Miriam and I are a little shocked at his firmness, but we shrug and smile. Our brother is a mystery. I wonder what goes on inside his head. How he thinks. Which thoughts are coherent and which are not. It's intriguing how articulate he can be about history. How broad his reading vocabulary and how simple his other actions. As though the connections are wired wrong or the synapses misfire at different times.

"I'll stay home, too. As long as you don't mind doing the shopping alone, of course." I'm a little concerned about Dembi but I keep this to myself. I'll try to get something out of him this morning. Besides, I'm still so tired.

"I don't mind a bit. It's not a huge list. As long as you guys help me into the house with it. Okay, Dembi?"

"I am strong," he answers.

"Good. I'll need your help when I get back. I should be a couple of hours or so." In her raincoat, she looks like Little Red Riding Hood as she heads off to her car.

"I'm going to get dressed, Dembi. Then do you want to visit Memé with me? We'll bring Dee some coffee."

"Maybe," he replies without looking at me. His hands flap nervously. I wonder briefly why he's so upset this morning.

"I'll see you in Memé's room in five minutes." I hope my statement will become a fact in his head.

I throw on jeans and a t-shirt, make Dee's coffee, and head down the hall to Memé's room. Dembi isn't there. The big woman bustles around the room. She cleans up the breakfast things and prepares medication. Then she stops to sip her drink.

"As you can see, Libby's sound asleep again," Melody whispers. "She's tired from all the recent activity, I guess."

Memé and me both, I think.

The woman looks proud of her patient. I impulsively kiss her cheek. "I repeat. You are wonderful."

She smiles and sips. I believe she's used to being called wonderful. "Have you seen Dembi?"

"No, he hasn't stopped by this morning. Kind of unusual for him."

I gather up Memé's breakfast dishes. "I'll go look for him. He seemed out of sorts earlier."

The kitchen, where I deposit the bowl and plate on the counter, is empty. Out in the hallway I notice that the side door is unlocked once more. Inspecting the mechanism a bit closer I note that, once unlocked, the latch is loose fitting. I hazard a guess that unless the bolt has been slid into place from the inside, a good strong wind could push the door wide open. One mystery explained.

"Dembi?" I ask the empty parlor, family, living and bed rooms. Nobody answers.

Back in the hallway I check the coat closet. Dembi's raincoat, a copy of Miriam's red one, is missing. I wonder if he's gone treasure hunting on his own. The weather is still blustery and wet but he probably doesn't mind. After all, he's oblivious to the heat.

I feel an urgency to check on him. Melody agrees. There's forest green gear in the closet that fits me nicely.

Immediately I regret my decision to follow Dembi. It's miserable out here. The rain pelts down relentlessly. Not a gentle tropical shower but a vicious cold front angrily usurps the space from the summer weather. I have to lower my head and watch my feet as I slip-slide along the sodden ground. The weeds and grasses are slippery. Heavily soaked branches slap lazily at my waterproof jacket, forcing the water to drip into my boots. I am soon shivering, but the determination to find Dembi doesn't abate. Thinking about his odd behavior the last couple of days propels me forward.

It's the red that I see first. Peering through the rain I catch a glimpse of his raincoat as he quickly races from the steps of the church. His head is down and I am hidden by a clump of trees. Dembi passes fairly close to me but is oblivious to my presence. I decide to see what he was up to inside the old building.

It's dry in here. The only sound comes from the pounding water outside. Even the birds are quiet, huddled in the grey misery of the day. Now and then they emit a feeble trill of protest at my intrusion.

I gaze upward at the choir loft, a small afterthought of a balcony constructed of dark wood. I wonder what it would have been like to stand up there singing for the congregation. The first thing I notice is the absence of the ladder. When I reach the altar, I can see the top rung jutting out along the floor. It's been pulled out of sight, just behind a set of pews at the side. Dembi's version of hiding it?

Now I have to follow his footsteps, or what I surmise were his movements. I settle the ladder against the crumbled staircase. Jam it into the crevices on the floor. It feels sturdy enough. When I am at the top I feel a bit dizzy. The floor looks intact but some of the rungs of the railing are rotting, so I wonder. Nevertheless I crawl onto the platform and gingerly stand. There is enough room up here for one row of choristers. Behind the wooden bench, the cupboards take up the rest of the space.

Dembi has left a fairly easy trail. One door is slightly ajar. When I open it I discover the papers and canvases that had been piled under his bed in the cave. Curious, I pull them out and spread them on the floor. I am astonished by what I discover. A chunk of our history falls into place.

Dear Diary,

Sorry for not writing much, but I have been in such a good mood lately. Isn't it strange that most people only write in a diary when they're mad about something? Like poetry. It's always sad. Well, I'm not mad any more. I've figured it all out. Things are going to be just fine.

CHAPTER 23

I don't want to leave these here, vulnerable to thieves and rats. But can I risk taking them out into the elements? Back inside the cupboard, I find two big empty garbage bags. Obviously Dembi thought of the rain, too. Alongside these, there's a beaten-up wooden rectangle that I recognize as a travel paint box. I take it, too. Everything fits in the two bags. I ensure the door is fully closed this time.

Getting it down the ladder is the hard part. Several times I almost drop the whole bundle. A couple of times I feel a dizzy fear that I will flop onto the stone floor any minute. But I make it down. I replace the ladder in its inadequate hiding spot.

Tossing the bags over my shoulder like Santa Claus I fight my way through the bushes and the weather back to the farmhouse. I have no idea what I will say to Dembi if he sees me.

Fortunately no one is around when I return. In my room I check the locks on the windows and doors. From the pantry I lift an old broom and wedge the handle between the sliding door and the frame. Once again I study the paintings.

They are various dimensions from small sketches to medium-size canvases. Thick paper to thin and delicate. They are immediately recognizable. Their color, lines and subject matter are identical to the 1940's sketches in the Vryheid book, not to mention to the painting on my living room wall in Los Angeles.

Opening the sliding door that leads from the back of the closet to the dark storage space, I bundle everything onto shelves or lean the larger ones against them. When everything is stored away I turn back to my bed and see with dismay that I have forgotten the paint box.

But now I hear Dembi's voice. He calls my name as he wanders toward my room. I shove the box under my bed, exit my room and lock the door.

I try to smile normally at him as he ambles down the hallway.

"Triplet Anne!" he grins. "Miriam needs us to help."

He seems to be in a better mood, as though his errand gave him some kind of relief.

We rush through the kitchen and out into the pouring rain. By the time we have hauled the bags into the room we are drenched and laughing heartily. Melody comes by to see what's happening. We sprinkle her with water from our dripping fingers. The silliness helps steady my thinking. Slows the pounding of my excited pulse.

"I'll make hot chocolate for you drenched rats," Dee offers.

Dembi skips off toward his room.

"Come with me," I urge Miriam, pulling on her sleeve.

While I change into dry clothes, she examines the cache behind the cupboard. I explain its significance quickly but we don't have much time.

"We have to talk to Dembi at some point," I say.

"Let's wait until tonight. I need to think first. And we need to talk."

"Agreed."

But my pulse has quickened again. I'm excited, almost greedily so. I try to tamp down the intensity of my exhilaration.

We rejoin Dee and Dembi in the kitchen. The hot chocolate is thick and creamy. Dembi appears to have returned to his old self, cheerful and good-natured. He and Rolly play with a string on the kitchen floor while we women sip our drinks at the table and talk.

"Is it supposed to clear up for tomorrow?" Miriam asks.

We have begun to assume that Dee knows everything.

"So the weatherman says," she answers, because she does in fact know everything. "The rain should stop some time during the night and the prediction is that the morning will be lovely."

"Do you think Memé is up to attending the powwow?" My turn.

"I do. I can't believe the progress she has made. And as I said, the organizers always have boards and planks spread around. There are lots of elderly people who come to the powwows."

For the first time in weeks Memé sits at her kitchen table for lunch. Although she is unable to say much—her voice is low and lacks the power of oxygen—she breathes out each of our names. Her eyes sparkle now. Life has crept back into them. Her crooked grin is a permanent fixture.

Afterwards, our mother has a nap while Dee cleans and fusses. The alarm company representative is scheduled to arrive later this afternoon and clearly she wants to be ready. Dembi and Rolly play in the hallway with a ball of twine that they roll back and forth. The only sound is Dembi's delighted laugh and the scrabble of the cat's claws.

Miriam and I take one of the bags of paintings from my cupboard and huddle in the parlor with the Bible.

Miriam points to the records in the Bible with one of her short, clear nails. I look down at my own fingers, aware that I haven't noticed them in nearly two weeks. They are no longer long and shapely. My hair is no longer L.A.-primped. It's more rural-woodsy. I wonder if Ethan will recognize me. Which suddenly reminds me...

"Miriam, Ethan is going to try and get a flight here for Sunday. Is it okay if he stays for a few days?"

She grins at me. "Of course it is! This is just as much your house as it is mine."

It is? My house? My home? I lower my head and look at my toes, which are also scrubbed clean of their bright pink nail polish. How can things have changed so rapidly? Am I still that shallow? Was I that unformed?

Miriam brings me back from the shadows.

"And besides, I can't wait to meet him. I feel like I know him already."

A bunch of goose bumps congregate on my arms. Miriam is a wonder.

"I'll prepare Memé and Dembi for his arrival." I add, "After the powwow."

Miriam nods. Back to business.

"Memé's brother, Cornwall the Third or fifth or whatever—Junior multiplied—was born in 1918. So he'd be 65 now. He disappeared around 1955. We have no idea if he was married or had kids because nothing is recorded here."

"And we don't have any pictures either. Vera is our source, obviously."

"If she even knows. You said she ran away when she was quite young. Maybe before Cornwall married or disappeared. The only time she returned seems to be when she came and got you."

"Yes and after that she pretended the farm and all her siblings didn't exist."

"Maybe she pretended way before that, too. She must've been ashamed of them."

"Or frightened of them? If we believe Melody's tales, Vera would've had reason to fear them. The parents and their gang were drunkards and abusers."

Miriam's face clouds with grief.

"Those poor girls. Memé and Vera probably had it worse than the boys. Vera could've been sexually abused, too."

I begin to feel even more sympathy for my adopted mother. Miriam is right. After all, Vera rescued me from probable abuse and gave me the best upbringing she could. Her limited emotional skills were likely a product of a dysfunctional childhood. She must have had to become callused to survive as a runaway, too.

I reach into the bag and haul out a painting.

"This is definitely a CoJon. It's so similar to the one we have on our living-room wall."

I notice the 'we' and the 'our' but that painting is still attached to Karoline in my head.

"Cornwall Johnston. CoJon."

Miriam's voice is a whisper of awe. She lifts another painting out of the bag and studies it.

"I didn't pay much attention when Karoline started buying paintings for her boss. But I do remember that CoJon was an enigmatic figure. No one ever interviewed him or had photographs of him. He was reportedly a native but they only based that on the style of his paintings. As it turns out, if we're right, which we are, he was part native."

"With black and white mixed in," Miriam says. "A hybrid like us."

I always thought of myself as a mongrel but I don't say that. Hybrid has a ring of pride to it.

"CoJon sold his originals exclusively through an agent. Karoline said there were always rumors going around about both the agent and the artist. Like they were same sex lovers or the agent was really the artist. Or CoJon was a drunk who lived on the streets and the agent exploited him. All that kind of sensational stuff."

"Probably helped to sell his art," Miriam responds.

We are so engrossed in the paintings and our theories that we don't notice Dembi come into the room. Not until we hear him. At first, his keening is a low rumble in his throat, but before long he flaps and probes. The moan builds into a screech. He's fixated on the paintings, so I snatch Miriam's and stuff both hers and mine into the bag.

My sister rushes over to Dembi and tries to gather him in her arms. He screams louder, the decibels so high that they vibrate in my soul. He turns on himself. Slaps and punches his head and face. He inadvertently slaps Miriam. I am afraid of him and for him. I remain rooted to my spot.

Dear Diary,

Do you think a person can fake insanity? I mean, there's abnormal behavior, and then there's psychosis. I wonder if a person could pretend to be nuts by their behavior. They could do bad things and blame it on madness. I've read about lots of cases in L.A. where they say they're not guilty by reason of insanity. Are they just clever? Or do you have to be crazy to even think about doing something horrible and then claiming to be insane?

CHAPTER 24

Melody lumbers into the room. Her face displays the same fear. She tries, along with Miriam, to pin Dembi's arms, but he gouges his skin. Blood spurts from his cheeks and arms.

I can hear Memé respond to his distress with a wailing of her own. Muffled by the oxygen tent, it's a loud rumbling in her chest. It sounds as though she pounds the bed with her legs.

At last I move. By now Miriam and Dee have wrestled Dembi's arms. They hang onto them like squirming snakes.

"It's okay, Dembi, I've got a safe hiding place." Inspired by some message from the air, I add, "Other Anne said for me to protect it."

Our brother's arms stop flailing. His screech becomes a quiet moan. His eyes are still wild, bulging as though he's consumed a psychedelic drug. Miriam and Melody hang on to both hands, murmuring soothing words. I continue to hear Memé's anguish in the background.

"Dembi, we have to go and see Memé. Listen. Listen. She's so upset. You have to see her so she knows you are okay now."

The moan stops. Dembi yanks his hands away from the other two women and disappears down the hallway. Miriam and Dee follow.

I pick up the bags and race to my room where I store the paintings on the shelves once more. When I arrive at Memé's door the scene continues to be dramatic. Dembi is curled up on the bed beside our mother, rocking and moaning. Dee straightens the oxygen tent and puts the covers back to normal. Miriam sits on the end of the bed, patting their legs. Her touch begins to calm them.

Melody looks up as I enter.

"What on earth happened?"

"We don't know, Dee, I told you."

For Miriam, this is a testy response. I follow her lead.

"Something upset him but we're not sure what. We'll find out."

Memé is quiet now. Her arm rests on Dembi's body as he rolls around beside her. Just then the doorbell rings.

"What now?"

Melody is not her usual patient, calm self. I'm surprised at how much this incident has unsettled her.

"It's probably the alarm company," I say, gently putting one hand on her elbow. "Will you go, Dee? If you handle that we'll take care of Dembi and Memé."

"Should I tell them to go away?"

"Why don't you sit with them in the kitchen and look at their information? Tell them what we want and ask for cost estimates. Ask all the details about installation, like when and how long it will take, and so on."

The big woman looks unconvinced but she disappears out the door. Miriam and I take long, shuddering breaths. Clearly Dembi's sighting of the paintings in the house instead of their church hiding spot has completely unhinged him, but we're not ready to share the discovery with 'not family'.

"Dembi, I'm so sorry I moved the paintings." I am close enough to him to whisper. "They are safer now. I have a treasure hiding spot in my room."

He stops rocking long enough to stare at me. "Hiding spot?"

"Yes, a really good one. Safer than the church or your cave. No one will find them."

Tears spill down his face. He puts his fingers in his mouth and mumbles. It sounds like 'drown' but I'm not sure. Then he closes his eyes and rocks, though more slowly. I think he is less upset.

Miriam and I gather at Memé's side. Her eyes blink up at us and she says, "Diable."

This time, the word feels like a message. Our mother wants to tell us something. Information? Or a warning?

"It's okay, Memé," Miriam says.

"We'll take care of you," I add. "You and Dembi."

The rocking has ceased and now we see why. Dembi is fast asleep.

Memé squeezes our hands and closes her eyes, too, her arm crooked over her son's huddled form. Tears sprout from the lump of grief in my stomach. These simple, sweet people do not deserve to feel so vulnerable.

"Who is Diable? Who is the devil?" Miriam asks and I see that her eyes are filled, too. "She's been saying that for three or four weeks now, every once in a while."

I gulp down a cry. Memé wasn't calling me Diable. That was my guilt, my anger and insecurity. She was telling me something even then.

"I remember you told me she was saying other weird things," I say as we head toward the kitchen, an unspoken agreement to see what's happening with the alarm system.

"She could speak when I first got here but as she got sicker, she gradually went to the one-word speech that you're used to. And she seemed to get scared."

"How long ago?"

"I'd say about a month, maybe six weeks. By then she was in a lot of pain. She'd undergone all the tests and some chemo. She just didn't seem to be able to handle it. She stopped speaking, though the doctors had no idea why. There didn't seem to be a medical reason. They thought it might have been psychological or a result of a loss of oxygen when the cancer started moving into her lungs. For all the tests and treatments, we had to make long trips to the hospital in Hamilton and she hated it. I chocked all her behavior up to stress. Then suddenly she started repeating single words again. Like Diable or knife. Punch or kick. Once or twice, she said drowned."

Drowned? Didn't Dembi say that, too? Is all this violence a memory of the past abuse that Memé suffered? Maybe she passed on her fears to him.

Miriam is silent for a moment. We stop in the hallway within earshot of a murmur of voices from the kitchen. She keeps her voice at a whisper.

"Larue. She called out for him a lot. There was another name, too, but I could never make it out, other than it ended with n. At the time I thought it was Anne. I thought she was referring to Karoline."

"That's something I don't understand. Why did Memé think Karoline was me? Obviously she knew that I was your triplet and ought to look like you and Dembi even in adulthood."

"I never knew to ask. Karoline was here well before I ever visited. I have no idea how she ingratiated herself. Memé seemed to accept that she was our sister Anne. And of course I never doubted it, so I didn't even think about it."

The layers of Karoline's deceptions threaten to overwhelm me again. I can't think about any of this right now.

"Dembi is terrified because I moved the paintings. Who is scaring him? Diable?"

Miriam looks at me. "It was smart of you to tell them they were safe. What made you tell him that Other Anne said to move them?"

"I honestly don't know. I started thinking that Karoline had to have something to do with the whole CoJon thing. I have no idea how she was involved. But there wasn't anyone else I could think of who might have manipulated Dembi. And maybe even brought home a painting or two."

"I see what you mean."

Miriam looks at me with eyes that show thoughts racing back and forth. Questions and doubts cloud her brown depths. It occurs to me that she has no reason to trust me.

"Miriam, I promise, I am as confused as you are. I truly have no real idea of what Karoline did or was up to or thought…I swear to you. I was kept in the dark and had my head too far up my own ass to look around."

My sister can't help but laugh. "Anne, after these last few days, my intuition tells me that you are completely trustworthy. To be honest, there was always a little voice in my head that warned me about Karoline. Something not quite right, a false note. But I ignored the signs. With you…we're part of a whole, you and I."

I turn and throw my arms around her. "I love you."

There's that L-word again. It's getting a little easier every time I say it.

"I love you, too, Sis," she says and I am filled with gratitude and joy.

"Let's go pretend we are interested in this alarm shit."

Several brochures and plans later, we make an appointment for the alarm company to return on Monday. We've decided to wire up the whole place and it's going to cost a fortune but I don't care. Despite her protests, we send Melody home.

"You've been working for nine straight days," I say. "And we need you for the powwow tomorrow. We can handle everything here for the rest of the day."

Finally, she concedes. Her car kicks up a huge spray from the driveway. A thick drizzle continues to plow into the wet ground. I wonder how on earth we're going to get to the powwow. Or if.

Miriam and I spend the rest of the day tending to our patients. Dembi sleeps through most of it, sucking on his fingers, regressed to infancy. Rolly curls up at his back. I am heartsick. My meddling has caused my brother's suffering. I wish I'd never found those fucking paintings.

We bring dinner but neither Dembi nor Memé eats very much. Miriam and I have sandwiches in the room as we watch them sleep. We are too overwhelmed and confused to even discuss the CoJon issue or Dembi's reaction or the powwow or Karoline. We just sit and stare off into our own spaces.

When it's dark I go to the parlor to call Ethan. The receiver feels even heavier when combined with tinny silence. The telephone is dead. I wonder if the storm last night has had anything to do with its malfunction. Miriam surmises that there's a line down somewhere. I feel so terribly empty, as though I am starving to death.

I go around the house checking locks before I head to my bedroom. Under the duvet I shiver and sniffle. My new awareness is not much fun. I try to remember if I ever felt depressed, sad or lonely in the past and I can't. I don't think I felt much of anything other than a flat level of satisfaction and smugness. I don't recall pure joy but I don't have any memory of this dreadful loss, either.

All at once I notice a profound silence. The rain has finally stopped. Now the creaks and groans of the dampened old house skitter back into my hearing.

I jump out of bed. My feet stick to the old hardwood and linoleum as I try to run on tiptoes up the hallways. At Memé's bedroom, I brake and peer around the half-open door. My mother and brother are sound asleep. The oxygen machine sounds like a third person.

I open Miriam's door. She turns over, blinking at my shadow, as sensitive to sound as I.

"Miriam," I whisper so she's not frightened.

She moves over and pats the other side of the bed. I crawl under the covers and snuggle up to her. She's warm and soft. I give a little mew of happiness. Being fully aware and fully alive is worth every low point. I am wrapped in my sister's arms, secure, loved. Strong together. I wouldn't trade places with anyone.

With a rush of insight I realize that I've never experienced this kind of relationship before. My 'sisterhood' with Karoline, or my friendship with Parris, never came close to my feelings for Miriam. When a sister is also your friend there is nothing like it. I know we didn't grow up together, but we shared a womb and that seems to erase all the lost years. My sister knows me better than anyone. She accepts who I am but helps me to aspire to my personal best, too.

I tamp down on the 'ifs', which threaten to keep me awake. If only Memé hadn't given us away. If only I'd never met Karoline. If only I hadn't gone out onto the balcony that night.

Once they are filed away, I drift off to a healing sleep, warm in the heat of my sister's body, wrapped in her unconditional love.

Dear Diary,

Do you believe in the devil? According to a bunch of religions the devil is an angel that's been turned. A fallen angel. There's often some head guy who convinces everyone else to become a devil. Does this mean that angels are gullible and easily led? Why are they called angels then? Maybe they should just be called human, since human beings are, essentially, very stupid and easily duped.

CHAPTER 25

The glorious morning speaks of a perfect day for a powwow. Not that I can truly picture what the word means. I step onto the porch with my coffee and breathe and listen. Squirrels rumble across the roof. Birds whistle and call from the willows and evergreens. It's a riot of noise, yet infused with a serenity that I've never heard from my balcony in L.A. I try to picture our apartment with Karoline alive in it and all I can see is a fuzzy glint. At my back the farmhouse pulses with life. With my new reality.

Dembi is quiet this morning, but his excited anticipation of the powwow appears to have overcome his anxiety.

Miriam and I tell him that we will take good care of the paintings. After the powwow we will all talk about them and decide what to do. We will protect him and Memé. He smiles slightly. Not his usual unabashed grin, but it's an improvement.

Dee arrives at ten and Memé is almost ready. The four of us are in her room, fussing over her dress, playing with her hair. Despite the paraphernalia that helps her breathe, she looks even more like herself, Elizabeth Johnston, the lovely Libby. Her face has signs of life that have been absent as of late. She has shape and substance again. Her eyes, a scant week ago sunken and dead, sparkle with joy.

Melody is astonished. She claps her hands and tears roll down her cheeks. I am amazed at her freely given emotions. It must be soothing to have such a gift. To never hold anything at bay.

"I can't believe the change in her," she says. "It's a miracle."

She puts a large, comforting hand on my shoulder. Her eyes say that she can't believe the change in me, too. I smile back at her and impulsively wrap my arms around her in as tight a hug as I can manage around her ample flesh. Dee is startled, but she returns the squeeze.

Memé wears a grey ponytail underneath a big red bonnet. The hat looks somewhat out of sync with her native dress, but it'll protect her from the sun. Her traditional garment's slightly musty odor speaks to the time it has spent unused in her closet. We have no idea where she got the outfit, but it's well made, hand-embroidered, and old. Squares of yellow, blue and white decorate the hem, sleeves and shoulders. A turquoise crest, bearing the outline of a bear on its hind legs, is sewn onto the front. She wears the turquoise moccasins that hung in the closet with the dress. Other than the oxygen tubes in her nose and the tank at her side, Memé looks resplendent in traditional native garb. She has crossed back into her matriarchal heritage.

Miriam and I wear sundresses, mine turquoise and hers pink. They're remarkably close in style considering we bought them in different countries. We represent the traditional mass consumer.

Dembi produces a fancy shirt that looks hand-painted. It's light cotton, streaked with red, yellow and white circles and flowers, matching Memé's colors. Accompanied by Dee in her voluminous green-leaf smock, I am sure we make quite the parade.

Dee has arranged for the rental of a large van to escort us to the powwow. It's well equipped for transporting a wheelchair. Our driver is a tall thin black man with long curly locks. The native influence is evident in his high cheekbones and long, narrow nose. His name is Viho, he says, as he effortlessly wheels Memé's chair onto the lift and tucks her skirts fastidiously around her.

"It means 'chief'," he laughs in response to our quizzical looks. "My parents really wanted to keep the native culture alive. Unfortunately, I'm not a chief in any way, shape or form."

We all laugh with him. Viho is immediately likeable.

Miriam decides to take her car, too. We are uncertain of Dembi. His behavior has not returned to normal. If he wants to come home early, or has a meltdown again, we want the freedom to return to the farmhouse. Or even race off to the nearest hospital.

Dee sits up front with Viho. Dembi buckles into the bucket seat beside Memé. I am in the middle. We wave excitedly to Miriam, turn left out of the driveway and take the new road into town.

It's quite a distance to the fairgrounds outside of Burford. All the fields we pass are full of puddles from the recent rains. Crops show their appreciation for the sun by pointing straight at the sky. Everything is a deep green, lush and thriving. All they need now is for the rain to go away for a while and let them grow.

There's a mix of beauty and ugliness in the scenery. A huge auto graveyard mars the land with rust and brokenness. Power lines thrust themselves through clumps of huge evergreens, cedars and pines, unsightly steel cable as umbilical cord to modernity. Purple flowers glow in the sunshine. Willow trees bow in their beautiful green dresses. A disused factory stares through leaded windows, its piles of brick, tin, rusted parts and empty trailers reminders of industrial hubris. Yellow wild grasses tickle the edges of the fields. Light green cabbages look like crayon lines. A small airport has shaved the land to replace it with strips of pavement. Yet the shiny silver bird that flies overhead through the rays of sun looks gorgeous.

I watch a graveyard whiz past my consciousness. Rounded, scraped, ghostly sentinels, the graves are spotted, aged, green with fungi. Maple trees, clover and dandelions paint the landscape. Somewhere a church bell rings. I am mesmerized and almost forget our destination.

A long line of cars on a dirt road alerts us to the proximity of the site. We're lucky with parking, however. A van for the handicapped has priority. Viho assists with the disembarkation. To my surprise, he plans to stay right with us, push the wheelchair over difficult spots and help with whatever we need.

I notice that he's especially interested in Miriam. As we follow Memé from the parking lot to the entry point, he maneuvers the chair so he is walking beside my sister. He talks animatedly about the powwow and its history. But I think he only does that so he can be near her.

The very large Indian fellow at the gate looks like an L.A. bouncer with his thick arms and massive head. I notice the signs warning against bringing alcohol into the park. I guess he's here to ensure compliance to the rules.

He makes a fuss over Memé.

"Libby! I'm Charlie's boy, Anton. Do you remember me?"

Memé nods and smiles her crooked grin. I'm not sure she really understands. Her lined brown hand reaches out to pat his, though.

Anton stares at the three-ness of us but he remains polite despite his obvious inquisitiveness. So it goes as we traverse the wooden planks that lead to the stands. Friendly Canadian greetings cannot quite mask the astonishment, shock and curiosity as our odd little group passes by.

Dee makes it easier. She knows everyone. Introductions are fast and numerous. I doubt that I'll remember any of the names or even the faces.

There is a huge crowd. Families, moms and dads with little ones, elderly parents, teenagers, young and old people are everywhere. Many are dressed in shorts and t-shirts but lots display traditional dress and wild colors. To my overloaded senses it's a sea of feathers, paints, beads and emblems.

The sun is already hot but it's not humid. The air is clear, rich and scented with damp flowers and leaves. Most of the water has run off this area, as it's surrounded by a dip in the land that leads to the river. The Grand rushes past, happily full, gurgling with contentment.

The stands form a circle around an earthen track. There are lots of entrances between the rows of seats, with one large one to our left. In the middle is a mound of very green grass and empty flagpoles. The bench on which we sit is in the first row, where Memé's wheelchair provides perfect sightlines without being in anyone else's way.

Viho sits next to Miriam with me on the other side. Dembi stays close to Memé. Dee disappears to find Tommy.

The air is charged. Everyone chatters away. The boards bend as more people hoist themselves onto the seats. Light little people spring all the way to the top, proud kings and queens of the castle. There's a feeling of anticipation that connects all of us.

Even Dembi is cheered by the excitement. Though he has not said anything, he stops flapping and his smile is genuine. Miriam points out that he has clamped a hand onto Memé's chair. As though he is anxiously hanging onto her. We are still worried about him. I feel that knot of guilt again.

Dee returns with Tommy. He's a foot shorter than she is, bald and bespectacled, but his smile is generous and fun. In his eyes we can see that he adores his wife.

Suddenly the ceremony transports us away from our worry about treasures or illnesses or the darkness of night.

First, the drummers enter the ring. One of them is a round, short native man. An aging wrestler who carries his drum like a featherweight. His fat fingers fly over the canvas, sending up a rhythm in perfect time with our collective heartbeats. He sports a beautiful white and orange-feathered circlet, cocked toward the back of his head. His vest, shirt, fringed pants and moccasins are lined with bright orange embroidery and beads. He looks fierce and magnificent. His face is a frown of concentration.

The second musician is a very tall black man who taps two bongos that add a lighter sound to the beat. He's scantily dressed, showing off his naked well-muscled chest already shiny with sweat. His only attire is a thick red and blue cloth that covers his rounded buttocks and obviously generous frontage. I try not to think of pulling on the string that holds these pieces in place. He is a breathtakingly beautiful male.

Next come two people who must be officials. One is dressed in a white t-shirt and modern grey slacks. The other is clad in a black t-shirt, pants and a baseball cap. Both are older but tall and trim, one black and one brown. Each of them carries an emblem perched on wooden poles. Next, a young woman in a red dress carries the Canadian flag.

On their heels come the dancers. They are all ages and shapes, male, female, black, brown and white. Babies in arms. Children traipse after parents or older siblings who know the routines.

The colors are astonishing, so vivid are they in the bright morning light. Deep reds, sea blues, fierce yellows. Bells and beads and shells and embroidery all mounted with artistic abandon. Feathers decorate heads or are carried as fans that are not just fans but part of the ceremony.

A melodious wave rolls into the circle, gathering strength as the number of people increase. I realize that they are chanting along with the drumbeat. The sound becomes a pleasant rumble that resonates in my blood. Miriam feels it, too. She grasps my hand in exhilaration. Perhaps everyone here experiences the same thing. The vibrations course through our bodies to connect mind and soul.

The dancers feel it most. They ride it. Dip forward in moccasined feet. Sway. Twirl. Tap the ground. Bring the chant from stomach to throat to air.

I close my eyes so the color doesn't sap any of the emotion. Every beat echoes in my heart. The wooden benches pulsate.

The parade spirals in on itself. There are layers of dancers now. They all follow the leaders. A chain that hops, leaps and steps. I open my eyes when the seats underneath us begin to spring up. People head for the track, summoned by both lead dancers. A deep voice reiterates the invitation through a microphone.

"Come celebrate with us. Join the chain. Join the dance of peace."

We can't take Memé's wheelchair onto the gravelly, muddy track, so the three of us stay near the benches. Viho, Dee and Tommy join the group. We're on our feet, though. We sway and hop around our mother. Memé smiles and moves her body from side to side as much as she can. We mimic the bend and step of the dancers in the center.

Briefly I wonder what my L.A. cohorts would think of me right now. Ethan and Parris would probably join in. As for the reaction of the rest of sin city, I put my head back and laugh with pure delight.

At first we don't notice that Dembi has halted all movement. He becomes a solid in our fluid motion. When Miriam stops and puts her hand on his shoulder, he goes into a frenzy again. This time he doesn't screech. His breath is pulled inward, mouth wide open. A mournful sound moans from his chest. He flaps and begins to slap his own face.

Goosebumps sprout all over me despite the heat. I look around for Viho but he has disappeared into the crowd. The chants and drumming continue to rise all around us. Dembi is frantic.

"Home?" Miriam asks loudly in our brother's ear. "Home?"

Dembi stops to look at her. She grasps his chin and forces his eyes to focus on hers.

"Home?" she repeats.

His head wags up and down in time with the beats. Continuous nodding replaces self-flagellation.

Miriam takes his arm and pulls her keys out of her shoulder bag. "Anne, I'll take him home. You stay with Memé. Take your time."

"As soon as I find Viho, we're coming, too."

I won't stay here while our brother is in distress. Especially since it's my fault.

She gives me a smile in return. The two of them disappear behind the benches. I look down at Memé and realize she hasn't actually registered the commotion. She's fixated on the dancers. She sways slightly. Conducts with her hands, thin arms in the air, a gesture of praise and joy. I decide she deserves a few more moments of happiness.

The chain of dancers forms into two large circles. Everyone faces the center grass where the flagpoles wait. I know that Memé can't see what's happening there but I'm unable to do anything about that. Until several large men, one of them Viho, arrive with grins and strength. They lift Memé, wheelchair and all, and carry her to the front of the crowd.

"Where's Miriam?" Viho asks.

He doesn't mistake me for my twin. The man is quick to notice the difference between my sister and me. He's definitely smitten. I have to put my mouth close to his ear to be heard.

"She took Dembi home. He's not feeling well. Once this part is over, I think we'd better head back, too. I hope you don't mind."

"Not at all."

And I know why he doesn't mind.

We're in the middle now. There are three poles, thin sentries high enough to reach above the stands. The entire crowd can hear because of the microphone attached to several overhead speakers. As the drummers become silent, the chants begin to die. That same deep voice from the previous announcement enters our ears with precise, rounded syllables, a sound that both soothes and captivates.

"Today we celebrate this historic gathering through the rituals of the powwow. Three cultures, three faces, join the dance of life as brothers and sisters."

The short native leader, who has been standing very straight with the flag at his side, moves toward the pole and begins to winch it. Slowly the bright blue and white cloth catches the sunlight and moves toward the sky.

"The Mohawk flag of peace is more than appropriate for this occasion. White is the symbol of peace and goodness. Blue to signify the importance of this meeting. The eagle sits atop the tree of peace to guard against those who would bring evil. The silver chain represents our circles here today. We are strong and powerful when we remain together.

We must continue to polish this silver with communication, respect and responsibility."

The flag now towers above us. A fluffy white cloud covers the sun briefly, bringing the colors and symbols into better focus.

Next, the tall black man clad in a loincloth begins to raise his flag. The voice directs our attention to the yellow wheel in the center of the purple cloth. Its spokes resemble the rays of the sun that is now almost overhead.

"The wagon wheel is the perfect symbol for today. Not only does it give tribute to the slave symbols sewn into quilts in the past, but it also represents our circle of peace and friendship in the present."

Lastly, the woman in the red dress begins to hoist the Canadian flag. She is tall, fair-haired and white.

"The Canadian flag proclaims our nationhood. We must all join together in community, law and good governance."

I notice that she says, "must all join", instead of "are joined". Even in Vera's 'perfect country', there are problems. People, I suppose, are flawed wherever we live.

"The inception of Vryheid was inspired. The African word means freedom. Former slaves and native people joined together to create a place where all men and women, black, brown, white and all shades in between…"

The crowd gives a collective chuckle.

"…could live in peace, freedom, and love."

Didn't exactly turn out the way they planned, I think.

At that moment I am astonished to see Mary Lou West step into the center. She is dressed in a traditional native outfit, a blinding white laced with turquoise beads and embroidery. With her light brown skin and wavy hair, she is the embodiment of the three cultures and races. I am taken completely by surprise when she walks up to Memé, microphone in hand, and crouches so they're eye-to-eye.

I am rooted to my spot.

"Elizabeth Johnston is an example to us all that we can make a difference. Past mistakes can be used as lessons for the future. Two years ago, before she was stricken with cancer, Elizabeth received a proposal from our town council."

Mary Lou straightens up and looks out at the crowd.

My heart hammers in anticipation.

"As many of you know, Ms. Johnston owns the land on which Vryheid once stood. After the fire in 1954 it was shamefully abandoned. Rumors and destructive gossip ruined any chances for rebuilding. Elizabeth agreed with the committee that the only way to reverse the errors of the past was to bring about something good in the future. She donated the land around Vryheid to the town of Burford, in particular, the cultural archives and museum. The transaction will occur after Elizabeth has left us."

There's a murmur in the crowd, sympathy or surprise. Someone starts to applaud and starts a wave of clapping that continues for several minutes.

Mary Lou waits for quiet. "Until today, I was sworn to secrecy. Today was chosen as the perfect occasion upon which to make our announcement."

She looks directly at me, asking forgiveness for her silence I guess.

No wonder Viho and the gang wanted Memé up front. No wonder Mary Lou West got so involved with Dembi's history and Karoline's machinations.

"We have already agreed to some strict rules that will govern the land use. Vegetable plots will be offered for lease to individuals who don't have room for gardens of their own. We will construct a ceremonial track similar to this one." She waves her hand to indicate the arena. "The church will be restored and used as a place to congregate, whatever faith you follow."

Cheers and applause accompany each of her announcements. I don't join in. I have no idea how I feel because I am numb with shock. From the detail, the agreement sounds altruistic, as though Memé understood all the nuances. I have only known my mother as a very sick woman so I really have no idea if she had been capable of following such concepts.

Did Karoline know about this plan?

Slowly I realize that the gang of men is lifting Memé in the air for everyone to see and praise. My mother looks very uncomfortable though she keeps her crooked smile in place. Her oxygen tank dangles at one point, pulling her head sideways. Though Viho readjusts everything, my heart races and I move close to her.

I notice that everyone is staring at me. Do they know that I am the witch who burned Vryheid to the ground?

I have to get out of here. I am afraid, confused. Ashamed. Fortunately, before I behave like a cornered animal, the group safely lowers my mother and carries her once more to anonymity at the back.

I can't see Melody or her husband or Viho. I feel abandoned. Memé continues to wave. People come up and clasp her hand in awkward shakes. They all look at me, smile and nod, but don't approach me. Might it be the look of terror and unwelcome on my face? Or the fact that I am the destroyer of the village of peace?

Viho is suddenly at my side. I try not to collapse with gratitude.

"I want to leave," I say instead, imperious Ice Queen slightly back in place. "I can't find Dee and Tommy, but that's okay. My sister and I can handle everything today."

"Of course. Turns out one of our drivers had a breakdown. I'm actually happy you have to go cuz now I can help him out. He's got stranded clients and our emergency mechanic won't get out there for a while."

He doesn't sound happy about leaving immediately but I figure that's due to the fact that he won't be able to hang around with Miriam.

"You should call my sister, Viho. She likes you, too. And she's quite single right now. Snap her up before someone else does."

He doesn't bother to deny it. As he pushes Memé along the wooden pathway, he turns to grin at me.

"Thanks, I will."

I can feel Memé's exhaustion. I can see it in the droop of her hands and head. We have completely tired her out. I can't wait to get her tucked into her own bed. I'm anxious to see if Dembi has calmed down. We'll have time to deal with the paintings, not to mention the donation of Vryheid. I don't notice the scenery this time. The roads feel rough and long.

At last we pull up to the farmhouse. Now baking in a sun directly overhead, the farmhouse is protected only by the lush leaves and fat branches. Once we are on the porch and have Memé through the door, Viho has to leave.

"You're sure you're okay?"

"Of course. Miriam and Dembi are here. Go help those stranded people. And don't forget to phone."

He flashes that grin again and charges back to his vehicle.

Memé's steady breathing tells me she's asleep. I try to be quieter than usual as I maneuver her up the hallway. I don't call out for my siblings so I won't disturb our mother but I do wonder why they haven't heard us. I also remember the malfunctioning phone. I'll have to go out again if it's still not working. I need to know when Ethan will be here.

As a result of the pleasure that tingles through me when I think about Ethan, I am smiling to myself as I near the parlor on my left. Preoccupied with my own thoughts my brain does not register the scenario at first.

Miriam sits on the sofa closest to my vision. Her face is pale and pinched. Her hands, clasped in her lap, visibly tremble. Dembi rocks beside her. His head appears intermittently as he bends forth, then back. The low keening would surely be louder if it weren't blocked by the large piece of duct tape over his mouth.

I don't react until I see the third person in the room. He overwhelms the crowded space. A big, flabby figure with jet-black skin, he's a classical menace as he waves the huge gun in my siblings' direction. I let out a screech as Glenn Simpson turns his attention on me.

Dear Diary,

Do you think certain traits run in families? Do we inherit madness or talent or goodness? Or is that our upbringing? I know some psychologists have talked about this forever. The old nature-nurture debate. I wonder if it's true that the reason no one can figure this out is because it's a 50/50 thing.

CHAPTER 26

Memé jerks awake. "Diable. Diable."

Her voice is louder than I've ever heard it. Even Glenn hears her.

"I heard that diss, Memé dear."

He notices my face as I step toward him. I put Memé behind me. She begins to rock, too. I'm terrified that she'll collapse from the stress.

"Hey, nigga, never thought you'd see me again, did you? I'm living proof that your sorry ass is nigga, too. I introduce my real self to you and the rest of the happy clan. I am Glenn Simpson, born Johnston, given away at birth to a New York cousin." He waves the gun.

"Annie, I got my finga on da triggah so sit your fine tight ass down heah and listen reeeeeal gooooooht."

"You don't have to use that stupid talk with me, Glenn. I know you're not stupid."

He puts his big ugly head back and laughs in a high-pitched, delighted guffaw.

This ugly asshat cartoon is our fucking bro?

"I'll sit down after I put Memé to bed. She's harmless. She's dying. What does it hurt to let her rest?"

The stupid grin doesn't leave his face but he drops the black slang.

"Oh, the lady has balls. Sweet Karoline was wrong. She figured you for a spineless self-absorbed idiot."

He steps close, his rancid breath in my face. He bends down slightly to touch Memé's hand. She flinches.

"Poor dear mother. Slut of the century. Nobody would wanna fuck that nowadays, would they? The old lady can see, though. She noticed my little nightly sojourns. Called me Diable right from the start. What a way to treat a son! No wonder I'm fucked up."

Open doors. Footsteps in the night. My mother's whispers about the devil. All warnings that I didn't figure out because I am still that self-absorbed idiot. But spineless I am not. I focus on the memory of Glenn's flabby ass as he fucked my friend. Ridiculous and repugnant in his nudity, he becomes a cartoon in my mind. Not a person to fear.

"Little sis, you must know I can't let you take Memé to lie down. It would be the gentlemanly thing to do but I'm sure you're aware I'm not a gentleman. However…" he draws the word out as he gestures for me to sit, "have a chair while we wait for my friends to arrive. Then maybe we'll talk about our dear mother's comfort."

Friends? What friends?

Without a word I obey. I wheel Memé by my side as I perch on the edge of a chair.

"I'm sure you know I can't let you go into a room by yourself. I'm your own bro but you still might bring back a weapon. Smack me over the head. Stab me. We are not a very nice family, are we?"

I look over at Miriam. Tears spill down her cheeks but her eyes are steely. She won't roll over easily either.

Dembi is terrified. He whimpers and rocks. I notice that he sits on his hands. Glenn probably forbade him to flap.

Now I can see that a fat chain winds through their legs and over their ankles. Bound like slaves a hundred years ago.

The gun is enormous. Although I am from L.A., where a gun can be had at the local department store, I am not familiar with them. I've never owned one. In Bell Canyon we had hunting rifles inherited from Granddad, but we never used them that I know of. Maybe it was the Canadian in us. I wonder how the hell Glenn got that thing over the border. Don't they check for weapons anymore?

I avert my thoughts away from its fearful threat. I can't allow it to silence me.

"You have friends? Somehow I doubt that."

"Oh you'd be surprised, little sis. In fact I am sure you'll be downright shocked when they walk through that door. Didn't Sweet Karoline teach you not to trust anyone?"

"How did you find Karoline?"

"*She* found *me*, my dear. Such a little ferret. She even looked like one, don't you think? Did all this research into slut mama's offspring. It was her idea not to tell you who I was. I didn't even know who I was until she told me."

He seems to think this is an enormous joke. Maybe it is. The joke's on me, as they say.

He gestures to something on the side table that I haven't noticed. When I recognize the paint box, my heart pounds. Not with fear—with rage. Ice Queen comes in handy now and then. She's got anger inside that has never fully been released. Not yet, I tell her, not yet. Though we have to do something before reinforcements arrive.

Glenn picks up a small blue leather diary from inside the box and waves it in my face.

"It's all here, Sisters. Karoline was a great little record keeper, I must say. She just loved dissing her friends behind their backs. You should read it some time."

He throws the book onto the floor and rests the cold barrel of the gun on my cheek. I can't stop the shivers from racing through me. My body wants to flee.

"Why'd you kill her, beee-atch? We had a good thing, Sweet Karoline and me."

"I didn't kill her, asshat. You did. You drove her to jump over the balcony."

He looks a little disconcerted. I must have hit a nerve.

"She wouldn't do that. She loved me. We had the whole scheme in place. The treasure. We'd'a bin rich. Being rich all alone is not as much fun. Karoline woulda bin my white slave."

He looks over at Miriam, who has stopped crying. She has her hand on Dembi's arm, comforting him. His rocking is less frantic.

Glenn leers at Miriam.

"Maybe a little sister love would work instead."

"Why did you have to involve Dembi in your stupid scheme?"

"You oughta know the answer to that one, bitch. You came here and looked for the treasure, too. All I had to do was tell Dembi I'd drown him and Memé in the river and he was more than willing to help out."

"I take back what I said before. You are stupid."

The cloud of anger on his face makes me wonder if I've gone too far, but I keep going. I bet on his cowardice. There is no way he'll shoot me. He's a fat lazy pig who couldn't be bothered with the mess. He might even be afraid of blood.

"There's no treasure. It's a myth. Dembi did it for fun."

I can see Dembi shift on the sofa. Now I'm somewhat happy that the duct tape prevents him from speaking. He looks as though he wants to contradict me.

"Not the gold, you jerk. The CoJons. They're worth a fortune. They're the treasure. Karoline made a mistake taking them a few at a time. She didn't want to flood the market and make the art world suspicious. I told her we shoulda taken them all and put them in storage."

"Why didn't you do that then?"

"When you killed her I went back to L.A. I had to see her one more time. Of course you had to take her off to that hick town she hated, so I never saw her. We had saved up some cash so I stayed in the city. For a while I just lost interest in everything."

Maybe in his own twisted way he *had* loved Karoline.

"Then you decided to take a little trip here. I was running out of money by then, so I figured I'd come up and have some fun as well as cash in on the rest of the loot. That's why I called our friends to help. I planned to get rid of the old lady and then we'd clear out the place. You had to mess things up when you turned the old crow's oxygen back on."

He waves his hand over the room.

"This place is thick with antiques. Don't tell me you haven't noticed. There's so much crap in here that Karoline and I took stuff and no one even noticed. Last week I made myself a nice bedroom in the back and nobody knew that either."

His flabby face is almost purple. I imagine the stress of trying to manage all this subterfuge without his master planner.

"I had so much fun these last few days. Hiding on you, behind you. All I needed to do was wear black, tiptoe on stockings and not smile. Nobody could see me."

He followed this statement with raucous laughter. The vibrations of his insanity zing through me. Glenn Simpson had been more of a catalyst in the destruction of Karoline than I'd even dreamt.

I consider the open doors, the sounds and shadows, my fears at night. My mother's constant warning about Diable. He was here all along. I shiver.

"But Memé saw you, didn't she? And Dembi knew you were here. He hid the rest of the CoJons on you. Memé forced herself to speak so she could warn us. Dembi kept changing hiding spots and leading you on a wild goose chase."

"I must've been a little lax with Memé's special medication. You can't give too much or it's game over too soon. I scared Dembi these last couple of days, though. Even at the powwow all I had to do was peek out from behind the benches. What a moron. Slaps himself in the head better than I ever could." Again, he laughs as though his remarks are incredibly hilarious.

"Face it. You were fooled by people you consider inferior! People you trusted to do what you wanted because they are simple and can be easily threatened. Didn't *Sweet* Karoline teach you not to trust anyone?"

He reacts violently to my sarcasm and slaps me. Hard. I have never been hit like that before. A high-pitched ring sears through my head. My eyes blur and my cheek stings.

Glenn's face becomes mottled with anger. His eyes blaze out at me. For the first time I am afraid that he might overcome his indolent nature and really shoot me.

"I loved her. We were going to be rich. Together. Don't blame hiding the paintings on our poor moron brother. You did it."

He kicks the paint box.

"I found this under your bed. When my friends get here, expect to show me the rest."

While he's focused on the box at his feet Memé surprises us. Somehow she pushes on the wheels. The slight incline in the old floor causes the chair to move abruptly forward. It catches Glenn in the back of his knees. He's already off balance, his kicking leg still bent. The weight of Memé and her chair pushes him face forward onto the floor.

I leap to my feet. Grab the first thing I see. The solid old statue of St. Joseph is so heavy that it falls onto Glenn's prone figure almost of its own accord. It glances off the top of his head. Blood spurts out but I know he's just stunned. Eventually he'll be able to get back up. I almost regret that I haven't killed him.

I kick the gun as hard as I can. It bumps up against the sofa.

"The key to the chain is in his pocket," Miriam yells. "It's the little one."

I quickly check our mom. She grins up at me. "Diable."

"You got him, Memé!"

Glenn writhes a bit on the floor, moaning, but I find his keys right away. The little one for the chain is one of dozens. Luckily its size gives it away.

Miriam and Dembi shake off the heavy shackles. Miriam's ankle bleeds a bit but she says she's okay. She bends and picks up the gun as though it has a disease. I gently remove the duct tape on our brother's mouth while our sister hugs Memé. I pick up the telephone. The same dead air greets me.

We don't hear the footsteps in the hallway but Glenn does. He's still not able to get up. He clutches his head and tries to roll to a sitting position. He must have felt the vibration of the floor as someone approached the parlor.

"My friends are here."

His voice is a squeak of pain. I'm right. He's a coward and a sissy. But will his friends be different?

The figure in the doorway is tall. His silver-streaked hair sticks straight up and his deep blue eyes blink at me from behind large glasses. He's ugly and beautiful at the same time.

I am about to run into his arms when a chill freezes me in my steps. Is Ethan one of Glenn's friends? Is that why he's been pretending to love me? Was it about money all along, cash that didn't belong to his parents, a way to be independent?

Dear Diary,

Is money the root of all evil? Or is it the lack of money that drives people to commit crimes? I've always thought that if you were already happy, a lot of money couldn't hurt. Like marrying for money, not love.

CHAPTER 27

"What the hell's going on here?"

Ethan's policeman voice thunders well above Glenn's moans and Dembi's whimpers.

There's something in his tone. Anger. Shock. Protectiveness. Love.

I get to him in two long leaps. He wraps his arms around me. How could I even have thought for one minute that he would betray me? Insecure with the new Anne, I relapsed into one huge moment of doubt. I burst into grateful tears.

Dembi begins to flap and screech. Glenn sits up.

Miriam hands the gun to Ethan. "This man tried to kill us."

"I did not." Glenn's voice is whiny. "I only had the gun so I could scare them. I wouldn't have shot them."

Ethan lets me go. He yanks Glenn up by the arm as though he is a featherweight and pushes him onto the sofa.

Dembi moves to stand beside Memé. He's quiet now. He can see that the other man, the one I've been hugging, is in charge and easily handles Glenn. Dembi's eyes are round and dilated but his hands are still. I quell my tears for his sake.

"Well, I imagine threatening with a gun is just as much against the law here as it is back in L.A. You go to jail for that, buddy."

There's a noise at the door. We all turn and gape at Melody and Tommy. In response they gape back at us. The gun in Ethan's hand captures most of their attention.

"You're a little late," Glenn says.

I glance at Glenn then focus back on Dee. I am breathless, aghast. We had welcomed this woman into our home. Betrayal makes my heart pound again. I work hard to replace the anguish with rage.

"*You* are Glenn's friends?"

"How could you, Dee?" Miriam's face is ashen.

At least Melody's expression is one of shame and fear. She might have some morals somewhere. She looks as though she's about to say something but Ethan doesn't allow her to speak.

"Nobody say anything. Dee, you sit over here. You—whoever you are—sit there."

Tommy is obviously weak with distress. He collapses in the chair. His wife sits straight, head lowered. Silent tears stream down her face.

"I'm a police officer in L.A. Though I've got no jurisdiction here I've certainly got the citizens' right to detain you until we can get the locals on scene. Has anyone called them?"

"The phone's not working."

"Ah, well, that explains a few things."

He smiles at me then snaps his official look back in place.

"I'll go and get them. The station's not far," Miriam says.

"Can we get Memé into bed first, Ethan? Her portable oxygen isn't as strong as the one in her room and she's been through a lot."

"I don't see why not. Dembi, I'm Ethan."

He takes two long strides forward and puts his hand out. I notice that he still has a good grip on the gun with his other one.

"I'm a good friend of Anne's. I'm here to help you."

Dembi nods. Once he shakes Ethan's hand he looks completely calm.

"I would like you to help me, buddy. Can you do that?"

Another nod.

"I want you to go and help Anne and Miriam put your Memé to bed. Then I want you to stay with her. Keep her calm and happy. Can you do that, too?"

"I am strong," Dembi says. "I can help Memé."

"Excellent. I knew that. I'll just stay here with these people and keep all of us safe."

We wheel Memé into her bedroom and lift her onto the bed. She's drenched, so I replace the diaper while Miriam adjusts the oxygen. All the while our mother strokes our hands. Murmurs our names. She's so exhausted she can barely lift her legs or arms, yet she's desperate to comfort us by her touch.

Once Memé is settled Miriam leaves for the police station.

Dembi lies down beside our mother. He curls into a fetal position against her body, exhaling with relief. Memé puts her arm over him.

Rolly pops out from his hiding place under the bed and snuggles into Dembi's neck.

"We'll bring you some food in a bit." I kiss Memé's hand.

"Anne." She sighs it. The word feels like a song inside me.

Even before I straighten up, she's asleep.

I make my way over to Dembi and kiss his cheek.

"You are a hero, Dembi. You are strong and smart and wonderful."

He smiles but doesn't open his eyes.

I stand and watch them for a while. I'm not sure what to feel. My body is propelled only by adrenalin. Emergency mode. My mind is blank. I decide to leave it that way for a while.

Ethan sits in the telephone chair with his long legs crossed, the gun propped on his knee. This is my lover as police officer. He's composed but there's an aura around him that speaks of strength and ferocity. Immediately I feel calmer, too.

He smiles when I enter the parlor. His eyes grin, too. Sparkle with love. I realize that he's been waiting for me. He wants to interrogate these three before the local police get here and take over. He wants me to hear.

I wiggle in beside him. There's plenty of room for two of us.

"Would someone get me a bandage or something?"

I notice that Glenn's head still bleeds a little. His hand and arm are covered in blood. Out in the kitchen, I find an ice pack and a clean tea towel. He mumbles thanks when I hand it to him.

"I'm a little confused. Who are you people anyway?"

"I'm her brother."

If Glenn thinks self-pity is going to bring him favor, he's wrong. His whiny pathetic tone only irritates.

"We haven't proven that yet," I say, wanting distance from this bumbling idiot in front of me. "You said Karoline found you when she was searching for our siblings. But I don't trust a word you say."

He starts to retort but Ethan cuts him off.

"And you, madam?"

Dee's tears have not abated. "My name is Melody Fischer. I'm a caregiver. Can I please explain?"

"In a minute. Introduce yourself, sir."

Tommy looks pasty and sunken. His voice is weak and belies his pompous response. "Dr. Thomas Fischer."

"All right. I'm Detective Ethan Byrne from the Los Angeles Police Department. You wanted to tell us something, Mrs. Fischer?"

"I want to explain what happened."

Dee clears her throat and wipes the tears across her plump cheeks.

"Our son is a gambler."

She sounds like a confessor at an AA meeting.

"He got himself involved with some very bad people. We never had much money because Tommy would not move from this little hick town. Somehow Karoline found out about our situation."

Glenn groans as he shifts the ice pack on his head.

"She was brilliant."

I had to agree with him there.

"She paid off his debts. In return, I helped her with her research and Tommy gave her drugs."

No wonder Dee knew so much about our history. The second thought that crosses my overloaded brain fills me with anger. I sit up very straight.

"Memé! Did you give drugs to my mother? Is that why she stopped being able to talk or move or…"

"We never gave her any drugs. That was Karoline and Glenn."

"What the fuck is the difference? You knew about it. You preyed on an innocent woman. A dying woman."

I am on my feet, fists clenched. Ethan reaches out to pull me back. I resist for a moment. Venom spills out in a long shuddering exhalation. I sit back down, but on the edge of the chair.

Tommy clears his throat.

"Your mother may have a lot more time than you think. The radiation and chemotherapy were very successful in shrinking the tumors. Her results were better than for most cancer patients, in fact."

"You knew she should be in remission, not sliding backwards. You knew she was being fed those drugs. And you're a doctor."

I spit out the last word the way my mother says Diable.

"As soon as Karoline was gone, Tommy made sure we took good care of her."

Dee is actually defending their actions.

"We figured out that Glenn here must be giving Libby the drug whenever he could. When he told us Karoline was dead we knew we were free, but we were still nervous about Glenn. That's why I offered to do the job of caregiver. You saw how she improved."

Her skewed logic is astonishing. Perhaps it's similar to ignoring your best friend's disintegration. Perhaps it's akin to manipulating all the people in your life for financial gain.

"You mean you were working against me? There are nothing but bitches in my life. Only Karoline…"

Glenn's ridiculous whine trails off into a weak mumble. He looks like a giant slug as he slithers further into the folds of the sofa.

Ethan moves his body slightly so that I can feel his warmth right up next to me. I want to dissolve. Disappear into his arms. Let go.

Either that or pummel the faces of these three lowlifes into bloody pulp.

"Let me get this straight," Ethan says.

He leans forward, the gun highly visible. His tone is measured and melodious. For that reason alone he sounds scary.

"Karoline found out about Anne's history. She came here and pretended to be a Johnston sister. Immediately she realized there was a lot of money in the paintings and antiques. She recruited Melody here to help with researching the family. I'm supposing she didn't have the time to do it herself. Mrs. Fischer did her bidding because Karoline offered to pay off their son's debts. As a result of the research Karoline found Glenn and began a love affair."

"They used to have CoJons hanging on their walls. They didn't even have insurance," Glenn scoffs. "Karoline dealt in art for her boss. Right away she knew their worth. Libby didn't even notice when Karoline substituted them for different prints or just left the walls blank. Slut mother didn't deserve that art."

Fortunately for both Glenn and me, Ethan moves his arm in front of me and holds me in.

"You are a bastard in more ways than one."

It's a childish retort but I feel better anyway. I have one more question that I need answered.

"Do people around here really think that I burned down Vryheid?"

Melody nods. "That was one of the theories, long ago. Karoline asked me to revive the rumors. Old superstitions kept people away from the farmhouse."

I draw in a shaky breath. Sweet Karoline. How could I have lived with this person my whole life? How could I never have known how controlling and evil she was? I am ashamed of my previous shallow existence. I was so self-satisfied that I took no notice. Never examined anyone or anything too deeply.

A loud noise at the front door interrupts my thoughts. Lots of heavy footsteps. Then suddenly a booming voice.

"Detective Byrne? Constable Miller here! Is everything all right?"

Ethan moves into the doorway, the gun at his side, talking loudly.

"I'm here, Constable Miller. Everything is under control. I confiscated a gun from the perpetrator and I have it here at my side. Just down the hall in front of you."

Three burly men and one tall thin woman all in dark uniforms follow Ethan's voice into the parlor. Behind them, Miriam looks tired and scared. She lights up when she sees me. We hover in each other's arms for a minute. Neither of us even tries to stop the tears, though I do tamp down on the sobs that want to scream out of my chest.

Things happen very quickly after that. The police constables question each of us separately, including Melody, Tommy and Glenn. They pretty much leave Dembi and Memé out of any heavy interrogation. All I remember about the officers is that they are of a size that could be intimidating but they are kind and thorough instead.

Miriam and I whip up some food for everyone at one point. Meat and cheese and bread. Soup for Memé. We sit with Dembi and our mother for a long time. All four of us are tired and numb. Miriam and I take turns holding hands with Memé, Dembi, or each other. We say very little. Rolly makes us smile with his antics.

At some point in time in the mid afternoon Ethan joins us in Memé's room. He's tired too. How could he have expected his vacation to turn into work?

"The police are reading Simpson and the Fischer's their rights. They've confessed to the crimes and will be held over in jail. A judge will decide if they get bail, I guess."

Ethan and I haven't even had a chance to talk. As if he's read my mind he asks if he can speak to me privately. Miriam smiles and tells me she'll be fine with Dembi and Memé.

I take him down the hallways to my room. We drag his suitcase, which had been left abandoned near the parlor.

As soon as I shut and lock the door of my room, we are in each other's arms. We tumble onto the bed. Without bothering to remove anything but his shorts and my underwear, we make frantic, passionate love. Two teenagers on a family sofa. We both laugh when we're done.

"Sorry, honey, that's not what I meant to do."

"That's what I meant to do," I say, pulling up my panties and snuggling into his arm. "Later we'll do it right. There are too many people in this house right now."

I help him with his shorts. Other than our flushed faces and satisfied airs, I'm sure we look normal.

"Hey listen. I found this on the floor in the parlor. I know we might have to turn it in later but I thought I'd look it over first."

Ethan pulls out Karoline's blue diary.

"In between interrogations I was able to read quite a bit of this. She wrote a lot in point form as though she couldn't be bothered to embellish. I don't think you should ever read it."

I feel sick to my stomach. How much longer would Karoline reach out from her grave to torture me? How many more betrayals might I uncover?

"I don't think I want to anyway. I don't think I can take any more. At least not right now."

"I hear you. I can't imagine what this day has been like for you. But I thought you might have some questions about Karoline. Some loose ends that you need tying up."

Reasons for her suicide, he means. To make me realize that it wasn't my fault. Except nothing in that diary will help. After the last few days immersed in my new family, I feel as though I will be plunged back into my former life if I hear any more about Karoline.

Yet there are so many questions.

"Does she explain anything? Does she say why?"

"I've skipped around and she records nearly every thought she had over her last few months."

I can hear that scribbling once again. The constant irritating sound of a pen ground onto paper. Thoughts so dark they had to be stabbed into existence.

"Karoline was a psychopath."

He's firm in his conviction, but feels he has to explain.

"In police work, you meet a lot of people with mental health problems. I've taken lots of courses. We're trained to spot psychopathic behavior because most of our criminals are psychopaths. From serial killers to corporate frauds."

"Aren't some sociopaths?"

"The thing about psychopaths is that they are organized and smart. Sociopaths aren't necessarily. Karoline planned everything. Sometimes her schemes were years in the making."

He sits up. With his head propped on one hand, he looks down at me. Strokes my arm to soften the punch of his words. I know his goal. He wants me to see Karoline's true nature so that I can put her suicide into context. Forgive myself for not curing her. She was crazy, beyond hope. He doesn't know that part of his theory is very wrong.

"She admits stealing paintings and antiques from this house. That's how she paid the mortgage on your apartment."

"What?" I have to sit up now to squeeze some breath back into my lungs.

"Her Boosha didn't give her any money. She stole the CoJons and sold them to her own boss. In her diary, she mocks him. She charges him more than anyone would pay and tells him the auction went higher than expected. Karoline literally amassed a fortune."

I won't cry. I *do* need to know it all. I make eye contact with Ethan, letting him know without words that I've changed my mind about hearing everything.

"What does she say about finding my family and not telling me?"

"She found them because a letter came for you from your mother's lawyer."

"Memé sent me a letter?"

"Yes. She wanted you to know that she was dying. She wanted to reconnect with you. Karoline decided to show up and pretend to be you. Of course she had no idea that Dembi and Miriam existed. She didn't know you were four years old before you left here, either. She wouldn't have expected Memé to know the difference."

"How did she make Memé cooperate with her?"

"She doesn't mention that. At least I didn't find anything. I haven't read it thoroughly though. If the explanation's not there, maybe Libby will be able to tell us someday."

I shake my head slowly. I wish I could shake the information like a kaleidoscope and come out with a different picture.

"Even before she became ill, before the cancer and the extra drugs, Memé was simple and trusting. I don't know how Karoline did it, but she either had them fooled or frightened."

I think of the threats of drowning Dembi in the river. Perhaps Memé was convinced it would happen. Maybe her brother had drowned all those years ago and his death had scarred her toddler's mind. She would be terrified by the thought of her son going into the river.

Ethan flips through the book. The writing looks like scorpions to me.

"This is how sick she was, Anne. To answer the second part of your question about why she never told you about your family. She convinced herself that she was protecting them by keeping you away. As though she bought that hogwash about you being the witch who burned Vryheid."

I lived with this woman. I loved her. I trusted her implicitly with every part of my life. How stupid am I?

"One other thing. In her research, obviously with the help of Mrs. Numbnuts out there, she stumbled across a man who just might be Cornwall Johnston the younger. The artist, that is."

"Wouldn't the art world like to know about that?"

"Wouldn't the *whole* world like to know?"

Dear Diary,

Living in L.A., I always hear the stars moaning and groaning about their loss of privacy. But isn't that the price of fame? Don't they know that they're embracing fame as soon as they take on that role? You're up there on the screen and people start talking about you, recognizing you. That's the very definition of fame. So I think they should suck it up or quit the job.

CHAPTER 28

The evening is warm and fresh. Soaked with the previous rain, the fields and forests give off a fragrance that could never be captured except by nature. Evergreen, sweet clover and flowers mix with the scent of rich soil. A soft breeze plays with our hair as we sit on the porch.

The sun disappeared in an orange ball. Overhead there's a three-quarter moon that outshines any stars. Even the cicadas are quiet, although a few crickets strive to replace their song with one of their own. Bats skim the darkness in search of mosquitoes. We hear their winged hunt and are grateful.

Miriam has lit candles all around the veranda. We've pulled out lawn chairs and pillows and snacks. Memé sits in her wheelchair with a blanket tucked around her thin knees and arms. Ethan stretches out his long legs in a worse-for-wear lounger that is nevertheless comfortable. My sister and I sit on the porch benches.

Rolly entertains Dembi by chasing an unfortunate grasshopper along the boards. Our brother is almost back to normal. He's still a bit quiet and prone to cuddling up with one of us more often than usual. But we're convinced that he'll recover faster than we will.

Memé is more alert than we've yet experienced. The doctor who replaced Thomas Fischer stopped by earlier to see her and pronounced her fine for now. We have an appointment at the hospital on Monday. He'll do a thorough examination and give us recommendations for her future care.

Miriam has a bandage around her ankle. I have a purple bruise under my eye and a red mark down my cheek. Other than that, we have no visible repercussions from our encounter.

I don't think I'll be afraid any more. Despite Glenn's efforts, no one was seriously hurt. We uncovered a lot of interesting facts. We did hand over the diary although the police officers weren't sure it would be of any use. We will all have to be formally interviewed tomorrow. For now, however, we are peacefully at home.

Over dinner and this sojourn on the porch, my family bonds with Ethan. We're all exhausted and somewhat shell-shocked, but that seems to heighten the connection. We talk about everything except Glenn, Karoline and Melody and what just happened.

In between conversations we sit in pleasant silence and think. Or at least I do. Mostly I contemplate Karoline, our life together and how the past affects my present. How it will affect my future.

I was a little girl in terrible circumstances. Even my mother, with her fierce love and simplicity, knew she had to send me away. Vera was a good choice in some respects but she nurtured my innate desire to protect myself. To insulate with distance and lack of emotion. No risk of hurt when you don't give away any piece of yourself.

Judging by the flood of emotions since Karoline died, I don't think I am a sociopath. Ice Queen Anne has mostly disappeared. I have to learn that some anger and aggression are justified as long as the actions that accompany the feelings are controlled. The real me can be sarcastic or upset or irritated. I just can't get up and walk away. I can't block out the rest of the world while I create my own universe where the sun revolves solely around me. Not if I love these people. And I most certainly do.

Was Karoline a psychopath as Ethan suspects? I guess so. She was certainly mentally ill. She carefully plotted her revenge when she thought her friends had betrayed her. Giulio with his determination to forgive me. I suppose I deceived her with Parris, but I think my sin was having a rich family who was as oblivious to that as I was to Karoline's real self. Thus her retribution included theft of both identity and wealth.

I know that I have to forgive myself. Under the canopy of moonlit comfort the thought of forgiveness is easy. Even acknowledging that I have to tell Ethan doesn't send me into hyperventilation. Instead I feel calm and relaxed. My confession will be the first step toward redemption.

When we have made love and are tucked into my farmhouse bed, however, I nearly lose my nerve. I cuddle into Ethan's arms and refuse to look at him. I can't tell him with those deep understanding eyes on mine. I ask him to listen without interruption and he does.

Dear Diary,

Do you think love and hate are on the same continuum? Or is hate still tinged with a bit of love? Maybe real hate of someone is indifference. The despised someone's name or face or something they said or what they really need rarely crosses your hateful mind. You never, ever think of them or have any strong feelings about them. If you are angry with them all the time or miss their presence in a negative or positive way, maybe you still love them.

CHAPTER 29

Karoline was in the kitchen when I got home from Cleveland. The apartment smelled of onions and spice. It smelled the way it used to. Alive and inviting. The dining room table was set for two with candles, our best cutlery and plates and bowls of steaming food.

Karoline came to the doorway and stared down the hall at me. Her eyes seemed larger than usual. Beadier. The smile on her face was one I recognized. Self-satisfied. In control of everything and everyone.

"Have a seat, dear friend. Supper's on the table."

For one last time I obeyed her. Despite the sarcasm and cruelty in her voice, in spite of all the information I had gathered, some part of me wanted her to be two people. One that was my Karoline, lifelong friend. The other a person who had nearly destroyed us but who could be vanquished.

We faced each other as Karoline poured us each a large glass of wine. I drank mine quickly and filled up another. I still couldn't bring myself to speak. I was engorged with rage and trauma. Choked into silence with bewilderment and pain.

Karoline chuckled at my need for alcohol as though she had won a round.

"So, Annie love, do tell me what you've discovered."

As though I had been on a journey in which we're both interested. Not one that would expose her betrayal. I took several gulps of red wine.

"Why, Karoline? Why would you do this to me? To Giulio?"

She shoveled some of the red meat into her mouth, masticated a bit and then opened in a huge guffaw filled with dead cow.

"Do you really think I did something to you?"

I poured another glass. My hand was trembling now as I lifted the wine to my lips. When I found my voice it was deep and strong from anger and disbelief.

"You lied to me about Giulio. He lived in the States for years. From the beginning he wanted to reconcile with me but you denied us both. You lied to him about me. You wrote letters and signed my name. You told him unspeakable things."

"I see."

She put down her knife and fork and poured herself another glass. A full minute passed before she spoke again. During the silence she kept her eyes on me. I wanted to scratch the smile off her face.

"Are you sure I wrote those letters? They were signed by you."

"You know perfectly well you wrote them. I never saw them. When Paolo sent them back you stuffed your dirty little secret in your closet."

"So you say."

"You also didn't tell me that Vera and Ian Williams are not my real parents."

"Not that I'm confessing to anything, but maybe I was protecting you. I've always taken care of you. Maybe I didn't think it was good for you to find out you're adopted."

"Oh my god, Karoline. My god. Listen to yourself. What is wrong with you?"

I was in danger of losing it. I was going to give into the rage and if I did that I'd have no chance of making any sense. Finding any answers. Knowing any peace.

"Giulio killed himself, Karoline."

I kept repeating her name as though I could break through the layers and find her. As though my friend was hidden under a smiling demon's skin.

"You told him horrible lies. You convinced him the love of his life was unfaithful. You picked on him when he was sick and vulnerable. Karoline, he died because of you."

She stood up and flung her glass of wine at me. Red droplets splashed all over the table.

"He didn't die because of me. He died because of you. He believed that you were evil enough to betray him like that. Because you are."

She was screaming by then. Spittle and bits of food spewed from her mouth along with her vitriol.

I got to my feet and shoved the plates across the table. Steak and potatoes and carrots and salad mashed together in a steaming lump at Karoline's feet. She laughed.

"You are a selfish cold bitch. I spent my whole life looking after you and that weakling. All I ever did was keep things nice."

Karoline pushed herself away from the mess and was instantly at my side. Though she was shorter than I, her eyes seemed to be even with mine. Their glow was terrifying. Waves of rage flew off her and slammed into me. I tried to take a step back but she fastened her hand around my wrist with a painfully strong grip.

"You would have been murdered by now if it weren't for me. Some man would have raped and killed you. Your stupidity is boundless. You think you can use somebody and they won't retaliate. I protected you."

Her voice was a screech. I couldn't move. I was a mouse frozen by a lion's roar.

"And how did you repay me? You fucked everything that moved when I wasn't looking. You brought home women you thought could be our friends. We didn't need anyone else. We were perfect on our own."

Karoline flung my hand away and stomped into the living room. I stood and watched. Some of what she said didn't make it to my brain. I couldn't process her mad diatribe.

"Giulio was worse. He left us for that wreck of a man who couldn't even decide if he liked boys or girls. They pretended they were Ozzie and Harriet in their perfect little house on their perfect little street with their perfect little neighbors. In Cleveland of all places. Armpit of the earth."

She paced up and down. Her arms flailed as though punctuating her sentences with exclamation marks.

"I couldn't make him come back. Even to make everything up with you. I figured if I got him back to L.A. he'd never leave again. But nooo…"

Karoline began to pull at her own hair.

"Then the asshole goes and gets cancer. Still he wouldn't come back to me. I would have taken good care of him. Even you would have taken care of him. I tried to make him leave Paolo but nooo…"

She turned to face me again. I saw the tears streaking down her face. Not tears of sadness but from a wrath so all-consuming that it spilled from every pore.

"He killed himself instead. I guess he had the last laugh, didn't he?"

I began to sob. My grief was a river that almost knocked me over with its strength. I stood in the middle of the furious water unable to move or do anything to stop the flow.

"Karoline. Karoline. You're making no sense. You need help. We can go to the hospital. We can get help."

She whirled around on me. Her face was mottled and swollen. She clenched her fists.

"I am so glad you're not next to me at this minute. I would scratch your eyes out. You are a stupid fucking bitch."

The balcony door reverberated as she shoved it open.

"Leave me alone. We will talk about this later."

Her tone was that of an annoyed parent. I almost heard 'young lady' after her directive. She had stopped crying. The muttering and pacing on the balcony was almost worse.

I cried for a long time. I had no idea what to do. The inertia was heavy. It seemed to take a long time to lift myself from under it.

I cleaned the kitchen. Put the ornaments back on the table the way Karoline liked them. Shoved the broken plates and bowls down the garbage chute in the hall. Took a shower and put on my nightgown.

All the while Karoline talked to herself and paced like the sentries outside a royal palace.

I was calmer now. I thought I had some clarity. Karoline was obviously suffering from a mental breakdown. Some kind of personality disorder had suddenly worsened in the last few years. Unbeknownst to the rest of us she had slowly gone crazy.

But things like this could be fixed. I went out on the balcony and sucked in my breath. Karoline sat on top of the balcony wall. She looked back at me and laughed.

"Talk me down, Annie baby. Go ahead."

"Karoline, you shouldn't fool around like that. You could slip."

I walked forward a few steps. She didn't seem to care.

"You don't think I'm serious? Why not?"

"Come down and we'll talk about everything. We can set this right."

"Listen to you. Little goody two-shoes. Set this right she says! Good lord. Shouldn't you be screaming at me for killing your precious Giulio?"

"I care about you right now. I'm afraid you'll fall."

I kept walking toward her.

She repeated my statements in a singsong voice.

"What a sap. You are stupid, Annie dear. Dumb as a post. You can't even tell when you've been outshone."

"Karoline. You're my best friend. We've meant so much to each other. We love each other. Come down and talk to me."

"Love you? I can't stand you! I have my reasons for putting up with you all these years. But none of them has anything to do with love. I cannot imagine anyone loving you. Not really. We all get attracted to your sunny little disposition and your good looks. But very soon afterward your true nature becomes evident. Stupid, selfish, haughty. Indiscriminate. Sex addicted. Oh, I could go on."

I took a step closer. Now I was fairly close. She twisted herself sideways so she could gaze at me.

In the distance I could hear the traffic. Car horns, a screech of tires, an emergency vehicle. The trees outside our building swayed slightly in the darkness. I couldn't see over the wall but it was unlikely that people were out in the garden at this hour.

"Isn't this fun? Isn't honesty just the best policy? You should be honest now. Tell me how you really feel."

"I don't like who you are right now," I admitted.

"Who I am right now. What psychobabble. I yam who I yam, girlfriend. Always was and always will be. Smarter than you, though that's not saying much. Better at manipulating people than you ever dreamed of. Everybody thinks you're the one who managed people and did that horrible job so well. Little did they know that you were my puppet at home. I pulled your strings, you did my dance."

I didn't mean to argue with her. I couldn't help myself.

"Obviously you didn't play your role of puppeteer too well if both Giulio and I defied you."

"Oh how little you know! I kept you in the dark. I have tied your strings so tightly around your life that you'll never recover. You are both the protected and the one people need protection from."

She bent one leg so she could look me straight in the eyes. She began to laugh again, that high hideous cackle that shook with crazy merriment. She stretched out her arms as though she wanted me to grab them. I took the last few steps until I was right beside her.

"You can't change me, Annie dear. I have completely screwed up your life and mine. Giulio never came back to me but he sure as hell didn't mind killing himself for you. You showed me that you never really loved me either. I failed at keeping you as my little Pinocchio, but I sure as shit messed up your life too."

"Maybe you should just kill yourself then, Karoline. If everything is so fucked up why don't you just do it?"

That was when she went over.

Dear Diary,

Have you ever thought about suicide? I'll bet nearly everyone has. Personally, I think it's a vindictive, cruel act. Splatter blood everywhere so the people left behind have to clean it all up and feel bad. When I think about it, it seems to be the purest form of revenge.

CHAPTER 30

"I don't think she meant to fall," I stammer through my tears. "I think she was so shocked by what I said. I think she wanted me to tell her it was going to be all right. That we'd work it out. That I'd stay with her forever."

Ethan moves around so he can see my face.

"No wonder you feel so guilty. Oh, Anne, that's horrible. So awful and traumatic. I'm not surprised you had your own breakdown."

My eyes burn and my throat is sore. There is so much anguish and guilt pouring out of me. My tears have turned to acid.

"I've been so afraid that I'm a bad person. I probably burned down Vryheid when I was four. I killed two of my uncles. I murdered my best friend when I shouted at her. Instead of calling emergency services, I was haughty enough to think I could deal with her. Then instead of talking to her nicely, I argued with her. I shouted at her. I dared her to do it. I obviously have this terrible anger. What if that monster is still inside me? What if I can't control her?"

We both sit up facing one another now. I am shaking but not with cold. Ethan puts his hand under my chin and forces me to look into his eyes. Those blue understanding eyes.

"Anne, you are not a bad person. You are loving and sweet and thoughtful and kind. You can't even see yourself. Karoline had you twisted around. She convinced you that you were worthless and heartless. That's what psychopaths do. They abuse and hurt and shame."

He puts his hands on both my shoulders.

"You didn't kill Karoline. She got up on that damn wall and she fell. Maybe you startled her with your honesty. But she was up on a railing seven stories above the ground and that was her fault."

He looks as though he wants to shake me. Ensure his words are driven home.

"And I do not for one minute believe you set that village on fire. You were a little girl. You might have dreamt now and then that you would get rid of the place by burning it down. But you couldn't have done the kind of destruction that resulted in two deaths."

I cannot stop crying, but I do hear him. After a minute or two I collapse against him and we lie back down. He caresses my cheek, wipes away the tears. His lips brush against mine. His hands feather my neck and my breasts.

I lean into him. I stop weeping.

"I love you."

"I love you, too," I answer and this time I don't feel reluctant or doubtful.

Ethan pulls me on top of him. Encircles me with his long sturdy arms. Our lips connect. Our tongues find each other's warmth and silk. I shift a little and open my legs. He enters me and we move in slow tender motions.

And the two shall be as one, I whisper to myself, and this time no one contradicts me.

Dear Diary,

I've read psychology books that say people's personalities are pretty much fixed by the time they are four. I think they're wrong. People can change. They can get better or worse. Maybe there are some things that are written in stone, like if you're anti-social or something. But the rest can be influenced by the situation. I can point to a few examples in my life, believe you me!

EPILOGUE 2013

In response to recent revelations, the reporters will be here in the morning. I have to get ready for them. Having spent my whole career in the television and movie business, you would think I'd be a natural. I can handle anyone else's book-to-screen press conference. Handling my own is turning out to be completely different.

Outside, the Pacific goes about her daily chores. Nothing will be different for her tomorrow. As for me, I will present a book to the world that will turn the light of millions of eyes onto our family.

I love this ocean. She is wild, untamable, beautiful and ugly. Every day she reacts to her natural rhythms without censure. Waves might be gentle and easy, immediately followed by aggressive ferocity. The water grabs at the sand, pulls it in to blend with the salt, capriciously throws it back again. I love the sound of its fists against the rocks.

I am still breathless when I look out over this vista. I can't believe my good fortune and never take it for granted. This house, these houses really, since there are three of them on the property, are beyond decadent. I reside in complete and utter luxury.

Sometimes the guilt washes over me, the same way my beloved sea covers my head with a wave now and then. I'll spend a few minutes giving to charity online.

Mostly, however, my days are filled with sunshine, water, laughter, extravagance and love. Perhaps I am not deserving of such things, but that's the way it happened.

Thinking once more about what led to this place, this unveiling, has made my past come alive again. That's good, because I must be prepared for questions. I must be ready to answer correctly. To never be exactly truthful.

As I wait for the reporters to arrive and snap pictures of the Book of Vryheid, I don't just think about those early events from the 1980's. I also contemplate the twenty years since Karoline died. I know time hasn't really gone by quickly. Sometimes it just feels that way.

Ethan took a leave of absence that summer of 1983 and we stayed in Canada at the farmhouse for several months. Throughout those long luscious weeks, Memé enjoyed a well-deserved remission from pain. It was a wonderful time. We laughed a lot. Played like children. Got to know one another for real.

Vera and Ian came to visit. So did sister-cousin Elizabeth. There was, eventually, forgiveness.

When Memé's time was over, Vera returned to the farmhouse. She was there with us at her sister's deathbed. She was helpful and kind in the aftermath, too. She wouldn't talk much about her early years, but we learned enough to become somewhat sympathetic.

Vera plays grandmother to my children, though she's slowing down in her early eighties. Ian is wonderful as a grandfather, too. They remain in Bell Canyon but they're in a retirement home now. We visit as often as we can.

Parris came to Memé's funeral and stayed a few days. All these years later she is still my friend. We've gone through a few life changes together, including marriage and babies. It's a great feeling to share life's joys and sorrows with someone who knows you so well.

I learned more in those months at the farmhouse than I had in thirty-three years. Memé, Dembi and Miriam modeled family for me. Ethan taught me love.

Memé never did fully recover her power of speech. She never told us much about what had happened with Karoline and Glenn. As for him and his cohorts, they did their time in jail. We haven't heard anything about them since.

By pointing at pictures and mumbling simple words, Memé was able to reveal that Larue was our father. Although they never married, she really knew a strong healthy love with him. I hope it's true that people reunite in the afterworld.

I became very proud of my heritage. No longer do I feel as though I have to pick sides. I am a hybrid. Years later I became a spokesperson for unity between races. Ironically, my face is well known throughout the country these days. Something I didn't want when I was younger. I am a television star. I am often a guest on talk shows. I'm the one in those ads from the state promoting understanding and community.

We found Cornwall Johnston. He lived in a hovel just outside Vancouver. Gradually we convinced him to come and stay with us. He hasn't left. He's one of the residents of our compound beside the Pacific Ocean. Of course no one knows that. An agent still sells his paintings. The art world is astonished every time a new one is 'discovered'. As a result, we are all insanely rich. Even his paint box was worth a fortune.

The Johnstons were, indeed, a talented bunch. Cornwall's forefathers had kept the Vryheid Book throughout the decades and every one of them was a great artist. CoJon was the best of them, but he says that's because he had the example of his ancestors. I think it's because the artistic gene just kept getting stronger. One of my daughters shows great promise. Maybe the talent will keep going into the future.

It wasn't easy getting Cornwall to tell us about the Vryheid fire. He was wracked with guilt because he hadn't paid any attention to the abuse and insanity within his family. A gentle giant with a huge talent, he kept to himself. Lived quietly in one of the village huts. That terrible night he was away in the cave—Dembi's cave—where he did his painting, when the smoke and screams drew him back. It was only after his two brothers died that he learned of the appalling treatment of their younger sister. He gave the farm to her and retreated from the world.

Although Cornwall is now in his eighties, he's still energetic and strong. Every morning he walks around the property. Every afternoon, until the light wanes, he paints. I think he's overjoyed at this second chance with Memé through her children and grandchildren.

Ethan left his job shortly after we were married. Ted and Teresa were ecstatic, both with the wedding and my husband's retirement. They are thrilled to be grandparents again. Ethan keeps very busy with a variety of projects. Three of them being our two daughters and me.

We kept the farmhouse but followed through, in a fashion, with the donation of Vryheid. Our lawyers negotiated a major change to the gift. The museum has a ninety-nine year lease. The Johnstons technically own the village. After all, the rumors about the gold still might be true. Memé wouldn't be expected to know all those nuances when she originally gave the land away.

The farmhouse serves as the Burford museum these days. Mary Lou West and her collection moved in with the antiques we agreed to leave behind. Dembi spends a lot of time there.

Every year we all return to Vryheid for the annual powwow held on the grounds. You should see the place now. It's dotted with little gardens. The church has been restored to its former beauty. The cemetery is well kept. There's even a real road right into the village.

The farm is now surrounded by huge homes that are architectural beauties. Miriam, her husband Viho and their children live in the loveliest one. They have a house here, too, more like a cottage, where they spend several weeks a year. Dembi has a room at Miriam's as well as a small cottage here. He has become close to Uncle Cornwall on visits to California.

Dembi hasn't been the same since Memé died. He lost some of his childlike nature. Now that we're all in our fifties, we're a bit more subdued, but Dembi is almost withdrawn.

In the last couple of years we decided to release the Book of Vryheid to the world. It will be a national treasure in Canada and a source of endless interest in the States. Its sale will also keep our children and future grandchildren in the style to which they are or will be accustomed.

As usual in L.A., there is talk of a documentary and a movie. Right now I am simply interested in getting through the press conference.

Initially it wasn't easy to move the book from its hiding spot. Dembi was terribly upset. He changed his mind when we took him to Dublin and showed him the Book of Kells. He decided our book deserved a similar place in history.

I still have the occasional doubt or run-in with the Ice Queen. However, I am living proof that people can change. On the whole I am gratefully happy with life. I adore Ethan and my daughters. I'm a very good mother. I miss Miriam and Dembi every day and revel in our long visits and vacations.

As long as I remember to never be exactly truthful, everything will be all right.

No one will ever know that my memory returned during my first stay at the farmhouse. Flashbacks of the night Vryheid burned gradually became clearer. Eventually, I saw my little girl self as plainly as though I had remembered all along.

I lit the dry grass around the hut where my uncles were working on their illegal home distillery. They'd told me to stay away from the equipment in the back. At the time I thought they said it was highly flappable, but soon I knew what they meant. I did stay away. I didn't get too close when I threw the smudging stick right into one of the open cans.

Those men didn't deserve to live. Filthy disgusting animals. I saw what they did to my mother when Larue was away. I saw how they got her drunk and crawled into her bed. Memé did love me, but she had to give me away for my own protection. And perhaps to protect the others, too. I don't know whether or not she knew the truth about the fire. She never asked and I never told.

No one will ever hear about the rather strong shove I gave Karoline the night she died. She would probably have jumped anyway. After all, she was responsible for Giulio's suicide and she kept my trio away from me. She was a psychopath. Ethan said so.

As for my husband, I will never tell him that I knew who he was the moment he set foot in our apartment. How could I not know? The upper echelon of money and stardom in Hollywood is surprisingly small. I was a little afraid my lifestyle might change once Karoline was gone. My creature comforts and travel budgets might have been cut drastically without her. As it turned out, I needn't have worried. My calculated pursuit of Ethan doesn't really matter anyway. I truly did fall in love with him.

I will never mention Glenn or the Fischers. As far as anyone is concerned, they simply dropped out of sight after jail.

Nowadays I can handle the Ice Queen. I only let her out when absolutely necessary. I simply keep her thoughts and secrets to myself, locked up safe in my diary.

~ * ~

If you enjoyed this book, please consider writing a short review and posting it on Amazon, Goodreads and/or Barnes and Noble. Reviews are very helpful to other readers and are greatly appreciated by authors, especially me. When you post a review, drop me an email and let me know and I may feature part of it on my blog/site. Thank you. ~ Cathy

cathy@catherineastolfo.com

Message from the Author

Dear Reader,

I sincerely hope you enjoyed the ride that was Anne's journey. I actually "met" her three years ago, but got sidetracked from writing by breast cancer. Fortunately I was a lucky woman; my experience was relatively easy. The women who survived, or did not survive, are my heroes.

Lots of people wonder why I write such dark novels. I don't usually consider them "dark" myself, because they always end with hope and love conquering all. In a way, that does happen with *Sweet Karoline*, too. I am simply fascinated with the human condition and all its facets, but I have a strong belief that we can overcome evil with goodness. Thus in my life I am quite a joyful optimist.

The best part about being a published author is getting to share what I have written. So please, don't hesitate to contact me and tell me what you think (politely please). Visit my website—and virtually, me. I would write anyway, but the delight is in knowing you've read my book.

Please do remember what I said about "never allowing the facts to get in the way of a good story". That's the motto I follow, so everything in this book has been brushed with a wild imagination. I hope you suspended belief and simply enjoyed.

Next up are a young adult book (a ghost story of course) and a cozy (not so dark this time). I hope you stay with me as a reader fan for a long, long time!

~ Cathy

cathy@catherineastolfo.com

Book Club Questions by Frances Daley

1. Who was writing the diary at the end of each chapter?

2. What betrayal did Karoline feel that caused her to inflict such pain on her "friends"?

3. Why do you think Karoline impersonated Anne with her birth family?

4. The passages set in Italy made Karoline seem "attractive" in Anne's eyes. She made a similar comment about the picture of her with Dembi. What was it that made Karoline attractive on those occasions?

5. Did the author convince the reader that Anne was as shallow and self-absorbed as the character continually focused on, or was that only Anne's perception of herself?

6. Were you surprised that Giulio and Paulo ended up together?

7. The confession Anne made to Ethan was only a half-truth. Or was it? If it was only partly honest, why was she able to be content with herself?

8. Why would Karoline have been involved with Glenn? Was the relationship intended to upset Anne or was it to keep him close because he was related to the artist CoJon?

9. What particular passage or image is most vivid in your mind after reading the novel?

10. Was time intentionally manipulated to keep the reader unsure of what stage Anne was in her "development"?

11. Is Ice Queen Anne a good description of her character when she becomes forceful? Why or why not?

12. Women dominate the storyline in "Sweet Karoline". Is it fitting that Memé is the one that brings down Glenn at the end of the novel?

13. Why did Vera create such a complex history for herself and inflict it on her children?

14. Could the relationship with the triplets have been just as effective with them being siblings only? Why or why not?

15. There seems to be a fixation on appearances in the novel. What is the author saying about physical beauty?

16. Family history plays a key role in the unraveling of the novel. Why do you think Karoline's background isn't more fully developed?

17. What is the significance that the CoJon paintings paid for the apartment?

18. What questions do you have unanswered at the end of the novel?

19. What role does setting play in this novel?

20. The blend of the three distinct racial groups in a town named for Freedom is very vividly brought out during the powwow. Is it significant that the Johnstons retain the land when they seem to be so corrupt? Why or why not?

About the Author

Catherine Astolfo retired in 2002 after a very successful 34 years in education. Catherine received the Elementary Dufferin-Peel OECTA Award for Outstanding Service in 1998. She was also awarded Dufferin-Peel Catholic Elementary Principal of the Year in 2002 by the Catholic Principals Council of Ontario.

Catherine is a past President of Crime Writers of Canada and a Derrick Murdoch Award winner (2012). She was a Zonta Club 2012 Nominee for Women of Achievement.

Writing is Catherine's passion. She can recall inventing fantasy stories for her classmates in Grade Three. Her short stories and poems have been published in a number of literary Canadian presses. In 2005, she won a Brampton Arts Award. Her short stories won the Bloody Words Short Story Award (second and first) in 2009 and 2010. She won the prestigious Arthur Ellis Best Short Crime Story Award in 2012.

Catherine's novel series, The Emily Taylor Mysteries, are published by Imajin Books and are optioned for film by Sisbro & Co. Inc.

Visit Catherine at: www.catherineastolfo.com.

IMAJIN BOOKS
Quality fiction beyond your wildest dreams

For your next eBook or paperback purchase, please visit:

www.imajinbooks.com

www.twitter.com/imajinbooks

www.facebook.com/imajinbooks

Made in the USA
Charleston, SC
21 July 2013